# The Shakespeare Conspiracy

TWO QUESTIONS HAVE ALWAYS PLAGUED HISTORIANS:

HOW COULD Christopher Marlowe, a known spy and England's foremost playwright, be *suspiciously* murdered and quickly buried in an *unmarked* grave – a grave which has not been found to this day -- just *days* before he was to be *tried for treason*?

HOW COULD William Shakespeare replace Marlowe as England's greatest playwright -- virtually overnight -- when Shakespeare had never written anything before and was merely an unknown actor?

*This is the historical novel* that intertwines the two mysteries to offer the only possible resolution. This story, a wild romp through gay 16th Century Elizabethan England, is a rapidly unfolding detective narrative filled with comedy, intrigue, murder and an illicit love story. It was made into a play which ran Off-Broadway in 2018.

Most importantly, all recorded events, persons, dates and documents are historically accurate. It's a scandalous view of the real William Shakespeare, with his sexual peccadilloes, illegitimate children and mistresses, wandering through the gay world of Christopher Marlowe, where it was acceptable to be homosexual -- like kings James I and Edward II. It's the battle of Inspector Henry Maunder matching wits with Marlowe -- one cleverly hiding the facts and other cunningly discovering the truth.

***It's the greatest literary deception of all time.***

# The Shakespeare Conspiracy

# The
# Shakespeare
# Conspiracy

*A Novel about the Greatest*
*Literary Deception of All Time –*
*Based Entirely on Historical Facts*

## TED BACINO

Printed in the United States of America

Library of Congress Control Number:    2020924233
ISBN:    Softcover                      978-1-64908-648-8
         Hardback                       978-1-64908-649-5
         eBook                          978-1-64908-647-1

Republished by: PageTurner Press and Media LLC
Publication Date: 01/21/2021

**To order copies of this book, contact:**

PageTurner Press and Media
Phone: 1-888-447-9651
order@pageturner.us
www.pageturner.us

For

*Geoff*
*Miki*
*Lara*
*And Jack*

## *To Christopher Marlowe*

*May he someday receive credit
for all his works*

## *And to the late Calvin Hoffman*

*Who kindled the flame
of inquiry*

# HISTORICAL STATEMENT

*All documents, persons, dates, Shakespearean quotes*

*and recorded events named herein are historically accurate except*

*for one date: that of the death of Sir Francis Walsingham, which was*

*changed for dramatic purposes.*

*Dialogue and events for which there are no records,*

*of course, had to be created.*

———————

*The supplement at the end of the book entitled*

*"Facts versus Fiction"*

*gives additional information –*

*referenced chapter by chapter*

*-- about the authenticity*

*of the information detailed in this novel.*

# HISTORICAL PERSONS

**CHRISTOPHER MARLOWE** – *England's foremost playwright until 1593.*

**SIR THOMAS WALSINGHAM** – *Marlowe's patron. Head of the Walsingham estate in Scadbury Park, outside London.*

**SIR FRANCIS WALSINGHAM** – *Cousin of Sir Thomas Walsingham and the head of England's spy service. England's first Secretary of State.*

**THOMAS KYD** – *Popular English playwright and Marlowe's former roommate.*

**CONSTABLE HENRY MAUNDER** – *Constable-Inspector of the Privy Council.*

**QUEEN ELIZABETH I** – *England's monarch: 1558-1603.*

**KING JAMES I** – *Successor to Queen Elizabeth I. Monarch: 1603-1625.*

**RICHARD TOPCLIFFE** – *The Crown's Royal Rackmaster at Bridewell Prison.*

**SIR HENRY WRIOTHESLEY** – *Earl of Southampton and friend of Marlowe and Sir Thomas.*

**WILLIAM SHAKESPEARE** – *An actor from Stratford.*

**ANNE SHAKESPEARE** – *Wife of William Shakespeare.*

**SIR WALTER RALEGH** – *Friend of Queen Elizabeth I and voyager to America.*

**SIR CECIL BURGHLEY** – *President of the Privy Council.*

**RICHARD POLEY** – *An employee of Sir Thomas.*

**INGRAM FRIZER** – *An employee of Sir Thomas.*

**NICOLAS SKERES** – *An employee of Sir Francis Walsingham.*

**WIDOW BULL** – *Owner of a tavern in Deptford, outside of London.*

**WIDOW DAVANANT** – *Owner of a tavern in Oxford.*

**WIDOW VAUTROLLIER** – *A resident of London.*

**EDWARD BLOUNT** – *Local printer and friend of Thomas Walsingham*

**MARY, QUEEN OF SCOTS** – *Mother of King James I and challenger to the throne of Elizabeth I*

**SUSANNA SHAKESPEARE** – *Older daughter of William Shakespeare*

**JUDITH SHAKESPEARE** – *Younger daughter of William Shakespeare*

**THOMAS SHELTON** – *Pseudonym sometimes used by Christopher Marlowe*

# PART 1

# Heresy

## CHAPTER 1

# BURIAL

The cheap wooden coffin pitched from side to side as the old wagon was pulled through puddles of mud and uneven ground.

Heavy rain the day before made the field soggy. And the blue-grey clouds overhead gave everything a dark and ominous look. It was going to rain again.

The old horse, pulling the wagon through the mire, was having trouble with every step, his hoofs sinking deep into the mud.

A solitary figure in a long black cloak slowly followed. He didn't seem to be concerned how the ruts and holes almost toppled the casket from the flat wagon. Nor was he aware how the wheels, going through the dirty slush, splashed mud onto his meticulously pressed garment.

Two men with shovels silently watched the wagon approach the gravesite. Unceremoniously they pulled the casket from the wagon and struggled to carry it to the open grave.

It was getting darker and cold; torrential rain suddenly began to fall.

With heavy ropes the two workers lowered the rain-soaked coffin to the bottom of the grave. One of them snaked the muddy rope from beneath the casket as the other began to shovel dirt and mud into the hole.

The icy wind blew more fiercely. But the solitary figure seemed in a trance, not hearing the splatter of each shovelful of dirt landing on the casket below.

The workers continued shoveling, nearly unable to see with the wind and rain scraping their faces. Rivers of mud began to wash over the bottom of the man's cloak and into the deep hole.

The solitary figure just stared at the grave.

# CHAPTER 2

# PANIC

*The same field.*
*Forty years earlier.*
*Outside London – May 1593*

he horse was in a heavy gallop, going as fast as he could over the uneven field—the bright sunlight in its eyes. But the rider kept spurring the mount harder and harder, one hand tight on the reins and the other holding a leather bag of papers. He used his arm holding the bag to wipe the sweat dripping into his eyes as he desperately kneed the horse. (Oh, please, just a little more speed.)

Across the bridge over the empty moat – dry for almost a hundred years – and onto the estate of Sir Thomas Walsingham in Scadbury Park, twelve miles outside of London.

Riding straight for the garden entrance, the rider leapt off the horse without bothering to tether. The horse, in almost complete exhaustion, wandered about the garden in a heavy pant, whipping its head from side to side.

Scadbury Manor was known for its peaceful, quiet air, far away from the turmoil of the city. Only the occasional breeze broke the usual country tranquility. The door of the study burst open, slamming against the wall. *That* was definitely more jarring than the occasional breeze.

"That son of a bitch! *That son of a bitch!*" the rider screamed standing in the doorway. "Where is that son of a bitch?"

Sir Thomas Walsingham, writing quietly at his desk, didn't bother to look up.

"Could you be a bit more specific, Mr. Kyd? That term applies to most members of my staff … and almost all of my friends."

"Where is Marlowe?" His voice was tinged with rage.

Walsingham turned to him, "Oh, *that* son of a bitch.

"Where is he?"

"I would think I should ask you that, Mr. Kyd."

"Oh, don't hand me that, Walsingham. All of London knows he moved in here months ago – as your new bed warmer!"

"Please, Mr. Kyd," Walsingham shielded himself with one hand. "You're desecrating these stately walls."

Kyd strode to the desk, yelling "*Where is Marlowe?*"

"Why?"

Kyd took the edict from the leather bag and threw it onto the desk.

Walsingham sat and read, suddenly becoming very serious. "When did you get this?"

No longer angry, Kyd was just scared. "This morning."

Walsingham waited for more details.

"Some Constable – or Inspector – named Maunder came looking for me."

Walsingham quietly began to read out loud. "By order of the Privy Council Thomas Kyd is ordered to appear before the Councilors on 11 May 1593 to answer charges concerning the discovery of *vile heretical concepts denying the deity of Jesus Christ our Savior*. Under suspicion of blasphemy, he will --"

"Walsingham," Kyd interrupted, grabbing the decree, "atheism is treason -- a crime punishable by death!"

Walsingham just stared at the edict in Kyd's hand as if he were expecting to learn more details. "What happened?"

"What happened? *What happened?* They searched my quarters – no -- *our* quarters. Marlowe's and mine. Well, what *were* Marlowe's quarters."

Christopher Marlowe and Thomas Kyd had lived together for more than two years. The English -- who seem to be able to come up with euphemistic terms for almost anything -- referred to them as "chamber fellows," a delicate expression. No one asked about the relationship; it was just quietly accepted. The conventional word about town was that "they had an affinity for each other."

In this period Kyd had written one of the most successful plays of the time, "The Spanish Tragedy," as well as a stable of other acclaimed works, becoming England's second most respected playwright – second only to Marlowe. They seemed to spark each other's creativity. It appeared to be the ideal relationship.

Thomas Kyd dropped the edict on the desk, walked to the door and stared out. "And they found all those bloody papers he left behind. Pages and pages. With all that crap he's always spewing about Christ being just a magician -- and St. John the Evangelist being a bedfellow of Christ." Here he did his imitation of Marlowe's cocky inflection, "and Christ using him as did *the sinners of Sodom*."

"Why did they search your quarters?"

"Read on." Then suddenly he crossed to the desk and said "No," grabbing the writ from Walsingham and reading it himself. "'There will be a reward of 100 crowns to the person who supplies information about such libelers'. *That's why.* A hundred crowns." Suddenly he was completely spent and slumped into a silver ornate chair and leaned on the nearby table. "Where is he?"

"Christopher? I haven't seen him yet this morning – but he's somewhere on the estate."

"And it isn't death that frightens me the most." He reached back to hand the writ to Walsingham, not looking at him. "Look at the end."

Almost to himself, Walsingham mumbled, "If Mr. Thomas Kyd refuses to afford the Privy Council proper information, officers shall put him to the torture in Bridewell Prison."

Kyd tried to stop his body from shaking. "And Richard Topcliffe, the prison's royal inquisitor." Then, asking no one in particular, "What do I do?"

"They think the papers were yours?"

"They know they weren't mine. They think they're Marlowe's -- or Sir Walter Ralegh's -- or someone the Council would like to get their polluted hands on. I'm just the link to catch them."

Kyd stood and started to pace back and forth across the room, glancing from side to side as if expecting to mysteriously find a solution somewhere. Walsingham picked up the edict and read it again, rubbing his neck. "There's a war with Spain. There's a plague in London killing a hundred people a day – and the Crown spends its time trying to find atheists."

"*No*, Walsingham," Kyd yelled. "The Crown doesn't. Your fat-ass cousin does. But this time *Sir Francis Walsingham* is going to find out the path leads to you, 'dear cousin Thomas' – *and* your new toy."

"Listen, Mr. Kyd --"

"No, you listen to *me*, Sir Thomas. Let me tell you how Topcliffe works his subjects over and over – well after he's gotten all they know – just to see if he can learn just a bit more. They say he can get prisoners to admit anything." Kyd sat there – almost collapsed – his mind far away, trying to think. "Is there anything you can do?"

"With Cousin Francis? If it concerns atheism -- probably little."

"And, when Francis finds out it was written by one of his ex-spies ...."

Going back to the desk Walsingham said casually, "Christopher was never a spy."

"Oh, *please*, Walsingham. It's hardly a secret. And do you really think I couldn't deduce that in two years?" A few moments of silence followed. "So, when Christopher joins me at Bridewell, I wonder if he will prefer the rack, the iron maiden, or maybe even the water chamber.

Thumb screws are always popular. And Topcliffe loves working over former spies."

"That's enough, Mr. Kyd."

"I thought maybe my plays might keep me out of the stink."

"Mr. Kyd, people put kings into prison. They lock up their own fathers or children. So a popular playwright has no more chance of staying out of the Tower of London than did the wives of Henry the Eighth. Make no mistake: The mood is ugly right now."

"Ugly? Oh, more than ugly. Her new Commission makes it really just a police state, doesn't it?"

Earlier that year Queen Elizabeth had created the Royal Religious Commission to "hunt down and punish all those who secretly adhere to our most capital enemy, the Bishop of Rome," as the Pope was known. She was determined to forge England into a solid Protestant nation.

"Then you haven't heard the latest, Mr. Kyd."

"What now?"

"The commission has announced that from now on it will – as the decree worded it -- 'incarcerate anyone who refuses to attend church and hear divine services.'"

"Oh, glory Jesus. So you can't just be a Protestant," Kyd murmured. "Now you have to be *good* Protestant."

For endless minutes the two of them just stared at each other. Finally, Kyd broke the silence. "He left without a word, without a note, nothing. He was just gone. For days I worried if he was alright."

Walsingham thought it best to remain silent. "Then I had to find out from rumors around town. It seemed all of London knew but me. Though it probably was a good trade, wasn't it? Love for money. Love for protection. The idea's been popular for centuries."

"Don't," Walsingham said, almost whispering.

"But remember, Walsingham, I wasn't Christopher's first – or even his second. He left Thomas Watson to live with what's his name? Baines. And he left Baines to live with me and left me to move in with you. Get the pattern, Walsingham? Who will he leave you for?"

"Was that remark meant to be advice for me or to hurt Christopher?"

"Both," Kyd said and headed for the door. "I'll try France … Spain … anywhere. And give my heartfelt thanks to Kit Marlowe. I'm sure he's next." But he stopped as he heard a voice coming from the garden.

"Thomas … Thomas … Sir Walter Ralegh is planning a meeting tomorrow and if the queen hears about it.…"

It was Christopher Marlowe.

# CHAPTER 3

# CHRISTOPHER

**M**arlowe bounded into the room and playfully roughhoused Walsingham's hair, obviously not seeing Thomas Kyd.

"Sir Walter Ralegh is planning a meeting tomorrow and if the Queen hears about it …."

Christopher Marlowe was his usual carefree self -- poet and prominent playwright -- jostling his way through life with little concern about any consequences. He had the reputation throughout England as London's hottest new writer and loosest cannon, shooting off his mouth about whatever crossed his very clever, and irreverent, mind.

And that mind was *frequently* irreverent. Christ was a bastard and therefore, he reasoned, his mother was a whore. John the Evangelist always rested his head on the bosom of Jesus. And with just a soupcon of projection, he reasoned that Jesus must have loved John and used him just as did "the Sodomites" (a word he enjoyed using since it gave that particular sex act an intellectual flair and bewildered those who didn't know the word's meaning).

So, it was not surprising that Christopher felt confident to do as he chose. He was 29 years old, tall, handsome, clever, and (as he was known at court) "so wickedly cute". His bushy black eyebrows, which almost joined on his forehead, and tousled black hair, gave him a hint of a devilish look that was only accentuated by his dark, deep-

11

set green eyes and fine-line moustache. Adding to his good looks and mesmerizing ways were a string of theatre successes unmatched in England at that time, including the haunting and fiendish *Dr. Faustus,* and the very successful *Jew of Malta.* Yes, he had reason to feel cocky.

Except for the circle of nearly 100 spies that answered to Thomas Walsingham's cousin, Sir *Francis* Walsingham, only a few people knew of Marlowe's jaded spying past which actually began when he was a student at Cambridge. He had gone to Corpus Christi College, Cambridge, on a scholarship designed to educate men of modest means for the ministry.

It surprised none of his friends that after graduation he never elected to take Holy Orders but instead chose the theatre – which at that time was considered barely a step above prostitution, thievery and vagrancy. Theatres were required to be built outside the walls of London (along with brothels, prisons, lunatic asylums and unconsecrated graveyards). To "the people of God," theatres were disreputable places and actually just dens of iniquity. If it weren't for the fact that Queen Elizabeth herself liked them (and occasionally stole away to a performance), they would have been banished completely.

And Marlowe was exactly in the heart of all this turmoil. People said he was mad, bad and dangerous. And this bold rascal loved it. So he was just being the usually devilish Christopher Marlowe -- bounding into the study, telling the world that "Sir Walter Ralegh is planning a meeting tomorrow and if the Queen hears about it, there'll be royal turds on the palace balcony." But the look on Walsingham's face made him suddenly aware that something was wrong. "Oh, no. What have I done this time?"

Walsingham nodded toward Kyd and handed the warrant to Marlowe who barely glanced at it. "They couldn't possibly believe that ...."

Kyd suddenly erupted. "Christopher, you knew your stupid antics would cause trouble someday," he screamed, throwing the leather bag across the room.

The bag hit Marlowe and fell to the floor. A stunned Christopher Marlowe stammered, "I'm...I'm really --"

"Sorry?" Kyd shouted. "Really sorry? You spew your spicy little remarks all over London, and everyone is dazzled at how cute and clever you are. Didn't it ever occur to you that someone — some day — would pass these vile remarks to the Privy Council, or the queen or somebody? Again, as is your style, *you* sin and *others* suffer."

Kyd slumped into the chair again and became very quiet for a long time. Finally, "Why did you leave?" Stunned, Christopher gave no answer. "One day. One day, your things were just gone. Two months -- not a word. Not a *word*."

"I ... I didn't know what to say."

"Maybe '*I'm leaving*' would have been a good way to start," Kyd went on sarcastically. "But Walsingham is rich -- and powerful, isn't he? And now you've got a patron. *And* a protector. A very powerful one." By then he was almost screaming. "Right? *Right?*"

Nothing from Marlowe.

After a long stretch of silence, Kyd calmed, "And, I suppose you're going to tell me 'But I really love him!' How we used to laugh at anyone who used *that* line." Finally, he stood, "I leave tonight."

"You can't," Walsingham quietly interjected. "By now Cousin Francis has offered a reward to every spy in London to find you; so you couldn't get half way to the coast. And my cousin would use that as the perfect sign of guilt."

There was more than sarcasm in Kyd's words. "Walsingham, people don't come out of Bridewell alive. And if they do.... "

For a long time the room was silent as Kyd's words echoed down the halls. Then he said softly to Marlowe, "Kit, the torture scares me. I don't know how much I can take before.... I'm afraid if they catch me, they catch you."

Marlowe looked at Walsingham. "Can you speak to your cousin?" His question got nothing but an uncomfortable stare.

"Then I leave tonight," Kyd repeated.

"You could hide here," Christopher looked for approval to Walsingham -- who nodded. "They'd never find you."

"For how long, Christopher? A fortnight? A year at the longest?" Then he added with sarcasm and hurt, "Living here with the two of you?" He stared at Christopher. "Prison would be less painful."

Kyd crossed the room, stood behind Christopher and held him close, wondering how all this could have happened. After a long moment he kissed Marlowe on the back of the neck and stepped away. He nodded his farewell to Walsingham, grabbed the warrant and quietly walked to the door. Stopping in the doorway, he didn't look back. "Christopher -- I really cared. It's a shame you didn't."

Marlowe almost squinted in pain, knowing nothing he could say would mean anything at that point.

Thomas Kyd left through the garden door and the room was once again silent.

## CHAPTER 4

# THE ESCAPE

"The carriage to Dover?" Thomas Kyd asked, as he stepped inside the coach and sat down. One of the two men facing him nodded. The other just stared at him intently.

Suddenly his fears gripped him again. His plan had seemed so safe the previous week when he had had been at Scadbury. Don't shave for a few days, wear some old clothes (that he had grabbed from the costume room at the theatre) and take only a few critical belongings in a frayed canvas bag (that he had found among some old props there). Get the carriage to Dover and the boat to France.

But now, sitting opposite the two stern faces, he wondered if a well known poet really could weave through the myriad of spies that Sir Francis Walsingham had certainly alerted across all of England.

The boots of the men across from him were shiny and military looking. That was not a good sign. And they said nothing. Just watched him.

This, he feared, was not going to be easy. He tried to look casual and calm his nerves. He picked up his bag and began to rummage through it intently. Anything to avoid their gazes. And, he thought, this would give the impression that he had nothing to hide.

But the ride seemed to last forever. Finally arriving at Dover, the driver opened the door to signal the ride was over. Kyd looked around for anywhere to avoid notice. Across the road was the Inn of the Two Foxes, the local rooming and public house. Without looking back he casually walked into the pub and watched from inside the door. The two men stood restlessly by the carriage.

Kyd waited until they got back into the carriage and it was well down the road. As his fears subsided a bit, he had to decide what to do next.

"The next boat across the channel?" he asked offhandedly going to the bar. "And a pint of ale."

"Tomorrow at daybreak," the chap answered. "Too early for most blokes. You'll probably want the one just after midday."

"I'll take the one in the morning. And a room for the night."

"Number three upstairs is open. Small. Only two shillings."

Kyd took two more sips of ale and decided to leave the rest. He just wanted to get inside a room, lock the door and slip onto the ferry to France in the dark before daybreak. By the time the Privy Council met the next morning, he would be far from London.

He put a few coins on the bar. The bartender handed him a large, heavy key. "Down the hallway past the storage room and up the stairs. Number three."

Grabbing his bag, he headed down the hall. At the other end of the bar, two men in quiet conversation exchanged glances and silently began to follow. As they passed, the bartender nodded and handed them a key.

Kyd walked into the small, cold room, locked the door, and threw the key onto the rumpled bed. Luckily there was an anemic blaze dying in the small fireplace. He took the warrant out of his coat and tossed it into the fire, not hearing the two men coming up the stairs and walking towards his room.

In the small fireplace the warrant began to blaze – much like the flames of the brazier at Bridewell Prison – the brazier holding the fire tongs.

## CHAPTER 5

# BRIDEWELL PRISON

The flame from the brazier below the fire tongs gave an eerie look to the bricked arched ceiling in the cellar of Bridewell Prison.

If the dungeon wasn't frightening enough, the flickering flames made the stone walls very red and filled the cellar with weird shadows. It had a dank and putrid smell.

Thomas Kyd was mesmerized by the iron tongs near his feet as the heavy iron pincers began to glow a bright orange color in the flames. He nervously tried to shift his body around but heavy ropes tied him – completely naked – to a splintering wooden slab. He worked to keep breathing as evenly as he could. The silence was driving him insane. (Why doesn't Topcliffe say something?)

Richard Topcliffe ("the Crown's Royal and Sadistic Rackmaster," as he was known around London) smiled soothingly -- just inches from Kyd's face. He knew his inquisitor should always appear relaxed and casual. Years had taught him that this worked so much better than badgering. In the flickering light from the flames and the grim shadows on the walls, Kyd could discern only Topcliffe, but he could sense movement in the darkness farther back. He tried to catch his breath.

Topcliffe's voice was almost comforting. "Once again, Mr. Kyd, whose papers were they?"

The inquisitor didn't expect information just yet. From experience he knew that always came later. Words alone got you nothing.

Bridewell Prison was far from the southeast corner of London where Topcliffe had grown up, a puny, scared child whom everyone pushed around. Everyone. The uncle who raised him, the bigger boys at school, even the head rack master when he first came to work at Bridewell.

But soon his boss, the head rackmaster, began to realize that, like himself, Topcliffe was fanatically anti-Catholic – and like himself, relished torture and torment. So, it wasn't long before Topcliffe became what his boss called "his assistant for *big* dungeon devices." Consequently, when his predecessor died, the queen named Richard Topcliffe the Royal Inquisitor of Bridewell Prison.

Then everything changed. People didn't laugh at him any more. No, they spoke to him with quiet, respectful tones. And across London, everyone knew his power and greeted him with a smile and a nod.

Yes, things had changed. On two occasions he had even been called upon to question former schoolmates -- ones who had bullied and hurt him years before. Life, he realized, can eventually be rewarding.

But today was no ordinary questioning. Topcliffe knew the papers were really Christopher Marlowe's. But with a little extra effort he just might be able to get the prisoner to actually implicate Marlowe or Sir Walter Ralegh. The Privy Council would appreciate that.

Ralegh was considered gross and uncouth; his only claim to fame was his travels to the new world and the tobacco he brought back. (But he *had* gotten a lot of acclaim from the Queen by naming a province in the new world "Virginia" for her questionable moniker "the Virgin Queen." And it also didn't hurt that time he dropped his coat over the puddle of mud so Queen Elizabeth would not get her slippers dirty. He sopped up the glory on that little ploy like the thick red cloak sopped up the muck.)

However, to the more prestigious members of the Privy Council, Ralegh was known as "Walt Stick the tobacco man." They definitely did not want him brought into their cozy, refined council -- but he had become too close to the Queen to attack openly. There were even rumors of a wild romance between the two of the them.

18

So Thomas Kyd was the way to Ralegh through Marlowe.

And, adding to Topcliffe's enjoyment for the evening, was the fact that Thomas Kyd was the number two reining playwright in London. Kyd's classic play, *The Spanish Tragedy* had had twenty-nine different productions throughout the city, a record at the time. His myriad of other scripts had been performed by four different London theatre companies. So this night's work was far from ordinary. It might not be Marlowe, but Topcliffe had a celebrity.

"Mr. Kyd, whose papers were they?" Topcliffe nodded to someone in the dark and a hand in a heavy leather glove picked up the handle of the glowing tongs from the fiery brazier near the prisoner's feet. Kyd looked from side to side as he felt the heat of the tongs traveling up just inches above his naked body, stopping so close to his face that it reddened from the heat. (No. Please! Not my eyes.) Topcliffe's subtle glance to a person in the dark holding the tongs went unnoticed by Kyd. But on cue the glowing tongs touched a loose end of rope near Kyd's face. The rope fibers flamed up for a second, burning a bit of his lip.

"Were the papers Sir Walter's? Maybe Sir Walter Ralegh's?" Kyd's eyes widened in panic. "Or maybe Marlowe's? Were they Christopher Marlowe's?"

Still no answer.

"Didn't poet Marlowe just leave you to live with a wealthy aristocrat, Mr. Kyd? Now, wouldn't that be proper justice if they were his papers?"

Kyd tried to breathe evenly and not stare at the tongs, which on cue were moved slowly back over his body, seeming to pause every few inches but eventually stopping at his feet. He closed his eyes and clinched his jaw.

"You say they weren't yours. Then whose were they?"

The glow of the tongs began to redden Kyd's bare feet and the heat grew more intense as they got closer and closer. "Think hard now. Try to remember," Topcliffe whispered as he leaned in, just inches from his victim

In the cellar of Bridewell Prison there was a long, long period of absolute silence. There was only the sound of the prisoner trying to catch his breath. And then a scream and the pungent smell of burning flesh.

# CHAPTER 6

# SCADBURY MANOR

**S**cadbury Manor, located in Chislehurst, Kent, was always beautiful in the spring. For months the gardeners had been planting the early growth and trimming the bushes and trees.

It was a lovely day, so beautiful that it seemed as if a madrigal should be heard in the background.

For generations this had been the home of the ancestors of Thomas Walsingham – all the way back to the year 1315, during the rein of King Edward III. Even Thomas's cousin *Francis*, now England's Royal Spymaster, had lived there for a while as a young boy after his father had died when Francis was only one year old. Until "Cousin Francis" was almost grown, he was raised as part of the Thomas Walsingham immediate family at Scadbury.

Thomas frequently scrutinized the grounds – encompassing more than a thousand acres – appreciating the heritage and family history contained therein.

Friends thought that Thomas Walsingham, more than any of his ancestors, probably best personified the traditions of Scadbury Manor. He had the reputation of being thoughtful, thorough, intellectual – and always the gentleman. His tall stature, erect carriage, and air of confidence gave him greater presence than his thirty-one years should have afforded. There always seemed be a master plan for every strand of his very light brown hair and every item of his clothing.

He was a bold contrast to his new ward, Christopher Marlowe, whose hair and clothing always gave the impression that he was in the midst of a wild rush to handle some crisis.

Walsingham and Marlowe made an odd pair standing next to each other in the courtyard garden, scrutinizing the large, overly embellished oil painting of Sir Henry Wriothesley. It was overdone, too ornate and too, *too* flattering for words.

After a moment to catch his breath, Walsingham spoke first. "How … how wonderful … and … beautiful." Trying desperately to be kind, he went on. "The right Honorable Henry Wriothesley – wealthy – ornament to the Court – a favorite of Queen Elizabeth. His portrait will be a focal point of beauty in this manor forever." Then, as a pronouncement, as if accompanied by a fanfare: "Henry Wriothesley, the Third Titled Earl of Southampton."

Wriothesley, standing there in the garden with his portrait in front of his face, peeked out from the behind the painting he held so lovingly and exhibited a grand smile. "And, remember: *also* the Baron of Titchfield." He adorned the salutation with a cute wink.

It took a lot of effort to tolerate Henry. He was always excited and London regarded him as the poster boy for the homosexual movement in England. Almost everyone considered gay activity – which was referred to at that time as "unnatural love" – to be acceptable (just so long as one stayed within one's own social class). After all, so many of the British kings had openly preferred men and *they* made no excuses for it.

(Really, people commented, "We have progressed. This *isn't* the dark ages, you know.")

But it wasn't Wriothesley's sexual proclivities that bothered the local citizenry; it was his behavior. So many stories about him abounded across London. There was that tale his fellow officers told about him when he was serving as a soldier in Ireland. Comrades in arms commented that "he spent his active duty in bed with Captain Piers Edmuns," whom he would "hold and hug and play wantonly." Henry always contended that he learned to love other men while serving in the military. (*That* must have set new standards for Her Majesty's Royal Service.)

When Wriothesley was seventeen, the Queen's prime minister, and the head of the Privy Council, Lord Cecil Burghley, made plans to have Wriothesley marry the lord's own granddaughter. At the final moment, the bashful bridegroom declined to proceed with the marriage and had to pay a forfeit of five-thousand English pounds (the equivalent of millions in today's currency). It was obvious that it was going to take more than money and social pressure to get Henry to the altar.

Wriothesley, who had entered University at age twelve and received his master's degree at sixteen, was younger than the other two but definitely didn't look it. He was on the paunchy side, far less attractive than either of the other two men, with long, light-colored hair that he wore over his left shoulder in a far too feminine way. When sycophants would flatter him on how his hair was much more beautiful than the garish, orange wig of the Queen, he would pet his mane gently and say, "And would you believe it; it's *real*." His big eyes and flamboyant hand movements seemed to magnify every colorful expression that came out of his mouth.

Most of all he loved to correct people who mispronounced his name. He would roll his eyes in disgust and say things like "No, no, *no*. *It's pronounced "RIZ-lee."*"

He cooed, trying to contain his excitement about the painting, "Don't you just love it? I knew you'd love it. Where? The grand hall? The library?"

The clothing, the pose and the look on the face in the portrait did little to help determine the sex of the subject. The word on the streets of London was that Henry spent more money on clothing than the queen herself. (Centuries later when this same painting would be discovered, it would be accepted – for almost 70 years – to be the rendering of one "Lady Norman," a rather outlandish-looking woman. The portrait was complete with rouge, lipstick, a double earring and tresses of hair flowing over the left shoulder. But, the world would one day learn: it *wasn't* Lady Norman. It was Sir Henry Wriothesley.)

Christopher's sarcasm was a little too thinly-veiled. "The Grand Hall or the Library? It's a shame you had only one painted."

Ignoring the derision, Wriothesley went on. "Well, maybe the artist could do another one." Neither Thomas nor Christopher seemed to get the caustic comeback. "Oh, what's the matter with you two today? I bring you a strikingly beautiful portrait of myself and you both look like a scene from the last supper."

Thomas waited a moment before breaking the façade. "Henry – Thomas Kyd is in prison, and --"

Pooh-poohing it, Wriothesley interrupted. "And ... and ... and ... Christopher's in trouble again. I heard. That's why I came here today with three ringlets still to be added on the forehead. But I told the artist, I'd gladly look less gorgeous when my friends need me."

Neither Thomas nor Christopher offered more details.

"So, Christopher, what have you done this time?" With a saucy twinkle Henry added, "Bedded the Queen's new lover, Sir Dudley? You *do* know that Earl of Leicester sometimes – well, you know," swinging his hand from side to side, "...swims both upstream *and* downstream? Not that I, myself, have ever really – you know – with *him*."

"Oh, just the usual, Henry," Thomas finally gave in, "leaving around papers that say that Christ was justly persecuted by the Jews because of his own foolishness, that Moses was just a magician ..."

"I hadn't heard that last one."

"...and that he made the Jews travel forty years in the wilderness when it could have been done in less than a year. The usual."

"Christopher, it's bad enough being a spy, but --"

Marlowe quickly defended himself, "Henry, why do you think writers become spies? Because if we didn't, we'd starve. That wonderful plague has closed every theatre in London. I've earned far more from spying than I ever will from my poetry ... or plays ... or...."

"But, Christopher –"

"Henry, I know I'm always saying stuff like that on the streets, hoping maybe someone will realize what a mockery the church is. But this time I don't even remember where I got those papers."

Marlowe felt obliged to promulgate the idea that the religion of Moses (like all religions) was designed "only to keep men in awe." The Old Testament – like the New – was "filthily written" and filled mostly with sexual scandals.

It was true that he considered these infamous remarks chiefly as "lessons" to be sprinkled throughout London, as he often said, "to free people from the shackles of a corrupt church."

As Wriothesley eyed both of them a bit suspiciously, Thomas came quickly to Christopher's defense. "Henry, it all began with a reward of 100 crowns to anyone who could give information about the latest thesis against the church. Since the Queen created the Religious Commission, it's been a feeding frenzy over rewards for exposing atheists *or* Catholics. When there's a lack of treason in the air, all the spies for Cousin Francis seem to find Catholics everywhere and create sedition where there is none. Or his spies starve."

"Yes," Christopher added. "Since the start of the war, spies have been going crazy – usually just accusing *other* spies."

Wriothesley seemed deliciously scandalized. "Now that's my idea of excitement: spies spying on other spies! Bizarre – but exciting, huh?"

"Most of the time you only have to accuse someone of *being* a Catholic, Henry."

Wriothesley seemed almost to raise his nose in disapproval. "Catholics! Those wonderful people who brought you the Spanish Inquisition!"

The charge of atheism in the sixteenth century did *not* necessarily mean not believing in God. In Protestant England, it meant secretly believing in the papacy or the Catholic religion. In Catholic Spain or Italy, it meant being a Protestant and therefore a heretic. It was revealing that Catholic priests who were caught preaching in England were not charged with heresy but with treason. Consequently the two terms were almost interchangeable and almost anything could fall into either category.

"And worst of all," Thomas gave in, "Christopher's name seems to be locked into that famous line that he uses all over town."

Christopher squinted. "What line?"

"'*All they that love not boys and tobacco – are fools.*'"

"What's wrong with that?" Henry asked naively.

"The prison at Bridewell maybe?" Walsingham answered.

"Ah – *ne pas – ne pas*," Henry dismissed it all. Then he whispered *sotto voce* to Christopher, "I'm learning French. It means 'never – never.'"

Christopher was confused. "I think you mean *jamais ... jamais*."

Henry scoffed, "Eh -- *je ne* give-a-shit *pas*,"

"Thomas Kyd is probably dead by now anyway," Thomas added.

"He's not," Henry's reply got double takes from the other two. "I have my sources. He's still at Bridewell, though I think he would be better off dead. But enough of that. All will be fine. You'll see. Now that my portrait has cheered you, I must be with the north wind, gone. Christopher, that's a beautiful line, so if you ever need it, you can use it in one of your plays."

"I would never steal from a true friend."

"Whatever you say. But parting is such sweet sorrow," Wriothesley replied and left with a flourish.

"You know, Thomas, that line I *might* steal."

Just as quickly, Henry returned, very concerned. "A very official looking carriage is coming up the front path."

"Who?" Christopher asked.

"Someone I've never seen before – but it looks official."

In his usual calm manner, Thomas took charge. "Christopher, wait upstairs. Henry, you may want to stay. The staff will bring him out here."

Marlowe went into the manor and up the steps to a balcony where he could listen, but not be seen, as Walsingham and Wriothesley waited silently in the garden.

It was Constable Henry Maunder.

### CHAPTER 7

# CONSTABLE MAUNDER

onstable Maunder was ushered into the garden by a servant. Maunder was tall and thin with a serious face, a long nose and high forehead, noticeably balding. Though only a few years in age beyond young Walsingham and Marlowe, he looked much older. His voice had a naive quality that kept people from knowing if he was fool or fox. As Royal Messenger for the Queen, it didn't take long for Walsingham's cousin, Sir Francis, to realize that this innocent looking "simpleton" could be a real asset to the intelligence world. Soon Sir Francis made him Constable-Inspector of the Privy Council.

"Thank you sir," Maunder said to the servant. Then turning to Thomas, he asked, "Sir Thomas Walsingham?" Thomas nodded and Maunder turned to Wriothesley. "Christopher Marlowe, I assume?"

"No," Thomas answered for him. "Sir Henry Wriothesley, Earl of Southampton."

"And the Baron of Titchfield," Henry added, helpfully.

"And the Baron of Titchfield," Thomas conceded. What could one do?

"Henry Maunder," the guest stated as his introduction. "Her Majesty's Royal Messenger."

Thomas gave him a thoughtful nod. "And, if memory serves me, also Constable-Inspector of the Privy Council."

Only the slightest hint of a smile on Maunder's lips gave any indication that he realized he had met a formidable but interesting match.

"What can we do for you, *Constable* Maunder?"

"I have a writ from the Privy Council for me to ..." he began, opening the document to read, "... repair to the manor of Sir Thomas Walsingham in Scadbury where it is understood Christopher Marlowe to be remaining, and to apprehend and to bring him to the Court for daily attendance to their Lordships."

Marlowe, listening at the balcony, took a step back into the shadows of the room.

Thomas didn't ask questions about the reason for the order nor did he bring up any arguments. There was never any questioning of an edict from the Privy Council. "Mr. Marlowe is not here at the present, but if you'll leave the warrant, I'll be sure .... "

"I am required to issue the writ only to him, Sir."

"Well, then, Constable, as the writ requires he shall appear at the Privy Council daily – beginning tomorrow. You have the word of Sir Thomas Walsingham."

Maunder looked from Walsingham to Wriothesley. "If he does not – "

Thomas nodded. The Constable just waited. No one said anything. Finally, Maunder handed the writ to Walsingham. "Then good day, gentlemen. The Privy Council meets at --"

"I know what time the council meets, Constable."

Maunder waited and smiled. "Then until tomorrow, Sir Walsingham." He nodded and left.

There was the silence of a caged animal as Christopher came down the stairs and entered the garden. He sat at the large circular table and slowly poured a large glass of a deep red wine but did not drink any. Thomas went over and stood behind him, putting his hands on the young poet's shoulders. Walsingham could feel Christopher shaking.

28

"At least it's not a summons to prison," he whispered. "Just to appear at Court."

"Until?" Christopher asked. But there was no answer. "Until I'm required to appear at Bridewell Prison for 'further questioning?'" Still no reply. "I'll flee to the Low Countries – or Italy."

Thomas was standing behind Christopher and turned the young poet to face him, his hands still tightly on Marlowe's shoulders. "Not possible. Think of Thomas Kyd. You'll appear before their Lordships until we can devise some plan."

Christopher looked at him incredulously. "A plan? What plan? Thomas, we're talking about a warrant from the Privy Council!"

Marlowe sat at the table and looked around the garden confused. The punishment for the charge of treason or heresy was quite standard. In the terminology of the Treason Act of 1570, the *accused* was to be "hanged, drawn, and quartered." (It was interesting that the act read "the accused" instead of "the guilty person".)

The law required that the person be dragged on a wooden frame to the place of execution. Then he (and it was always "he," since this was the punishment for men only; women found guilty of treason had the lucky fortune to be burned at the stake) – *he* would be hanged until "*almost* dead." At that point the law required that the prisoner be "disemboweled and emasculated" (two words that, in spite of their technical sound, could instill fear in the minds of the heartiest) and then the man's "entrails and genitalia are to be burned before his eyes."

The finishing touch was the "quartering" which entailed first beheading the person (while he was still alive) and then having the rest of the body cut into four more pieces (hence, the "quartering.") These four pieces were nailed at various places around town as a graphic reminder of the consequences of heresy. Finally, the person's head was jammed onto a pole at the southern end of London Bridge. That, it was assumed, would be a lesson to those Catholics (-- or heretics – or traitors – or whomever.)

Christopher knew what he faced because he had seen it so often. Probably death. Definitely torture. With a great amount of luck and intervention from Walsingham, the charges might be reduced to the minimum: puncturing and then cutting off his ears. And Christopher knew better than most people: there were no acquittals in Elizabethan state courts.

Suddenly his composure broke. He began to pound his fist on the table as if to make Walsingham understand, repeating "A plan, Thomas? A plan? It's the Privy Council, Thomas. The Privy Council!" He unconsciously kept banging on the table, his eyes wide with the visions of the usual torturing – the ultimate death. It was one thing to watch local citizens being butchered alive. But this time, he realized, it was not someone he knew. It was Christopher himself. *His* head, *his* guts, *his* blood. He seemed to be almost in a fit, hitting the table.

Marlowe's banging sounds seemed to be still echoing in Walsingham's ears the next morning. But this time it was the sound of a huge gavel as the two of them waited outside the massive carved doors of the Privy Council.

## CHAPTER 8

# PRIVY COUNCIL

While Marlowe paced, Walsingham stood waiting with his hand on the ornate door handle to the entrance to the Privy Council.

They could hear the Council President, Sir Cecil Burghley, inside, banging the huge gavel on the wooden block, now almost in shreds from decades of abuse.

"Let the Council Recorder show that today is 20 May, in the year of our Lord 1593," Marlowe could hear Burghley saying from within the chamber, once it was finally quiet, "Is Poet Marlowe here?" Then he heard the bailiff reply, "Yes, Your Honor".

As Christopher heard the bailiff unlocking the door, he crossed to join Thomas.

"Remember," Walsingham whispered, putting a hand firmly on Christopher's shoulder, "present fears are never as bad as our horrible imaginings."

The bailiff swung open the heavy oak doors. "Mr. Marlowe?"

Both Christopher and Thomas started to enter. The Bailiff stopped Walsingham. "Only Mr. Marlowe."

"But I am...."

"Sorry, Sir Thomas. Only Mr. Marlowe."

Marlowe entered, trancelike, and the bailiff closed the massive doors. Even though he knew it was locked, Walsingham pulled at the handle, then turned and began running down the Council steps.

Inside, Marlowe looked down the long aisle between the rows of wooden-carved seats lining each side of the room – every one filled with elaborately dressed Lords, each like a minor god staring out from an oak cocoon.

The seemingly endless walk to the front of the hall with the bailiff was a journey that had unnerved many others before. The long narrow design of the chamber wasn't accidental. When they reached the high platform at the other end of the hall, the bailiff reached over with one hand and stopped Marlowe. Sir Burghley sat with a Lord on each side at an ornately carved desk.

What a difference, Marlowe was thinking. Sir Burghley was the one who interceded for him years before when Marlowe was a student at Cambridge. In 1587 the ministers at Cambridge College unexpectedly withheld Christopher's master's degree.

The charge was that Marlowe had disappeared and they feared he had defected to the Catholic seminary at Rheims, in France -- a common enough occurrence at that time when Catholics and Protestants were spying on each other. But, just as unexpectedly, the Privy Council intervened to point out that "in his absences from Cambridge he has done the queen good service and deserved to be rewarded for his faithful dealing."

"Good service" was a common code expression for spying. And so, Christopher got his master's degree. Obviously, he had simply been part of another common occurrence at the time – being a *double* spy --"defecting" to a Catholic seminary while actually spying *on* them for Protestant England. Sir Burghley, who was very fatherly to Marlowe at the time, was the one who had written to the College and explained that when this student disappeared, he was doing spy work for England. This rectified the problem, and Marlowe had gotten his degree.

But now, Marlowe stood before the same man, about to be condemned to death.

"Christopher Marlowe?" the echo reverberated throughout the hall.

"Yes, Milord."

"You have been called here on charges of heresy," Burghley began. The words echoed in Marlowe's mind. (Heresy? Was it really heresy, he wondered? Or just politics? So easily interchangeable in England in 1593.)

Everyone accepted that Henry the Eighth's newly-formed Church of England was actually just an excuse to legitimize his series of marriages and divorces. However, the new Protestant religion certainly wasn't any better than the traditional Church of Rome. They were both obsessed with deeds like spying on each other, selling indulgences, buying the papacy, or offering bishoprics to the highest bidder.

The Catholics in France, Italy, and Spain felt that England's queen, Elizabeth I, was nothing but a bastard child of Henry VIII and Anne Boleyn, the woman the king married after he had "divorced" his first wife. This severed ties with the Pope when King Henry declared himself Head of the Church of England. Catholics believed that Elizabeth's cousin, Mary, Queen of Scots, should be the real ruler of England.

This, of course, would be a bit difficult since Elizabeth had insisted on keeping Mary in prison under the contention that Mary had plotted to kill Elizabeth.

Then, when the Queen had Mary executed, Spain, in retaliation, sent a fleet of ships to capture the English throne and try to replace Elizabeth. But a brutal storm resulted in the Spanish Armada being defeated and hence began the ongoing war between Protestant England and Catholic Spain – and all the spying each did against the other.

To add to the clashes between the two religions, the Pope had first excommunicated Elizabeth I and then openly called for her assassination. So every precaution was taken to protect the Queen. She was never alone outdoors, closely guarded when in the castle, and even insisted sleeping with an old sword beside her bed.

Consequently, the war was ripe for any fodder – and Marlowe had frequently been boldly in the middle, as spy, as a counter-spy, or even counter-counter spy.

And now he stood before the council knowing that his double dealings could technically make him guilty of heresy by *either* side.

Sir Burghley now sat before him, droning on and on. Accusations Marlowe had heard so many times before. He closed his eyes. His mind was becoming numb.

Outside the chambers, Walsingham was dodging carriages and pushing past people as he rushed to his cousin Francis's London chambers.

## CHAPTER 9

# SIR FRANCIS

Walsingham had only one prayer on his mind, as he pushed his way through the streets. "Please, please, make cousin Francis be in his chambers."

Past building after building on the noisy London streets, and finally into the massive, overly-decorated structure that held the chambers of London's key authorities.

Up two flights of steps and into his cousin's office. As Thomas headed directly for the closed double doors, a guard, standing there said "I'm sorry, Sir Thomas, but Lord Francis is --" But the guard made no attempt to physically stop Walsingham as he charged ahead and into the private office.

Sir Francis Walsingham, sitting at a dark, wooden desk, looked up. He was the very soul of warmth. "Dear Cousin Thomas. How are you?"

Thomas was accustomed to this façade. Cousin Francis *was* Cousin Francis, and no one was going to change him.

Sir Francis was seven years older than his cousin, shorter and heavier. Queen Elizabeth had nicknamed him her "little Moor," though there was no obvious basis for the Moorish reference.

Even though Sir Thomas and Sir Francis referred to each other as cousins, the two of them were actually only second cousins. When

Sir Francis was only one year old, his father died and Thomas's family raised him. Since they were so close in age and since Francis had lived at Scadbury with Thomas for years, they always referred to each other as cousins.

In spite of the age difference the two of them had spent many hours together when Thomas was a young boy and Francis a bulky teenager. With no other companions nearby, the two wasted hours discovering all kinds of mischief in the Scadbury Manor. Francis would amaze his younger cousin with feats of magic and daredevil tricks that always seemed to get Thomas into trouble but resulted in no repercussions for Francis. The older boy knew secret hiding places all over the cavernous Scadbury Manor. Hiding places even the adults had never found. Their favorite was the small crawl spot under the floor in the West Tower.

But as they grew older, Thomas saw less and less of his cousin. Thomas inherited wealth and position as Francis was accumulating power. Soon they were almost strangers; and Francis was no longer the older cousin that Thomas had so admired.

Sir Francis Walsingham was known for his booming, threatening voice that seemed even more frightening when he lowered it to a softer tone. He had headed the Royal Intelligence Service (a euphemism for the spy network in England) for almost twenty years. He was quickly becoming the architect of modern espionage. As a fitting reward for his "unswerving" service, Queen Elizabeth had named him England's first *Secretary of State* in 1573 -- a position not quite structured yet -- giving Francis the opportunity to do pretty much as he wanted with the position. He had the reputation of being the archetype of Machiavellian political cunning with tentacles to fathom out the smallest detail in the country. He knew he was courted and needed by everyone.

He was also hated by everyone.

(He was the inspiration for the line that would someday be written into the play *Measure for Measure*: "It is certain that when he makes water his urine is congealed ice.")

"Thomas. What can I do for you today?" The question was ripe with irony. Of course, Francis knew about the summons from the Privy Council. For all practical purposes, Constable Maunder was his foremost assistant.

36

But everyone had to play the game exactly as Sir Francis dictated, so Thomas went along with the façade – the pretense that his cousin knew nothing about the ordeal taking place at that moment in the Privy Council chamber room.

"Francis, you have to be our salvation from heaven."

Francis went back to his paperwork. "With an opening remark like that, the problem has to be Christopher again."

"I know, Francis. But he's --"

"But *he's* ...?!" Francis quickly interrupted and began reviewing his mental list, "... been *convicted* of brawling in the streets of London ... been *deported* from the Netherlands for his part in a counterfeiting scheme ... been *jailed* for being an accomplice to murder and ...."

"And often accused of '*even being a spy*".

"His only saving grace, Thomas. And actually, I never really knew if Marlowe was spying for us – or on us." Francis grabbed some papers on the desk, as he tried to find the exact words he wanted. "He's a smart, wild animal that has all the talents to be a great spy. But he brings with those talents a despicable desire to find trouble at every fork in the road." Then he added the coup, "And his life always seems to be entwined with the scum of the netherworld."

"Isn't that what has made him an effective spy for eight years?"

"And caused us problems – for eight years." Thomas said nothing. "And now he's added blasphemy. So we keep ignoring all his sins since his work was so important."

Thomas knew better than anyone else the reports of filth and muck that stained Marlowe's reputation. "Those weren't his papers, Francis."

"But, *coincidentally*, those were the same charges made against him last month by Richard Baines."

Years before Marlowe had been living with Baines. But the relationship got ugly when Christopher decided to leave and move in with Thomas Kyd. For years his former "chamber fellow" had been waiting for a chance to return the hurt.

"And didn't Baines receive eighty crowns for that attack?" Thomas quickly countered. "Isn't it possible that that simpleton earns his bread by passing lies to you – and then blackmailing his victims?"

"Thomas, you know they weren't lies." Sir Francis cocked his head, smiled and asked, "And the Chomley Report?"

When he got no argument, Francis went on. "That was quite flattering for Christopher really. Richard Chomley claimed to have been converted to atheism by Christopher and…" he picked up a report and began reading, "…alleges that Marlowe is able to show more sound reasons for atheism than any divine in England is able to prove divinity." Francis gave a look of "now isn't that damning?"

"Written for money, too."

"Oh, really, Thomas," Sir Francis seemed to be tiring of the games. "We have a list of eighteen separate complaints about your young ward. Shall I read them to you again?" Then his stare iced. "And Christopher seems to be spending a lot time with Sir Walter Ralegh. I hear he's joined all of Ralegh's infamous groups, the School of Night, the Durham House Bunch -- one of them," he tossed off hastily, "even rumored to be a coven for warlocks and witches."

"All groups that have members of some of London's most respected names," Thomas replied. Then he remembered and added, "And it was the Queen herself who gave Sir Walter that infamous 'Durham House' -- just last year, wasn't it?"

The tone in Francis' voice was losing its pleasant tone. "It would be hard to find any group that Christopher belongs to which doesn't suggest you spell the word "God" backwards – *or* doesn't promote devil worship – *or* hold black Masses. Come on, Thomas. One accusation?! Maybe two?! But now Thomas Kyd makes the third charge."

"Under torture."

"One charge too many, Thomas."

Without an invitation, Thomas sat in an antique 14th century Provincial settee. "You know the Council isn't looking for Marlowe. They want Ralegh. They don't want Sir Walter to be elected to their almighty Privy Council. Except now the tobacco which he brought back from the *new* world has almost taken over *this* world. Aren't there

7,000 tobacconists here in London alone? *And* he's too popular, too famous, and too close to the queen to go after directly, isn't he?"

Francis just sighed, picked up a quill and began to look through papers on the desk. It was obvious the meeting was over.

"Francis, you can't let him go to prison," Thomas's voice had a pleading tone as he stood and crossed to the desk, looking down at this cousin he used to admire so much.

There was a long pause while Francis considered if he should continue the conversation. Finally, he looked up and added offhandedly, "I have no intention of letting him go to prison. Christopher knows too much — too much about you, me, everyone. And the hot pincers at Bridewell can really loosen a man's tongue." Thomas just stood there, afraid to speak. "He's served his purpose to the state and to the Queen, and so now, ..." Sir Francis paused searching for the right words "...I've been told we will have to arrange some ... sort of accident."

Thomas was stunned. "Francis, *you've* been told?! Nobody tells you to do anything except the Queen herself and she's not about to have Christopher killed. It's your fellow councilors in that bloody Privy Council, isn't it?"

"It has to be done. Because of the embarrassment he's caused you."

"Embarrassment to me? Francis, he's my *life!*"

"He's *not* your life, Thomas; he's a toy." Francis put down the quill and added with a cavalier attitude, "And like all toys, one day we must put them aside."

Thomas sat — almost collapsed — in the overstuffed chair opposite his cousin. He glanced around the room and, without looking at Francis asked "What are you going to do?"

Sir Francis was casual. "I'm not going to do anything. It's what *you're* going to do." He casually looked over to Thomas and continued. "Thomas, I'm telling you that *you* will have to kill your young lover. You'll be able to do it so much more easily -- and without the attention we'd get from a trial for England's foremost playwright." Sir Francis put down his quill and whispered, "I'm really doing, of course, is giving you the chance to have it done more humanely." He smiled and his voice once again became warm and pleasant. "See? Our bonds of blood do give you privilege."

"Francis, if these are the benefits of our bonds of blood, then pray I should be thankful we were not born brothers."

"I leave it to you. I *could* make it look like someone that Christopher spied on was going to even the score – very painfully and very messily."

Thomas sat, his hands folded, elbows on the chair armrests and his face on his hands. Sir Francis was going to rid himself of a sticky problem with neither risk nor sweat. And all under the guise of privileges from the bonds of blood. Finally, Thomas made a decision and raised his head. "I will handle it."

"And my friend Nicolas Skeres will be there when you do."

For the first time, Thomas's voice was tinged with sarcasm. "Skeres? To make it painful?"

"To make it certain."

"Christopher has such a gift. Why waste it?"

Sir Francis replied sanctimoniously. "Then you should ask, why should this gift be so squandered that it not give glory to its Giver. He's got to die."

"London's number one poet? The city will be outraged."

Ending the meeting with pomp, Francis went back to work. "London will see it as cheap little street brawl and say a wrathful God has taken His rightful revenge on a vile blasphemer. *And*, there will be no blood on our hands." Not looking up, "Thank you, Thomas."

Thomas stood slowly and headed for the door.

"Thomas, I'm giving you only ten days," Francis said. This, he felt was soon enough so his cousin could not back out of the arrangement or devise some way to avoid doing it. Thomas turned to protest, but without looking up, Francis raised a hand to stop him. "I said: ten days."

Thomas walked out of the building and onto the steps in the street, leaning on the doorway to catch his breath.

But he was still too confused to see Marlowe running toward him.

# CHAPTER 10

# THE PLOT

**M**arlowe ran up the steps. "Did you see Francis?" Thomas didn't seem to hear him. Christopher shook his arm. "What did he say?" Thomas was slowly coming back to reality. "Thomas, what did he say?"

Walsingham started to run through the streets, saying, "Let's get out of here."

Christopher ran after him.

As they ran past fruit stalls and vendors, Christopher yelled to Thomas, a few feet ahead. "But what did he say? What did he say?"

Thomas kept running. "He said to kill you."

Christopher grabbed Walsingham's arm, stopping him. "He said what!?"

"He said I had ten days to get you killed – or he will do it."

Marlowe was speechless; then suddenly he started to run. "I'll leave for Spain."

A few steps behind, Thomas called after him. "Christopher, you know they must be watching you. You run and Francis will have us *both* in prison. No. We have to fake something. Convince them that you've been killed."

Christopher stopped and turned to him. "Oh, *that* would fool everybody," he said, sarcasm deep in his voice.

Thomas had to think fast. He had to conclude a way to keep Marlowe from being arrested – and to keep him from running away. "We need to fake a death. Something on the estate. Make it look like a --"

"On the estate?" Christopher said. "Are you crazy? Francis is not that dumb. He might believe it if it were something at a very public place – maybe a local pub or ..." He started to run again.

Suddenly Thomas knew he had his partner hooked. Give a playwright a premise and he'll give you a plot. "There could be a fire," he called after Marlowe.

"Come on, Thomas," Christopher stopped to face him again. "It would have to be something that could be staged more easily. A fight with some cohorts -- and they stab me."

"We could use Cardwell and Phillips."

"No, no, no," Christopher disagreed, starting to run again. But by then he was completely wrapped up in the scheme "Cardwell is too smart for this. And Phillip's face would give it all away," he yelled to Thomas behind him.

"Maybe Frizer and Poley."

"That's better," Christopher said stopping. "Two coins without too much shine."

"Yes," Thomas acquiesced. "Frizer and Poley." After all, they were *not* his two sharpest employees, but they were his two most trusted. "Sure! Frizer and Poley. They stab you --"

"I secretly slip out and they a steal in a body."

"A body?"

"So they have proof," Marlowe said, "that there was a murder."

Walsingham played innocent. Naively, he suggested "Well, we *could* dig up a body from some grave and --" He timed his remark to the exact moment one of the death carts, piled high with dead bodies was crossing the street. Thomas looked away to keep from smiling.

"Dig up a body? Thomas, London's in the middle of a plague. Every morning a hundred bodies are thrown on the threshold for the death carts to carry away." He nodded toward the cart. "We grab one of those bodies -- carry it in -- I cry out -- and steal away."

"Think we could make it work?" Then Thomas suddenly looked troubled. "Oh, but what about a coroner's report?"

Of course. "The Queen's royal coroner," Christopher beamed. "Coroner William Danby – who guarantees results for every shilling."

"Who is so firm that can not be seduced?"

"But what about Skeres?"

For the first time in the conversation, Thomas was honestly thinking of a possible solution. "Cousin Francis will pay him well. But I know Skeres. He'll boast to me about how much he's being paid, probably lying and doubling the amount he's really getting. I'll have to top that. Sir Francis is willing to pay well to get rid of you." Thomas looked Christopher right into his green eyes. "But I am willing to pay more. Far more."

"Thomas, do you really think this could work?"

"We have no choice. And besides, I think you've just written the perfect murder scene."

"Yes," Christopher replied, suddenly realizing he had been duped. "And I wrote it just the way you wanted, didn't I?" The smile on his face was turning into a hearty laugh.

Thomas beamed. He enjoyed the fact that he had outsmarted Marlowe for his own sake, and also that Marlowe had seen through the charade. The laughter became infectious, as Walsingham leaned on a building to maintain his control.

"Well," Thomas said, "you're the master of the scenes of murder, my friend. But this had better be the best one you'll ever write. Or the hangman will quickly show us this is no laughing matter."

Marlowe was still smiling and confident. "*If we succeed*, it will be the greatest deception ever pulled on Cousin Francis. So screw your courage to the sticking point and we'll not fail."

Thomas stood tall and mockingly echoed Sir Francis's booming voice, "You have ten days. Only ten days."

Christopher leaned in to whisper, almost forehead to forehead with Thomas, "Mischief, thou art afoot ... and may Zeus and Minerva be with us." He smiled and tendered one of his wicked winks. "The plot begins."

They stepped back as another death cart rode past.

# CHAPTER 11

# MURDER

There had been only a few days to plan this, but there was no way to delay any longer. Sir Francis had specifically stated: get the "task" done within ten days, and it was day ten.

The man on the back of the death cart lay upside down, his head dragging in the street, his eyes open and glazed.

The death cart rolled along slowly, stopping at every doorstep that had a body lying there. The driver with the full gray beard plodded along with nonchalance, as if he were delivering vegetables.

Twenty meters behind the cart, two of Thomas Walsingham's intelligence-challenged employees, Ingram Frizer and Robert Poley, stealthily followed. If their sharp glances from side to side weren't enough to arouse suspicion, their hoods pulled murderously over their heads completed the picture. This, they felt, was going to be "murder at its finest".

But, because of the plague, there was practically no one on the street to see their splendid performance. The two of them created an odd-looking couple: Frizer, very tall, skinny and mustachioed, towered more than a full-head above stubby Poley with his baby face, long hair and waddling gait. The two of them begged to appear suspicious.

The ridiculousness of the scene was not lost on Sir Francis's stooge, Nicolas Skeres, who walked a few steps behind them. As a professional spy, he marveled at their "expertise," almost rolling his eyes at their awkward attempts to appear casual.

Skeres was a bulky, muscular man with a stern look that made him appear sinister and sneaky. He had tight lips and an explosive temper. He spoke with his fists. He had arrived at Scadbury Manor two days after the Walsingham's meeting with Sir Francis. His only statement was "I'm supposed to help you with some murder."

Walsingham remarked to Skeres that Sir Francis must be paying him well for such an assignment. This met with a curt "Real, *real* well." After that there were no discussions of ethics or loyalty – only price.

The cart stopped at the next doorway and the driver headed to the threshold to pick up a body lying on the doorsteps, a body draped in a coat too expensive for the neighborhood clientele.

As the driver stooped to lift what he thought was a dead body, it suddenly sat up, grabbed him around the neck and planted a big, sloppy kiss right on the driver's mouth. It was Marlowe.

In utter panic, the driver ran back to the wagon and shouted to the horse, "Go! *GO!*"

As the wagon pulled away Frizer and Poley each grabbed an arm of the body hanging over the back of the cart. They had their corpse.

Marlowe, sitting on the stoop of the house, shook with laughter as Skeres rolled his eyes in reaction to what this "magnificent team" must have considered a polished and professional style.

A short distance down the next street awaited a horse and wagon piled high with straw. Frizer and Poley sat and pulled the body up onto the wagon and covered it with loose straw. Skeres grabbed the reins and Marlowe sat next to him on the driver's bench as the wagon pulled away.

A few minutes down the road, the body began slowly slipping off the wagon. Frizer and Poley, enjoying the ride and sipping from a bottle, noticed nothing until they were all startled by the sound of the body hitting the cobblestone street.

The two jumped from the wagon, and, as they lifted the body under each arm, another wagon came down the road. With no attempt to appear drunk, the two of them, staggering down the road, dragging the dead man, a bottle in Poley's hand, gave the impression of a trio of drinkers enjoying an early binge. Why not? It was London and it was ten in the morning.

Skeres buried his head in embarrassment.

After re-loading the corpse, the wagon finally arrived behind the rooming house of Widow Eleanor Bull, in Deptford on the Thames, three miles outside of London. Frizer and Poley lifted the body, one at the feet and the other under the arms. Going up the steps to the back door, Frizer went to one side of a wooden support and Poley to the other. Looking at Marlowe, Skeres slowly shook his head.

As they entered the door, the collar of the dead man's blouse caught on the handle. With utter disdain, Skeres gingerly lifted the collar and gave the two a weak smile.

The back room of the inn, which was intended for eating and drinking, was empty. Trying to be as quiet as possible, Skeres lifted a tankard from the table to clear it. He looked around for someone to hand it to. Both Frizer and Poley reached out to grab the tankard and the body dropped to the floor with a loud thud.

Misses Bull, in the next room, heard the noise and called out, "Hello? Hello? Is that you, Mr. Marlowe?"

In a scene of panic, Frizer and Poley scurried to drop the body into a storage bin under a bench and the two of them, along with Skeres, quickly sat innocently on the bench. There was a problem, however. One of the dead man's arms didn't quite make it into the box and his hand extended right between Poley's legs. Skeres saw it and lifted the lid – with the two men sitting on it – and quickly tucked in the hand – just as Misses Bull entered. Poley's look of surprise revealed that he had no idea what Skeres was doing between his legs.

Missus Bull was a portly woman, well over fifty, but still had flame-colored hair and a pinch of red in her cheeks. She was always smiling.

"Mr. Marlowe. How nice to see you again. Sir Thomas sent word that gen'lmen would be 'ere today."

The three benchwarmers smiled back sheepishly. Marlowe said, "Why, it's good to see you again, Missus Bull."

"I've got a nice surprise for you gen'lmen today. I've arranged for the four of you to spend the day in m' own parlor instead of this small back room. You'll be a lot more comtable and it's a mite warmer upstairs too. So just grab yer things and follow me." She smiled.

Skeres looked at the bench with the body barely tucked inside and opened his mouth to answer her.

"Now, that's very thoughtful of you, Missus Bull," Marlowe broke in, "but we'll just stay here in the back room. No need to fuss over us."

"Why no fuss there. I had another bunch of blokes coming today from Brighton but they's comin' no more. So you can have the parlor. I 'ready set some food for you there."

"Missus Bull," Skeres said rather forcefully, going to the door and looking out. "It be best we stay right here. I borrowed that wagon and nag from my neighbor and I should keep a watch on it."

"Are you sure you don't want --"

"No," Skeres said forcefully and sat on the bench again.

The smile on her face faded a bit and she seemed a little disappointed. "Well, fine then. You gen'lmen jist make yourself comfy and I'll get you some nice hot tea."

Frizer and Poley looked as if they'd been shot.

Skeres suggested innocently, "And, maybe four tankards of ale?" Missus Bull gave a look of "whatever" and headed into the next room. "Large ones?" Skeres called out as she left.

\* \* \* \* \*

It was hours later, as they waited for supper, when boredom began to set in. Skeres was playing a solitary game, balancing a dagger on the finger nails of his closed fist. He would then flip the knife, sending the dagger into the air and landing with the blade sticking into the table. Each time he would decide on his points depending on how close he came to the pile of wooden splinters in the center of the table. He would then grab a few of the sticks and repeat the knife toss.

Frizer and Poley sat, chatting and drinking with each other. Marlowe was reading from a small sheet of paper.

The body was beginning to give off a faint but peculiar smell.

Missus Bull entered with a large plate of sausages and placed them proudly in the center of the table. "I'll be right back with some bread and spinach."

As she turned to leave, she sniffed and turned her head questioningly. Without turning their heads, Skeres and Frizer gave a knowing glance toward Poley, who was not at all pleased with the implication.

\* \* \* \* \*

It was almost two hours later. Skeres gave the dagger blade one last flip into the table top and scattered all the wooden splinters onto the floor. *It was time.*

Frizer and Poley tried to pull the body from the storage area as quietly as they could, but kept bumping the head and almost lost a leg. Skeres's cold stare told them how disgusted he really was. He was shielding the body from the door in case Missus Bull should hear the noise and walk in again. The body now had on Marlowe's cloak, scarf and cap.

Guarding the door, Skeres reached for the dagger behind him and handed Poley the knife, indicating to him to "do it." The look on Poley's face conveyed clearly that he was not at all comfortable with that. So Frizer grabbed the dagger and appraised the body, trying to decide where best to stab it.

Frizer looked confused. Here? No, there? In desperation Skeres grabbed the dagger and just plunged it aimlessly into the body, stabbing directly into the right eye. Blood splashed everywhere. Without a second thought, Skeres took his hand and smeared the blood all over the dead man's face.

Then he nodded to Marlowe who headed for the back door and started screaming, "No, no, get away from me. I said get away from me."

Skeres kicked over bench after bench as Marlowe let out a loud cry and left the back way. Skeres and Frizer added to the mayhem by yelling at each other as Poley knocked over the table.

Missus Bull swung open the kitchen door and stood in the doorway, gaping at the three men and the bloody body.

"Oh, no! Mr. Marlowe! *Mr. Marlowe*!"

She began to scream hysterically as Skeres threw the bloody knife across the room, sticking it into the top of the table.

Missus Bull kept screaming. And screaming. And screaming.

# PART 2

# The
# Investigation

## CHAPTER 12

# SUSPICIONS

"The details of the murder? Well, they were – to say the least – very peculiar," Constable Henry Maunder was saying as he picked up and examined a large metal portfolio. The word "XTOFER" was hammered into the cover.

"Peculiar?" Walsingham looked puzzled.

"Very."

Walsingham didn't seem to be distraught. "Well, I don't suppose any murder would seem ordinary."

"But this one, Sir Thomas, is the most unusual murder I've ever investigated," Maunder said, his voice echoing throughout the Grand Hall.

"And that's why you're here today?"

"Well, yes. To check on some of the facts of the case."

"So, you must be here today not as the Queen's Royal Messenger but rather as Constable Maunder – to investigate a murder?

"Well, yes -- officially."

Walsingham smiled. "What other reason would you be here – except officially?"

Being a fair gamesman, Maunder gave Walsingham a faint you-got-me-there smile. "And this is …?" he asked, indicating the metal portfolio.

"A portfolio I had made for Mr. Marlowe before he was killed. He kept leaving sheets of writing everywhere." The constable looked quizzically at the word "XTOFER" hammered into the cover, and Walsingham went on. "It says 'Christopher' – the way it's often spelled."

"And pronounced?"

"Christopher." Thomas raised his eyebrows as if to say, "How else?"

"Oh," Maunder added, still trying to digest the spelling. "But didn't you call him 'Kit'?"

"All of his close friends called him 'Kit'. He liked the name," Thomas said, adding no further details. "Now, then, what can I do for you, *Inspector* Maunder?"

The Constable looked around the Grand Hall – banners hanging on every wall in tribute to major events in the history of the Walsingham family. He took a small document from his pocket and examined it for a moment. "There are some details I thought maybe you could help me with."

"Why me, Constable? I wasn't even there."

"Well, you were Mr. Marlowe's patron. And If I understand correctly, he was living here at the time of his death."

"To avoid the black plague in London."

"Uh -- yes," Maunder mumbled, indicating he knew better. "And two of the witnesses there that day were both in your employ – including …" he stopped to look at his notes, "Ingrim Frizer, the man charged with the murder."

"Coincidentally," Thomas said casually.

"A quarrel between your ward and one of your employees?" Maunder asked, feigning slight surprise. Walsingham said nothing, giving the question the aura of being inconsequential. "An odd group, don't you think, Sir Thomas? Poet Marlowe with those three rather rough gents?" Thomas shrugged innocently. "So, if my facts are correct,"

Maunder began, consulting his notes again, "the four of them went to the public house of the Widow Bull, a friend of yours." The Constable looked up for agreement but Walsingham just smiled. "At about ten o'clock in the morning?"

"So I was told."

Maunder checked a note and asked innocently, "Don't you ordinarily use Mr. Poley as your courier?"

"Yes -- usually."

"It seems Mr. Poley had just returned that very morning from Holland where you had sent him as a courier, correct?" Maunder began.

"How did you ever learn that?" Thomas asked, sincerely surprised.

Maunder didn't bother to answer. Instead he asked, naively, "Since he returned early that morning, there must have been an urgent reason to send him all the way to Widow Bull's in Deptford."

Thomas took a moment to think, completely unconcerned. "Oh, I remember. There were some chores I wanted Frizer to do for me and forgotten to tell him. So I sent Poley with the message."

"But, Sir Thomas, Mr. Frizer didn't leave Deptford that day to handle any chores."

"They were chores for the next day."

"Oh," Maunder said, realizing he had been bested, and then went back to his notes. "It seems that these men had been involved in other murders previously."

Walsingham looked as if he were trying to remember. "I think I've heard those rumors, too."

Maunder smiled and went back to his notes. "They had lunch, sat around talking, drinking, and smoking throughout the afternoon. Then, let's see: Widow Bull served them dinner about six in the evening. Then after dinner, Mr. Marlowe and Mr. Frizer began quarrelling ...." He checked his notes and went on, "...about the payment of the bill and the reckoning thereof. Mr. Marlowe grabbed Frizer's knife, gave him some small cuts on the arm. Then Mr. Frizer grabbed his knife back and stabbed Mr. Marlowe in the right eye, killing him instantly."

Thomas shrugged as if to add "so I've been told."

"You don't seem too upset by this, Sir Thomas."

"I'm terribly upset," he said casually, his demeanor belying his words.

Maunder smiled. The game was getting better. "Uh -- yes, of course. Now, Widow Bull's place is in the small village of Deptford, about three miles outside of London, isn't it?" he asked, consulting his notes.

Walsingham smiled. "Constable, you know where Deptford is as well as I."

"Uh -- yes."

Thomas took the metal portfolio from the Constable. "Well, then, Inspector, I imagine you have many other informed people you want to talk to."

As Thomas placed the portfolio down, Maunder continued, "But there were those 'peculiarities' I was talking about."

"All right," Thomas said and sat down in a dark green 200-year-old ornate chair with a velvet seat. It gave the Grand Hall a stately air.

Maunder sat on a bench near him and looked puzzled. "I've been wondering, what the four of them could have been doing there for eight hours."

"Well, as *you* just told *me* a few minutes ago, they had lunch, talked, drank, smoked and then had dinner."

"Oh, yes, that's right." Maunder enjoyed losing a point in a good game almost as much as winning one. But, he went on. "I read the report of Coroner Danby. It's hard to believe but *it's identical – word for word* – to the burial records at Saint Nicolas Church. The same errors and irregularities in each. The church record must have been copied directly from the Coroner's report."

When Walsingham said nothing, Maunder went on. "The killer's name is wrong. He's listed in each report as Francis Archer – not Ingram Frizer." Walsingham shrugged. "And the date is listed as the first of June instead of 30 May. And the victim is listed as Morley –

not Marlowe." Here he checked his notes. "...though the coroner did correct that later."

"Well, we both know William Danby," Walsingham said mockingly, "... the infamous 'Coroner to the Household of our Lady the Queen.' That's probably the closest he's ever come to getting things correct."

"Though it's a bit confusing and quite inaccurate, the coroner's report is so very, *very* detailed and really amazing in many respects. Pages and pages about who was sitting where, and how they all moved about the room during the quarrel, and that Frizer's wounds were only a quarter inch deep, and Marlow's stab was about two inches deep but it killed him instantly. One wonders how the men were able to remember such details during the excitement of the fight and murder. And the report is very specific that the killing was really self-defense."

"Hmm," Thomas said thoughtfully. "Then I would agree: really quite detailed." He stood up. "Well, if you have no more questions, we could --"

"Just two more items, Sir Thomas, if you don't mind."

Walsingham nodded and sat again. "Mr. Marlowe was buried in an unmarked grave in the St. Nicolas churchyard." Maunder looked up from the paper. Walsingham said nothing. "I went by the church and could see no recent grave. Old pastor Collins seemed to remember being told about the quick burial, but wasn't quite sure when it was or where the site was." Maunder looked at Walsingham incredulously. "Is it possible that Christopher Marlowe, England's most famous writer, was quickly buried *unceremoniously* in an unmarked grave in some insignificant rural village churchyard?"

Echoing the words of his Cousin Francis, Thomas replied as if he were delivering a homily. "Well, as Sir Francis worded it, 'It appears that a wrathful God has taken his rightful revenge on a vile blasphemer.'"

Maunder seemed confused by the remark, but went on. "And the second thing: yesterday my office received a Writ of Certiorari pardoning Ingram Frizer. And it was witnessed by the Queen herself."

Walsingham tried to look impressed. "How kind of the Queen to recognize the injustice of imprisoning an innocent man."

"It was less than two weeks," Maunder protested. "I receive pardons all the time – but they always take many, many months."

"Well, it's nice to know that the Queen is right on top of things." (Thomas savored how quickly Cousin Francis had gotten the pardon issued; realizing Cousin Francis obviously had not told Maunder about this.) Finally, Thomas stood and said, "Once again, if you ever have any more questions, Constable, consider Scadbury your second home."

Henry Maunder smiled at the gentle jibe and nodded. "Sir Thomas," he bid goodbye and headed for the door.

"Uh, Constable..." Walsingham stopped him. "Did my cousin Francis suggest you drop by today to get more information?"

"Well, actually, Sir Thomas," Maunder slowly turned back, "when we were discussing the case, Sir Francis thought it might be wise to clear up some of the facts before the record was finalized." He had an innocent, noncommittal air.

There was a moment of silence before Thomas nodded. "Of course."

"Good day, Sir Thomas," the inspector replied as he turned and left.

Christopher, who had been listening from the balcony, walked down the steps. "Well, Maunder the Marvelous was after the pound of flesh nearest the heart."

Walsingham stared out the door wondering. "And Cousin Francis suspects that there is something rotten in Scadbury."

Christopher walked to the doorway to stand beside Thomas.

Walsingham looked at his young lover and could tell he was frightened, worried, and anxious. Thomas pulled Marlowe close and leaned Christopher's head onto his own shoulder.

## CHAPTER 13

# OMENS OF TROUBLE

They stood there silently in the Grand Hall, Christopher's head on his partner's shoulder.

"Cousin Francis suspects something," Walsingham finally said.

"Why do you think that?"

"Well, by now Skeres has told Francis far more than the Constable knows. And if Cousin Francis didn't suspect something, he wouldn't have sent the Constable to fish for more information." Thomas began thinking it through. "And Francis can't tell the Constable that he ordered the killing or that he's been busy getting the Queen to set Frizer free – which he did in less than two weeks."

"Do you think you can trust your servants to say nothing about my being here?" Christopher finally asked.

"Worry not. They have all been part of this household for years."

"And why did Maunder keep asking what we did all day," Marlowe wondered walking to the huge window overlooking the garden.

"What *did* take so long?"

"Well, first of all we had to ride three miles into town to find a body. Then we had to wait for Widow Bull to leave us alone long enough to get the body dressed in my clothes. I thank all the gods on

Mount Olympus that I will never have to use those two idiots to do a murder scene on stage."

"Did you really bury the body?"

"Frizer and Poley said they dug up a little dirt but I think they finally threw the body into the Thames – right behind Widow Bull's place."

Walsingham was still analyzing. "Right now the main issue seems to be the overly zealous coroner's report."

"I think Coroner Danby tried to give you your money's worth and overdid it a bit."

Thomas was confused. "He was told the murderer was to be Ingram Frizer. Where did he get that *other* name, somebody Archer?"

"Where he gets everything. He pulled it right out of his arse. But he must have put every brainless detail he got from Poley and Frizer into the report. Could be a problem."

Thomas worked to allay Christopher's fears. "Probably not. The coroner's been paid; Skeres has been topped off rather generously; and Frizer and Poley work for me. What can the Constable possibly prove? Nothing," he said confidently, not quite believing it himself.

Christopher did not seem to be buying the argument but took the opportunity to change the subject -- to *a very sensitive issue*. He began harmlessly enough. "By the way, I finished *All's Well that Ends Well*."

Thomas was familiar with that "innocent" tone of voice. "And – so?"

Christopher was matter-of-fact. "And, so -- I'd like to see the Rose Theatre present it."

"Well, that's no problem," Thomas agreed. "You just walk over there, hand them the script and then check into Bridewell Prison on the way back."

"We can say I had written it before I died and you just found it." It was clear that Christopher was waiting for that argument.

"We could say that ..." Thomas seemed to agree, "... for one play. Maybe two. But then those would have to be the last you could write.

I can't keep finding new scripts every month in old drawers in the anteroom. Wouldn't that make Constable Maunder suspicious – not to mention Cousin Francis."

"Thomas, writing is my life."

"And could just as easily be your death."

Thomas thought for a few moments and then suggested "Perhaps – if you want – we could try to find someone else to take them to the theatre and say he wrote them."

"Are you out of your mind? Let someone else take credit for my work. I wouldn't give them to anyone else. Not even that traitor Thomas Kyd. He certainly has been afraid to come around here since he got out of prison."

Thomas had been trying to shield Christopher from the facts, but could do so no more. "He hasn't come around because he's dead." Then, deciding it would be best to tell Christopher everything, he added, "Before he was released he got the 'writer's special.' They broke all his fingers."

"He's dead?"

"Topcliffe did his work well, even making sure he didn't die until after he got out of Bridewell."

Christopher leaned on the table trying to comprehend all this. "He was only thirty-six." He walked to the open door, leaned on the doorway and stared at the piles and piles of fallen leaves. After a long, long time, he said, "Thomas, those were *my* papers."

"I know, Christopher. I know."

"And I blamed *him* for my arrest. I was the one who got those papers and he ...." Marlowe stared out the open door. "He was right, wasn't he? I sin and others suffer."

Thomas mind was scrambling for any topic that would change the subject. "That's why you can never make anyone suspicious that you may be writing. Yes, he was only thirty-six. But imagine what people will be saying about you. Marlowe was only twenty-nine." But Christopher didn't seem to be listening. "So now, Kit, you have three choices: stop writing – or let someone else present the plays -- or die."

61

Christopher wasn't really listening. "Thomas, aren't all three options the same?"

"Kyd was only 36," Thomas repeated quietly.

Christopher put down the script and silently left the library.

## CHAPTER 14

# THE REPORT

onstable Maunder waited in the outer office of Sir Francis. This was not going to be easy.

At a meeting three days prior, Sir Francis had told him, "Something is wrong, here, Constable. No, that's not right. *Everything* is wrong. That stupid coroner's report, the unmarked grave, Frizer's back working for my cousin Thomas. Yes, everything about that bloody murder is wrong. Does Thomas think I'm a fool?"

Of course, Sir Francis couldn't tell Maunder that he was the one who actually ordered the murder.

And sending the unknowing Constable to "check the details" would certainly give the impression that Sir Francis had nothing to do with it.

But something was bothering Sir Francis. Something wasn't right.

He had sat there, tapping his stubby fingers on the desk, thinking it through. "Here's what I want you to do," he had finally told Maunder. "Get out to Scadbury. Check every detail about that day. *Every detail!* Thomas is clever, but, if there's anything wrong, he'll slip up somewhere."

So, this report was not going to be easy. Sir Francis was not going to want to hear what Maunder's visit to Scadbury the previous day had uncovered: nothing. Nothing really.

At their meeting Sir Thomas had been relaxed, and as smooth as the marble statues in the Grand Hall. He had just casually shrugged off most of the Constable's questions and nonchalantly agreed with almost everything else Maunder brought up.

*Yes*, he was upset that his new ward and one of his employees had obviously been fighting.

*Yes*, he was astonished that the coroner's report and the church burial records were identical -- word for word – and yet almost completely erroneous.

*Yes*, he found it was weird that the murderer's name was wrong on both documents and later changed.

And, *yes*, it was rather shocking that the Queen had issued a Writ of Certiorari pardoning Frizer so quickly. Maunder mulled that last fact over and over in his mind wondering if Sir Francis didn't already know about the pardon when he sent him to see his cousin. Yes, obviously Sir Francis already knew, but was pretending ignorance about it.

Even the Constable's two surprise cards he played had gotten no reaction. Certainly, Sir Thomas was amazed when he had learned that Poley had returned that same morning from a trip to the Netherlands. But he had an unruffled explanation that defied any attacks.

And to explain the unceremonious burial, Thomas had cleverly dodged the question by quoting Sir Francis, "It appears that a wrathful God has taken his rightful revenge on a vile blasphemer."

Though none of that made sense, it did not give Maunder anything to work on.

And Sir Francis was not going to be thrilled with what little his visit had gleaned.

The Constable was about to learn that "*not going to be_thrilled*" was a bit of an understatement. He waited a bit nervously until a newly-installed member of the Privy Council, looking red-faced and very harassed, walked slowly out of the inner office, leaving the massive doors opens.

As he did, Maunder heard Sir Francis thunder, "And send the Constable in."

No, this was certainly not going to be easy.

## CHAPTER 15

# POSSIBLE SOLUTION

Christopher was sitting on the balcony of the tower off the west wing, writing furiously. The sun felt warm and the ink was drying quickly as it flowed from his favorite writing tool -- the white swan quill with a bright red tip.

Christopher felt that the west tower was the ideal place to write. The windows on all sides made it the brightest place in the manor. And from the top, one could see the entire estate and all the countryside.

He was aware of how different he felt since he had moved in with Thomas a year before. His plays had become more sensitive, and even lighter and more humorous. And Christopher was finally learning to write more complex roles for female characters. He had begun to write soliloquies not only to advance the plot but also to relay to the audience what the actor was thinking or feeling. This opened up a whole new way of developing characters.

Thomas had taken off some of the edge from his life and made living a little more even keeled. And Thomas would lightly admonish him for using any references about men loving other men.

The plays Marlowe wrote (once he moved in with Thomas) were far more subtle – nothing like what he had written under his own name in his play *Edward II*. (True, homosexuality was considered to be an acceptable predilection of "the noble and well born". But even sophisticated Londoners were not ready for this *on stage*. And, so graphically presented.)

Marlowe had *not* been very discreet. It was the last play he had written before he "died." Even though it was based on historical facts of England's King, Edward II, it was still ground breaking to portray a monarch who casts aside his wife, Queen Isabel, for his lover, a man named Gaveston. And the thinly-veiled but obscene parody at the end didn't fool anyone either. The King is killed on his own bed with a red-hot spit forced up into his bowels. (Even Christopher admitted: this was *not* the kind of performance one wanted to see immediately before dinner – and, of course, the end did parody the King's illicit love making.) But *Edward II* had become an instant success and there seemed to be no backlash from Marlowe's honest but brutal adaptation of the story.

But there was one element of the play that continued to haunt him. When the King is separated from his lover, Gaveston, his love ebbs to a younger man, Spencer. He remembered Thomas Kyd's remark to Thomas. "*But just wait, Walsingham. He'll do the same to you someday*." He hoped the implication of a man going from one lover to the next would never occur to Thomas as an ominous foreboding of their own relationship.

His thoughts were so intense that he hadn't heard Walsingham come to the door and stand there, watching him. Finally Thomas said, "Kit, we have some guests downstairs."

Christopher returned from his reverie and leaned over the balcony to look into the garden.

"And hiding, I notice," he said suspiciously. "From whom? Me?" Walsingham always found it challenging to try to deceive Christopher. "I see Wriothesley and his French cat in the garden. Who else?"

Thomas grinned brightly. This was going to be a real challenge. "An inspiring, young thespian from the Rose Theatre by the name of Will Shakespeare."

"The guy who holds horses for the gentry while they're in watching the plays?" Shakespeare, who occasionally did appear on stage, was better known at that time for the horse-sitting job he did more frequently.

"Please, Kit, he's had three stage walk-ons. *Three*."

Marlowe could smell when something wasn't right. "What do you want with him?"

"He's, uh… well …" Thomas began. "He's about to offer his two new plays to the Rose Theatre."

"What plays? He doesn't write plays."

Thomas's reply was straightforward, "*King Lear* and *All's Well That Ends Well.*"

"Have you taken leave of your senses, Thomas? *My plays?*"

Marlowe was turning purple and showing the veins in his neck and forehead.

Thomas quietly walked over to him and seated Christopher directly in front of him, his hands firmly on both of Kit's shoulders. He began to explain very, very slowly and very, very carefully. "Now. You told me you wanted a way to get them staged."

"Let someone else take credit for my work," Christopher fumed and tried to stand up. "Oh, no. No -- *No* -- *NO!*"

Thomas pushed him down into the seat again. "Then stop writing because they'll never be performed."

Christopher was livid. "This thing with Shakespeare would never work. At the theatre he's known as Horsy Will the Pony Man. You could have picked anyone but him."

"Like who?" Thomas asked. "Ben Jonson?"

"Well, no. People could tell my plays weren't written by Jonson. But how about someone not so well known?"

"Like Thomas Nashe?"

"Well, no …"

"Or Robert Greene?"

"He's dead, just like me."

"You see? Not only would your style be so different from any other writer, but the combined output by both of you would appear to be too much coming from one human being."

"But Pony Bill Shakespeare? He's never *written* anything."

"That's it exactly. He has no works for others to compare to your writing. He's an unknown and will certainly stay that way. Anyone better known would only draw attention," Thomas countered, sitting down next to Marlowe. "He'll be just one more unknown who's writing for one of the many theatres of London. Who is *ever* going to remember a name like William Shakespeare?"

"I don't know, Thomas. Really? Hitching Post Willy?" Then after a second, he added "And Wriothesley?"

Thomas smiled innocently. "Well, it would have looked suspicious for me to sponsor young Will after I had been your patron. We don't want to raise suspicions. So Henry has generously agreed to be his sponsor."

Playwrights and actors needed patrons, not only for financial reasons but because of the law. The various troops of actors wandering all over England were considered to be vagrants and often the cause of every problem in the country from thievery to the plague. Consequently, the Second Act of Congress of 1592 – the Vagrancy Act -- laid down all kinds of laws not really designed to regulate actors so much as to try to drive them away. (It read: "Unlicensed vagabonds, common players, and minstrels, not belonging to any baron or other personage of greater degree can, by law, be whipped, have their noses cut off or burned through the ear.") As a result, most actors, playwrights and theatre companies searched out a patron, who afforded them a measure of protection. The patron benefited by having his name carried throughout the country, offering him free publicity and prestige. Thomas Kyd was one of the few who frequently did not have a patron and the eventual effect on his life only emphasized the importance of having one.

"Wriothesley?" Marlowe asked with sarcasm. "You want Wriothesley to be his patron? You don't think that would make it even *more* suspicious? Henry's got a reputation for sleeping with boys as young as fourteen." Here he waved a finger, correcting himself, "No -- *twelve*."

"*Well, look at the righteous bigot casting the first stone,*" Thomas said knowing that Christopher's outrage was beginning to wane and was veering away from the subject of the plays.

Christopher took the bait. "Lord Walsingham," he proclaimed pompously, "You're going to give people the idea that theatre is populated by men who sleep with other men. Are you one of those who believe that – as it's worded -- 'actors have ambiguous sexuality'?"

Walsingham turned to Marlowe with a look of shock. He stood tall and looked around. "Mr. Marlowe, *theatre is a rough, tough profession.* I promise you, it will never get the reputation of being clustered with lewd lovers…" he added, haughtily surveying the scene, "…lewd lovers of other men."

Christopher concurred with macho mock disdain, "I pray not, Milord. I pray not."

With that they smilingly descended the spiral staircase and entered the library, almost like two proud monarchs.

At that moment, the garden door opened and Henry Wriothesley bubbled in – *avec le chat.*

# CHAPTER 16

# SHAKESPEARE

"**T**homas ... Thomas ..." Henry seemed frustrated as he entered, combing the fur of a brown and white feline named Jacques. Wriothesley didn't have cats. He had felines. All with French names.

Thomas looked around. "Henry, where is young Will?"

Wriothesley look flustered and glanced into the garden. "I told him to wait a moment." Christopher caught the glimpse of exasperation on Thomas's face. "Thomas ... Thomas ... how do I say it? Couldn't we have found someone a bit more -- 'receptive?'"

Christopher rolled his eyes and became very formal. "Henry, would you define the term 'more receptive' for me?"

"He's really not that --"

"Attractive?" Christopher finished for him. "Oh, my poor Henry Heartbreak. I've been told Will the Horse Man has been sleeping with every wench in London. And probably some horses too. So, I'm sorry but I think he'll *only* be interested in presenting his writings to you in the parlor." Christopher let the tone of his voice drop an octave. "And not in the boudoir."

"Really, Kit. You know what I mean."

"I think I do, Henry," Christopher mused, and then turned to Thomas. "Me thinkest the lady protests too much, Milord."

Thomas ignored the petty repartee. "For the record, Henry," he began, consulting a sheaf of notes at the desk, "Shakespeare has had little schooling. He left when he was fifteen. He has a wife, Anne, and three children that he seems to have left and almost forgotten in Stratford. At the time he married her, he was also seeing another woman. But when he learned that Anne was three months pregnant, they married. He was only eighteen and she was twenty-six -- eight years older than he, and ... uh ... there seems to be no information about what he's been doing for the last eight years." Walsingham mumbled a bit, skipping over most of the rest, finally adding "... and, yes, he *is* sleeping with anything and everything in town."

Christopher sang the next line, "Just so long as it's female." Wriothesley ignored the remark. "And there you are, Henry," Christopher added with mock seriousness. "Finally a chance to do some actual good for a needy and lost individual."

"The way Thomas is doing for you?"

Christopher gave him a fake smile. "May the sparks from our fireplace ignite your cod piece."

Thomas had had enough of the banter and opened the garden door. "Won't you join us, Will?"

"It's William," he said entering.

Thomas corrected himself. "William."

Shakespeare and Marlowe were both born in 1564: so they were the same age: twenty-nine. True, no one considered Shakespeare to be good looking, but that wasn't what really made him unattractive. He had a wide neck, big thick hands, and an expression that made people feel he either wasn't paying attention or didn't understand what was being said. His forehead receded all the way back past the top of his head, and he wore the bushy crop of black hair beyond that point in a fluffy orb that reached down to the back of his neck. His tiny mustache and miniature goatee seemed to drop his facial features noticeably lower and made the forehead look even larger. For some reason, he had the air of someone who should hold horses at the theatre rather than write plays.

Christopher was too, too charming for words. "A joyous pleasure to meet you, William. I'm the late Christopher Marlowe." He tilted his head and proudly smiled at Thomas.

"Yes, I know," Shakespeare said. "I've been in three of your plays. Well ... two."

"How wonderful. Big roles?" Marlowe oozed interest.

"Nothing special."

"Will," Walsingham began.

"You can call me William."

"William, you left Stratford rather suddenly." Shakespeare nodded. "Why?"

"They said I was poaching deer from one of the local estates. But it was a lie."

"Yes, from the estate of a Mr. Thomas Lucy. Were you convicted," Walsingham asked.

"It was all very confusing, Milord."

"Yes, I'm sure, Will – William," Thomas decided to skip the rest of the questions and put the sheets down. "But let's make sure we've got everything clear. First of all, as I told you yesterday, you will receive all instructions from Sir Wriothesley. If you have any questions, he will get the answers from us and give them to you." Thomas could see Christopher seething at the phrase "as I told you *yesterday*." There obviously had been collusion. Marlowe gave Thomas a frozen smile. The meaning was not lost on either of them.

Thomas went on. "Then you will receive manuscripts of two or three plays a year from Sir Wriothesley. Henry grinned, a little too broadly. "These you will copy in your own handwriting and present for presentation to the Rose Theatre." He took two from the table and handed them to Shakespeare. "Here are the first two."

Looking at the scripts, Shakespeare read, *"King Lear"* ... and *"All's Well."*

"*That Ends Well*," Marlowe added, not to be edited.

"If the copying becomes too much work, we have a scrivener who will help you."

"Oh, don't worry about that, Milord," he said proudly. "I write good." Christopher rolled his eyes.

"When the Rose Theatre has produced them, you will receive one fifth of all payments for these plays."

Marlowe glared at Walsingham, who continued hurriedly, mainly to cut off Christopher from any tirade. "And, of course, you will receive the glory and recognition for having written them."

Marlowe walked to the garden door to fume and calm himself.

"Are we clear, William?"

"Yes, Milord."

"Most importantly, you are to discuss this with *no one*. Not theatre owners, cast members -- and especially not with Constable Maunder or anyone connected with the Privy Council." He took a moment to let this sink in. "*No one*." Walsingham looked to Shakespeare for agreement.

"Of course, Milord."

"If you get any inquiries – no matter how simple or obvious – you simply tell them that, out of respect, you graciously defer to your sponsor *all* questions about your plays."

"And poems," Christopher added, in a tone to goad Thomas.

"Poems?" Walsingham looked undone.

Innocently, just to irritate him, "A few."

"We all have to remember: if anyone would learn of this, we all will probably die." The sound of Thomas's voice conjured up images of public hangings and spikes driven into the ears. There was a uncomfortable moment of silence as no one looked at anyone else.

"Oh, William," Henry finally broke the spell and chimed in. "I'm so excited that you will be my new … ward."

Christopher cleared his throat.

"Most important," Thomas said, "and this is for all of us – we are the only four people in the world who can ever know about this pact." With this, he took the hand of Shakespeare on one side and Wriothesley on the other.

"Agreed?"

"Agreed."

"Agreed."

Thomas looked at Christopher and said firmly, with meaning, "Agreed?"

Christopher answered so sweetly. "Oh, *agreed*." Mischievously Kit took the other hand of Henry on one side and Shakespeare on the other making a full circle. Slowly he raised all their arms to the heavens in mock ritual. Solemnly, he intoned, "And when shall we four meet again? In thunder, lightning or in rain. When the hurly-burlys done. When this deception's lost or won …"

Marlowe raised his gaze to the heavens in exaltation.

To Christopher's surprise the gods gave no answer. No thunder. No lightning. Nothing.

# CHAPTER 17

# INTERROGATION

There was a knock on the door of Sr. Francis's private chambers. "Yes?" he asked.

Nicolas Skeres stepped inside and stood by the door. "You wanted to see me, Sir Francis?"

"Oh, yes, Skeres. Come in." Sir Francis nodded to a chair and Skeres sat. "I wanted to talk to you about that little job I sent you to do almost a year ago."

"Little job?" Skeres felt uncomfortable. He *knew* what little job.

"Yes, the one with Poet Marlowe," Sir Francis continued slowly, carefully. "Now I realize that my cousin, Sir Thomas, was very fond of Mr. Marlowe. And knowing my cousin as well as I do, I'm sure he took every precaution to try to preserve Mr. Marlowe's – what shall I say? – '*safety*' perhaps?"

Skeres was beginning to sweat. He saw what was coming.

"And, so it would be only natural for my cousin to do anything he could to protect Poet Marlowe. I'm sure he considered even, how shall I put it, '*pretending*' to have him killed … and offering you a hefty bounty to – how should I word it? –'to just ignore the doings?' I ask this only because Constable Maunder tells me he keeps finding so many peculiarities connected with the poet's death."

Skeres' puzzled smile contrasted with the small bead of sweat he could feel forming on his forehead.

"So I thought: it's been such a long time that I'll just ask Mr. Skeres about this? I could assure him that there would be no repercussions and – most importantly – I could ... I could ... '*reward*' Skeres with a very nice bounty?"

Sir Francis smiled. "Yes, that's it. A very *substantial* bounty."

Skeres smiled weakly and tried to look interested. But, inside, he just wanted to evaporate.

\* \* \* \* \*

It was less than two hours later and Skeres was in a similar inquisition in the study at Scadbury. "And what did *you* say?" Thomas asked.

"Well, I remembered that you had warned me that Sir Francis might do that. So I jist said, 'Sir Francis, I han't heard nothin' of what yer talkin' – the unmarked grave and that crazy coroner report and all that stuff. You told me to jist be sure he was dead and so whin I saw all the blood and his brains all over the place, I jist left." Skeres smiled now, breaking character. He was rather proud of his performance.

"Fine, Skeres," Thomas began. "And, as I told you, if this happened, your efforts should be justly rewarded." He reached into the desk drawer and counted out silver coins. "You're a good man, Skeres."

He gave the money to Skeres who started to leave. "By the way," Thomas called after him. "Tomorrow or the next day, you're going to be thinking, 'Why not make the most of this and admit to Sir Francis all the things that happened?' That would certainly clean up everything, probably get you a nice reward, and make sure you'd never have to worry about Sir Francis learning the truth.

"But let me suggest you think about both the good from that ... and the bad." Skeres was definitely paying attention as he turned back, standing in the doorway. "The good is that Cousin Francis would probably double everything you've gotten so far from both of us."

Skeres face was a blank page, waiting.

"And the bad," Walsingham concluded, "is that you'd be dead within twenty-four hours. You've seen him do things like that before, haven't you?"

Skeres face had no expression. He left and closed the door.

## CHAPTER 18

# LITERARY DESECRATIONS

Walsingham, Wriothesley and Shakespeare all stood quietly in the library as Marlowe paced and read. Complete silence; all three spectators were afraid to move lest they make a sound. It had been more than a year in which Shakespeare had been presenting "his" plays to the Rose Theatre.

Suddenly Christopher broke the calm, exploding.

"No, *no, NO,*" he yelled. "You may *not* make changes in the plays. Not the lines. The titles. The characters. *Nothing!*"

Shakespeare seemed nonplussed. "Even if it improves it?"

Christopher let out a low groan and grabbed onto a book case to keep from killing him.

"You see, Will," Thomas got a sharp glance from Shakespeare and corrected himself. "uh… William. Christopher has written them exactly as he wants and we have to respect the author's wishes in this case."

"Well, I only thought …" Shakespeare explained.

"Renaming it 'Like You Like It'?" Christopher shouted.

"I thought it had a nice … ring."

"And in 'Macbeth', Duncan looks at the bleeding sergeant and is supposed to say '*Go*, get him surgeons.'"

Shakespeare looked surprised. "Isn't that what I copied?"

"*No*," Marlowe fumed. "You misplaced the *comma* and so it came out 'Go *get him*, surgeons.'"

"What's a common?"

"A comma, William," Marlowe said as he pointed to a line on a sheet of paper. Christopher was trying to be patient and Shakespeare was not really interested. "For the last thirty years we've using these hooks to help readers understand the meaning of what's written. Now I realize you've only had three decades to pick this up, but...," and suddenly Marlowe began to yell. "It's a comma. A COMMA."

"Glory, Jesus. So, I forgot the common."

"Comma," Christopher shouted.

"It's not what's written on a page that impresses women," Shakespeare said brazenly. "It's what's between your legs."

"Or your ears," Marlowe muttered to himself. Then, he went over to the desk and picked up a page of script. "Look at this, William. The line was supposed to read 'They stole our dogs and raped our women.'"

"That's what it says."

"Read it."

"They stole our women and raped our – oh!" Shakespeare shrugged as if to say "who cares."

"Really, Kit," Henry said, combing the fur on another of his cats – a black feline named Francois -- "you're being entirely too sensitive. They're only *plays*." Darling, theatre is for the *low* classes. After all the Church considers it really merely a form of lying."

"It's not like you're trying to create literature or something," Thomas added, trying to be conciliatory.

"Oh, a plague on both your houses," Christopher cursed, glancing from one to the other. "And, William," he went on, "the production that opened last week was supposed to have the title *Henry VIII – All Is True.*"

"That last part was supposed to be in the title?"

"Yes, William, I wanted the play to impress the Queen. Maybe make her father appear a little more noble and honest."

Wriothesley looked from side to side and rolled his eyes. "Well, Kit, you greased the old babe on that one. Hardly a mention of the divorce … and nothing about the breakup with Rome. Looked right up her skirt that time."

Thomas was enjoying the gentle jibe when Shakespeare chimed in, "And do you know *how much work* it is copying all those lousy lines?"

Christopher's eyes widened and he mouthed the word "lousy."

Thomas interrupted the conversation before it could become bloody. "But, William you're not copying that much any more. There were so many errors …"

"A few."

"…that we had to get a scrivener to recopy every line."

Shakespeare was sullen. "But, really, what do I get?"

Thomas looked befuddled. "Well, you get paid by me, you get recognition, and you get choice roles to play."

"A few lousy lines in my own plays," Shakespeare pouted.

Christopher turned to him with fire in his eyes. "_YOUR_ plays?"

"_The plays by William Shakespeare_," he said pompously.

"You were the ghost in *Hamlet*," Marlowe shot back.

"Oh, great part."

"And Adam in *As You Like It*."

Shakespeare scoffed. "Three scenes. A total of eight lines."

"You had the opening line of the play."

"Oh, and what a classic: 'Yonder comes my master, your brother.'"

"Oh, what delivery." Christopher feigned. "What style!" Shakespeare was starting to fume, so Marlowe went on. "Not a few lousy lines, but rather some small – though succulent -- roles."

"You're a bastard, Christopher."

"And you, Will --"

"It's *William.*"

"*William,*" he added, so sweetly, "are a dedicated and true actor."

"And you, Christopher, are an arsehole."

"And don't you ever forget it." Christopher grabbed a few more sheets of paper from the desk and began to pace and read, confident he'd find more errors.

Walsingham and Wriothesley exchanged glances, communicating clearly that it was best to stay out of this.

Shakespeare sat on a large, overstuffed bench and leaned on one of the armrests. What better place to pout? ("Yonder comes my master, your brother." What a lousy line. I could write better than that.) After a few minutes, Shakespeare decided it was time to get his revenge. He said casually, "By the way, the Queen sent a special note to me after she saw the second part of *Henry IV.*"

Mention of the queen got everyone's attention. "She was so fascinated by Falstaff," and here he took out a note to read, "'that wonderful, overweight, hard-drinking rogue' that she respectfully requested that I write a play just about him."

Christopher grabbed he note, but Shakespeare grabbed it back, and read, in a sing-song voice "in which ... he falls ... in love." He turned to Christopher and with a low bow majestically presented him with the Queen's note. "There's no rush. The theatre doesn't have an opening for *weeks.*" Having won the battle, he started for the door.

"William," Thomas said, "Constable Maunder has been asking many questions lately. No matter what people ask, you tell them nothing."

"But what if they --"

Henry put his arm around Shakespeare's shoulders. "Then I will answer them for you, my dear."

"Of course," he said with a "who cares" attitude, gently removing Henry's arm. Then I take my leave." His nod was almost a bow. He wrinkled his nose and left.

Christopher indicated the door where Shakespeare had just made his grand exit. "If we ever have another murder to fake, I've got the perfect candidate for the body." Suddenly remembering, he asked, "Have you heard what he's been doing? He's been nibbling at the nipples of the Widow Vautrollier."

"The ugly Widow Vautrollier?" Henry looked truly shocked.

"Yes. Quill Will has supposedly been so busy writing comedies and tragedies that he hasn't had time for his almost-forgotten wife and children in Stratford. So he occasionally pays Vautrollier's new husband to take a few shillings to them." Here Marlowe's voice went up an octave. "And – *AND* – while he's gone, William spends the fortnight in the new wife's bed!"

"*The ugly Widow Vautrollier?*" Henry repeated.

"Now, here's the best part. When he *does* occasionally venture to Stratford, he stops overnight each way in Oxford at Mistress Davenant's Tavern."

"Also ugly," Henry gasped.

"Well, the word is out that Will-Nil-The-Poet-Still has sired a son, whom the mistress has named William -- *not Will* -- after you know whom."

Henry found it disgusting. "Well, he seems to be sleeping with everyone in town except his patron."

Christopher grabbed Wriothesley's nose and tweaked it. "Some people have '*ole*' the luck, 'Enry." Then he turned to Walsingham. "Thomas, that 'Stratford Stud Stallion' has got little bastards running around all over London." Here he began to scream, "He's making a mockery of my works."

"Then, if you're lucky, people will remember your plays, and not the author." Thomas's voice got pedantic and firm. "And maybe then they will *not* remember things like your famous statement that: '*all they, who love not boys and tobacco, are fools.*'"

"My dear Thomas," Christopher argued, "in ten years no one will have heard of that statement," and then added a second thought, "-- or my plays." Then he concluded, dejectedly, "or even Christopher Marlowe."

There was a silent beat. And then, Thomas, Christopher and Henry all shrieked at the same time, "*Or William Shakespeare.*" Thomas was chuckling and Henry was snorting heartily.

Christopher resumed his pacing and reading. In a very offhanded way he added, "But when I finish the sonnets, they're being dedicated to you." Thomas stood, ready to protest. Christopher raised a hand and said, "I'll code the dedication." A few steps later he made a bold statement, "Either I publish them or I burn them."

"Then you'd better burn them," he heard Thomas say.

"What do I care? I've died once already, remember? After all, Thomas," and here his delivery became very grand, "a coward dies a thousand deaths, the valiant die but once." A moment's thought and then, "Oh, that was *good.*" In a flamboyant style, he grabbed a quill from the desk. He took a thoughtful pose and jotted down the quote.

## CHAPTER 19

# THE ENIGMA

enry Maunder walked down the dark street, the beautiful lines from the performance still ringing in his ears.

*The Merry Wives of Windsor* had run a little longer than some plays at the Rose Theatre and, after some steak and kidney pie at the Broken Horseshoe, the daylight was gone as he headed to his small flat on Marylebone Road.

He felt perfectly safe. Candles being lit in the flats above the shops gave enough light for him to find his way.

His mind replayed the fanciful plight of Sir John Falstaff, a loveable buffoon of a knight, as he hatches a scheme to get to the money of two local men, by seducing their wives.

But, of course, the plan goes awry and the feckless knight endures the revenge of the two women. He is hidden in a basket of dirty laundry, cast into the River Thames, dressed as a woman and then beaten. Finally, the women tell their husbands about their secret doings, and they all plot one last humiliation for Falstaff.

"Really enjoyable," he mumbled to himself. "Yes, a jolly midweek afternoon."

Maunder reached his building and entered the dark, narrow hallway. As he opened the door and climbed the two flights of steps to his flat, he was lost in the humor of the afternoon as well as some of the beautiful lines.

He lit two candles, poured himself a small cup of wine and carried a small taper to light the dried leaves under the branches in the fireplace. He sat, watched the fire and replayed some of the beautiful lines.

One short verse seemed to be imprinted in his memory:

*To shallow rivers, to whose falls*

*Melodious birds sing madrigals...*

Now what was the next line? Oh, yes,

*There will we make our bed of roses*

*And a thousand fragrant posies.*

The rhyme of the final two lines wasn't perfect but the thought was beautiful.

He sipped the wine and played the line over and over in his mind. "And a thousand fragrant posies..." he whispered.

The beautiful words rang in his ears.

But something was wrong. What was it? He said the lines aloud, again and again.

Was it possible? he wondered.

He picked up the candle and wandered over to the desk. "Where was it?" He had bought it about a fortnight ago and put it somewhere.

There it was, right there on the shelf above the desk. Christopher Marlowe's very popular poem "The Passionate Shepherd to His Love." It had been written just before the poet died and had become so popular that it was already in its second printing.

"Could it be here," he wondered. Thumbing through the fragile pages he came upon the verse he was looking for.

*By shallow rivers to whose falls*

*Melodious birds sing madrigals,*

*And I will make thee beds of roses*

*And a thousand fragrant posies.*

He knew he recognized it. But what was going on? Except for the words "and I will" (instead of "there will we") they were identical. He double checked his memory of the lines he indelibly memorized that afternoon – and the words on the paper before him.

His thoughts were going in a myriad of directions. Why would the man who was quickly becoming London's favorite playwright use the same exact lines from a dead poet?

I wonder, he thought, if there could be other passages where ....

He grabbed a few more sheets of paper from the shelf and began to rifle through them.

## CHAPTER 20

# FILE THIRTEEN

Sir Francis sat at his massive desk in his inner chamber. All the dark wood in the room (desk, furniture, window frames); the somber draperies, shutting out much of the outside light; as well as the few insufficient tapers burning on the desk; all gave the room an ominous feeling. And the air in the room was oppressive.

Constable Maunder stood across the desk from him, holding a tied bundle of papers and was aware he had not been asked to sit.

"And, Constable, what is the object of our visit today?" Sir Francis asked without looking up.

"Sir Francis, I was just going over some details in this file and I came up with some concerns," he replied, uncomfortably shifting his weight.

"This file?" Sir Francis put down the quill and looked up.

"Yes, The one on the late Christopher Marlowe. It's file number 13 at the Constabulary. Well, actually we start each year with number one again, so it's really file 13 from year before last when Mr. Marlowe disappeared."

"Was murdered."

"Yes," Maunder said flatly.

"Inspector, it's been almost two years. Shouldn't you have closed that file by now?"

"Well, Sir Francis, every time I do, something rather unusual seems to come up."

"You mean *besides* the odd incidents connected with Poet Marlowe's death?"

"Yes."

"And this time?"

"Well," Maunder rushed headlong into his thesis, "I've been doing some background work and I suddenly began to notice something very odd."

"What?"

"Well, there are many similarities between the works Mr. Marlowe wrote before he died and those of Mr. Shakespeare."

"Could it be just a coincidence?"

Maunder shook his head. "I've check hundreds of lines from each of them. There are so many similarities and identical references. And some lines are actually word for word," he said. The Constable could see the anger building in Sir Francis, who began to breathe audibly through his nose and gritted his teeth.

"You're sure?" he asked. The constable slowly nodded.

Sir Francis's face was turning red. "Spend what time you need, Inspector."

"By the way, Sir Francis," Maunder asked delicately, "I'm going to have to get some information from your cousin Thomas. Do you think we can trust him?"

"Let me put it this way, Inspector: would *you* trust a Walsingham?"

Maunder turned and started to leave. At the door, he heard Sir Francis say, "Inspector … good work."

As the constable quietly closed the door, Sir Francis shook his head and gave a sigh of resignation. He tried to concentrate and go back to work. But he couldn't. Yes, something was definitely rotten in Scadbury.

## CHAPTER 21

# ODD COINCIDENCES

The Scadbury Armory was a small room filled with remnants of suits of armor, breastplates and chain mail -- now all dusty and beginning to rust. Constable Maunder entered and said nothing.

"And, Constable Maunder, what is the cause of your journey to Scadbury today?" Thomas asked.

Maunder was his usual noncommittal self, giving the impression that he was merely wasting his time on some interesting but really nonessential details.

"Well, Sir Thomas, I began to notice something very odd. There are a number of similarities between the writings of Mr. Shakespeare and the late Mr. Marlowe."

"Maybe just a coincidence?"

"I think not, Sir. The lines aren't just similar. Many are identical. Virtually word for word."

"Really, Inspector?" Thomas tried to sound authentically surprised.

"Yes. I have a hundred or so examples here, and --"

"*A hundred or so?*" Thomas was genuinely shocked.

"Yes." Maunder beamed, slapping the word across the room. "Quite amazing, isn't it?"

Walsingham didn't bother to hide his distaste for this. "Like?"

"Well," the Inspector began with a naive air, "here's a speech from Shakespeare's play *The Merry Wives of Windsor*." He handed Thomas the sheet of paper with the four lines he had unearthed that night in his flat. They were beautifully written in a little-too-cursive style.

"And now look at this from Marlowe's poem "The Passionate Shepherd to His Love." He passed across the printed copy of Marlowe's love poem, opened to the identical verse.

Walsingham was stunned. They were virtually word for word. He knew that Christopher had used a line or two of the shepherd poem in two of the plays written under his own name. But to use a whole verse in a play supposedly by Shakespeare? "Are you sure those are both correct?" he asked incredulously.

"Oh, yes, Sir Thomas. I checked the exact reading of each." Walsingham was trying to put all of this together when Maunder went on. "I had heard that the queen herself had requested Mr. Shakespeare write a play about Falstaff getting married. So, I made it a point to attend the first performance of *The Merry Wives*. Maunder seemed to have lost his train of thought. "Very enjoyable," he reminisced.

But then, as if coming back to reality, he went on, "But something about that speech kept haunting me. It had a familiar flavor. And then I remembered Mr. Marlowe's beautiful poem. And when I compared them – lo, and behold!"

"Lo, and behold?" Thomas repeated with just a hint of mockery.

"Yes, lo, and behold," Maunder intoned – knowing full-well he was being mocked.

But Thomas's thoughts drifted elsewhere. Christopher had written that simple poem after Walsingham had sent him a note following their first few meetings. In a daring and impetuous move, Thomas has sent off a short missive, cryptic and bold. It contained one sentence: "Come live with me and be my love." The next day he regretted being so foolish.

Thomas had been audacious beyond his wildest imaginings, having never done anything so daring before. But every time he had an assignment with Christopher, he found that the rakish young poet was all he thought about for days afterward. And worst of all, the attraction didn't lessen as days went by; instead the fascination seemed to shade his every thought. And although he realized that he might be fooling himself, he felt that Marlowe was enjoying the relationship as much. After he dispatched the note, however, he felt foolish, old, and stupid. Out of nowhere, an invitation to 'come live with me and be my love." What would this young poet think?

But Christopher's reply was an astonishment. There *was* no reply. Instead Christopher answered within a few days by penning a short poem for publication entitled "The Passionate Shepherd to His Love." It was a delicate, loving verse that began with Thomas's line "Come live with me and be my love," and went on to list all the joyous things their life together would entail. The poem quickly became very popular; and Walsingham had his reply: *yes*. As Thomas's thoughts came back to the armory, he could hear the Constable continuing.

"And in Dr. Faustus, Mr. Marlowe wrote about Helen of Troy … I'm quoting now --"

Thomas almost said it aloud, "Oh, joy, he's quoting now."

"Mr. Marlowe wrote, '*Was this the face that launched a thousand ships?*' And then in Mr. Shakespeare's new play *Troilus and Cressida* there's the line about Helen of Troy: '*She is a pearl whose face hath launched above a thousand ships*.'"

"Wasn't that just two poets who happen to find the same phrase to describe the same woman?"

"Well, yes, that's what I thought at first. But I kept finding more and more identical lines like the one by Marlowe in *Tamburlaine*," and here he read from a note, "'*Ye pampered Jades of Asia. What can ye draw but twenty miles a day?*' And in *Henry IV* there's Shakespeare's line '*Pampered Jades of Asia, which cannot go but thirty miles a day.*'"

"Well, one was twenty miles and the other thirty miles," Thomas said with a touch of annoyance, telling him he was not going along with all this. "So, the miles are different."

"Well, Sir Thomas, here are two lines that *are* exactly identical, one from Shakespeare's sonnets and the other from Marlowe's *Edward II*: '*Lilies that fester smell far worse than weeds.*'"

The Constable looked up as if quite proud of himself. Walsingham was not buying the innocent act. Maunder started going through more papers. "And I have over a hundred more."

Quickly, Thomas grabbed the papers. His tone was irritated, "You needn't read them all."

"I've check other playwrights. I can't seem to find any of their lines identical to either Marlowe's or Shakespeare's."

Check and checkmate?

Thomas took a second to collect his thoughts. "And so, this leads you where, Inspector?"

Maunder continued, a little too simply to really believe what he was proposing. "Well, sir, I've become a little suspicious that Mr. Shakespeare may be – let's not say '*stealing*' – but maybe '*borrowing*' from the works of your late ward."

Walsingham knew that once again, Maunder was playing the fool. He had not come all the way out to Scadbury merely over concern for one author "borrowing" lines from another. No, he had the scent of blood.

Thomas went along with the ruse. "And so?"

"Well," he began, "although it's not a crime against the Crown, Sir Thomas, it is a bit unfair and all."

"Constable, writers have been using each other's plots for centuries."

"But, Sir, I'm not talking about ideas for plots. I'm quoting identical lines." Maunder took the sheets of paper back from Walsingham and said, "Marlowe wrote '*Yet Caesar shall go forth. Thus Caesar did go forth.*' And Shakespeare wrote '*Caesar shall go forth. Yet Caesar shall go forth.*'"

The Constable waited for confirmation, but Thomas said nothing.

He obviously was getting nowhere with Sir Thomas Walsingham. He had no trouble, however, a few hours later getting the avid interest of the lord's cousin, Sir *Francis* Walsingham.

93

## CHAPTER 22

# TROUBLING CLUES

Jt was just hours later. Sir Francis sat at a huge wooden table in his overly-embellished dining room at home, devouring chicken, bread and vegetables. Maunder stood to his side and placed the same sheet of paper he had read to Thomas earlier that day at Scadbury.

"Marlowe wrote '*Yet Caesar shall go forth. Thus Caesar did go forth.*' And Shakespeare wrote '*Caesar shall go forth. Yet Caesar shall go forth.*"

Sir Francis stared at the sheets. "And what did Thomas say?"

"He said 'Well, at least Shakespeare moved the word 'yet', so he wasn't exactly stealing.'"

"My dear cousin enjoys playing the fool.

"The Constable felt it necessary to firm his case a bit more. "So then I pointed out Marlowe's line '*The moon sleeps with Endymion*" compares exactly with Shakespeare's '*Ho, the moon sleeps with Endymion.*"

Sir Francis looked at the Constable showing his disgust. "Identical," he spit out the word, losing a bit of chicken.

"And I've got pages more, Milord." Maunder put a pile of sheets on the edge of the table, trying to avoid a spot of oily drippings. "And I've been wondering how Mr. Shakespeare is able to write so rapidly, so many plays a year."

Sir Francis was fiddling nervously with his knife.

"And Shakespeare keeps acting," Maunder added. And, also, he writes with such knowledge about foreign countries, the military and courtly manners. And yet – and I've checked – he's never left England or been in government service or had any occasion to learn about manners of court."

Maunder picked up a different sheet of paper to read another quote; but Sir Francis took his knife and stabbed through the sheet and into the table.

"Thank you, constable. You've made your point."

As Maunder went to speak, Sir Francis removed his knife and shoved the papers back at him.

In disgust, he repeated, "Constable, *you've made your point*. Thank you." The Constable looked taken aback. "Keep checking."

The message was obvious. Maunder gathered his papers and, without a smile or acknowledgement, left.

Sir Francis watched him leave and hoped his minor outburst would convince the Constable how upset he was with this ridiculous game his cousin -- or Shakespeare -- or someone -- was playing.

# CHAPTER 23

# SONNETS TO ANOTHER MAN

It wasn't long before Shakespeare was becoming known as one of London's most popular playwrights.

In 1603 Queen Elizabeth had died and the new king, James I, had given a healthy boost to the theatre world. Suddenly, theatre wasn't the low class dregs it had always been. Though still not legitimate or respectable, the crown at least found the performances "tolerable." And for the average Londoner they were becoming *very* popular. ("If you like that sort of thing," the respectable said.)

Shakespeare was becoming more prominent, confident, and more successful each day.

Not that there wasn't an occasional small concern in his life.

"*The Sonnets were written to another man?*" he screamed at Christopher.

Though the two of them were alone in the Scadbury study, every servant in the manor could hear them and assumed the entire household was probably in there.

"I thought you knew," Christopher replied calmly from the desk. "I wrote them to Thomas."

"*They were written to Thomas? Love poems to another man!?*" he repeated, turning a shade of royal purple. "All of London is laughing at me."

"I'm sure Sir Wriothesley isn't."

"And everyone in town seems to be able to tell ..." and here he took another breath and almost shuddered, "... *that they were written to a man!*"

"Of course, people can tell, William. They were intended to be homoerotic," Christopher argued.

Shakespeare paused momentarily, but refused to show his unfamiliarity with the word. So he went off on another leg of his tirade. "Do you know how people are referring to them around town? *The Sugar Sonnets!*"

"Oh, how sweet," Christopher said. "Sugar Sonnets, huh?"

"Don't be funny. I was half-way through a tankard of ale at the Owl and Raven when the bloke across the room shouts, 'Hey, William, who is your beloved fair youth?' I yell back to him, 'What are you bloody talking about?' And he says, '*The chap* you keep calling my beloved in your new sonnets.'"

Shakespeare paused and took a deep breath. "I went and checked. Some bloody fellow is called *my beloved* about seventeen times."

Marlowe was enjoying this but refused to let Shakespeare observe just how much. Instead he feigned a thoughtful look as if he was trying to remember the exact number of times that the phrase was used.

"I was just living down that dedication to your bloody poem 'Rape of Lucrece,'" Shakespeare shouted. Then he recited from burning memory, "*The love I dedicate to your Lordship is without end.*" Now he was really angry. "My wife wrote to me. Even she was suspicious."

"Remember what you always say, William: It had a nice ring."

"Why '*love*'?" Shakespeare was pleading now and appeared to be almost on the edge of tears. "Couldn't you have said '*respect*' or '*loyalty*'?"

"Hmmm," Marlowe seemed to be weighing the idea. "Not the same ring," he mulled over the idea, quoting Shakespeare's own words, trying to get to his very soul. "Oh, come on, William; you're famous and you're making more money than you've ever had before. Your family's getting a crest and you've bought a part interest in the new Globe Theatre they're building. What have you got to worry about?"

"A Constable that lurks around every corner. That's what I've got to worry about. And the tower prison."

Marlowe went back to work. "Thomas will take care of everything."

Shakespeare went to sit in his favorite bench for sulking. He fidgeted and fumed. Finally, he said, "I forgot to mention. King James really liked *Macbeth*. The new King himself came backstage after the performance."

Christopher kept working. "The new King is a big fan of witchcraft. That's why I started *Macbeth* with the three witches."

No reaction from Shakespeare.

"The three witches? In *Macbeth*? You did read it!?"

"Well, kind of."

"And our King is a descendant of Duncan." Christopher could tell that Shakespeare was still not with him. "Duncan? The King? In *Macbeth*?"

Shakespeare quickly changed the subject. "King James is planning to sponsor our company at the Globe now that the plague is over and the theatres are open again. He's going to call the company 'The King's Men'."

Christopher stared at him unbelieving. "'The King's Men'? Why that's absolutely clever. And so original," he mocked, going back to work. "But I wouldn't get too intimate with the King," he warned. "He doesn't use tobacco but he *does* sleep with boys."

"Not the new King?" Shakespeare was staggered.

"Oh, god," Christopher cringed. "You didn't say anything, did you?"

"Of course not." From the tone of his voice, it was obvious he was trying to remember.

The new King, James I of England, was the former James VI of Scotland and the devotedly Protestant son of Catholic Mary, Queen of Scots. At the time of his coronation he was thirty-six years old and already had an array of stories circulating. Though married, he had the reputation of nibbling at the ears and fingers of young attractive men while holding court, a habit that astounded his ministers. Not that anyone would comment on it to *him*. That, however, did not hinder them from quietly mentioning their bemusement about this to the rest of the court – who, in turn, mentioned it to all of London. And his finger-nibbling was not the worst of his traits. He also was known for not bathing and the constant habit of playing with his codpiece. Who knows? Maybe all of this was designed to give the new king a more human image.

As Shakespeare sat trying to play back his comments to the King, Christopher decided to give just one more prod. "The word on the streets of London is that, as it's *worded* around town, 'Young men lie in his bedchamber and are his minions.'"

"What are 'minions'?"

Christopher's voice registered shock. "Oh, don't ask." He loved to goad him, noticing Shakespeare was trying to assimilate all this. "His royalty gives him great priority with the young men of London." Christopher smiled sweetly to increase the discomfort. "That's why he's called *James the First*. He gets first crack." Then, trying to sound concerned, he said "Oh, am I shocking you, William?"

"No. Actually, I'm very comfortable with that sort of thing."

"Oh -- what sort of thing?"

"You know," he said, getting angry. Shakespeare hated to be goaded.

"No -- what?" Christopher asked innocently.

Shakespeare squirmed.

But the next minute his discomfort became intensified and, more significantly, it spread to Marlowe. Constable Henry Maunder unexpectedly entered, unannounced, through the hall door.

"Oh, excuse me," the Constable said. "I was told Sir Walsingham was in here." It was obvious, however, that his *accidental* entrance was anything but accidental.

For the first time, Marlowe was face to face with the man championing his arrest. And death. "He's in the garden," he said carefully.

"Then, if it's permissible, I'll just wait." Looking at Shakespeare, he said, "I know we've met, Will …"

"William."

"Oh, yes, William." He turned to Christopher, obviously probing for information. "But I don't think we've met."

There was a cautious pause by Christopher just as Thomas entered from the garden.

"And, you haven't," Thomas picked up the conversation, cheerfully. "Inspector Maunder, this is my Cousin Winston Walsingham from Warwick." He seemed to be pushing the alliteration a little too heavily.

"Another Walsingham?" the Constable asked.

"Common as horseflies."

Maunder turned to Marlowe and gave a slight bow. "Lord Walsingham."

Thomas corrected him, just to annoy Christopher. "Oh, no. Not 'lord.' He's never been knighted. Just 'mister.'"

The Inspector and Walsingham eyed each other with a self-satisfied look; both were "playing" the game. Though the Constable wasn't sure what was really behind that smirk on Thomas's face. Or what game Walsingham was playing.

"I apologize for barging in. But a member of your staff suggested I look for you in the study," Maunder explained.

The grin on Walsingham's face conveyed that he knew better. "I'm sure he did."

"The staff member who admitted me was Ingram Frizer, wasn't it?"

"It could have been," Thomas said evenly.

"He still works here? Four years after the incident?"

"The incident?" Thomas asked, laying it on a little thick. "You mean after murdering Mr. Marlowe? Well, it *was* self defense." Then he added a little too naively, "And he really *is* a very good worker."

Maunder was enjoying the mental chess match just as much as his opponent.

"Well, if you'll excuse us, Constable," Christopher said. "Mr. Shakespeare and I have some business to attend to," and headed for the stairway.

As Shakespeare followed, Maunder stopped him. "Mr. Shakespeare, I've had the opportunity to see some of the original copies of your plays. And I've admired your beautiful scrolled lettering. Almost like that of a professional scrivener's." Shakespeare smiled uncomfortably. "I wonder could you tell me what your next exciting play will be?"

Shakespeare took a breath and said, "Well, of course," which gave him a few seconds to think. "It's, uh, called *Cymberline*."

"What an unusual name," Maunder said. He picked up a quill from the desk and dipped it into an ink pot. "Would you mind writing the title for me?" he asked. "I certainly dare not miss it."

Shakespeare looked at the pen, seeing the trap: his handwriting compared with that of the scrivener's. There was panic in his eyes.

"Of course," Thomas said, offhandedly. He took the quill from the Inspector and wrote on a scrap of paper. That was *Cymberline*, William, wasn't it?"

Shakespeare nodded in relief.

"Thank you," Maunder smiled, but was not fooled. Something was rotten in Scadbury. He just didn't know what yet.

Christopher went up the stairs; Shakespeare right behind, his lower lip quivering ever so slightly.

"Now, Constable," Walsingham asked, sitting. "What can I do for you today?"

# CHAPTER 24

# SONNETS OF LOVE AND PAIN

Maunder watched Marlowe and Shakespeare go up the stairs and into an anteroom. "I'm sorry," he replied. "What did you ask?"

Walsingham grinned. "I said 'Now, Constable, what can I do for you today?'"

"Well, I was passing your estate and thought I'd drop by."

"We're two hours' ride from London."

Maunder didn't mind acknowledging a win. "So you are, Sir Thomas. So you are."

"So what was it? More similar quotes?"

"Well, that wasn't the main reason," Maunder began, "but I have just found … oh … maybe a few dozen more."

Thomas sat, making sure he gave the impression that he was neither very interested nor very shocked. "Uh-huh."

Without asking if Walsingham wanted to hear them or not, Maunder began, "In Marlowe's *Tamburlaine* the line '*The sun, unable to sustain the sight, shall hide his head*.' It so similar to Shakespeare's '*The sun for sorrow will not show his head*.'"

102

"Close. But not really a perfect match," Thomas argued.

"Well, maybe you're right," Maunder mischievously conceded the point. He took the quill from the desk and scratched it out. "But, how about this?" He handed Thomas a sheet of paper. "This line in Marlowe's poem 'Hero and Leander' is exactly like one in *As You Like It*. '*Who ever loved that loved not at first sight?*' Word for word."

"Yes, I can see it is," Thomas added noncommittally. Handing the sheets back to the Constable, he said, "and so what can I do for you today," indicating he had had enough of this game.

"Oh, yes," Maunder got back to the subject of his visit. "It's about the dedication of Mr. Shakespeare's wonderful new Sonnets. They're dedicated to 'W.H.'"

Walsingham was ready for that one. "Well, Constable, even though authors often try to keep the dedication cryptic, it's obvious, isn't it, that W.H. is his loving patron: 'Wriothesley ... Henry.'"

"You think so?" Maunder asked. "I just happen to be visiting the Earl's estate last week when ...."

"You were visiting Wriothesley?"

"Well, of course, at the time, he ... well ... didn't happen to be at home." Maunder realized that Walsingham had caught the gist of the visit and went on. "Mr. Shakespeare obviously lives only to write plays. He has no family here, no life of his own."

"Isn't that why it's called dedication?"

"Yes, but from what I could see it appears that Mr. Shakespeare definitely is *not* sharing the pillow of Lord Wriothesley." Thomas just smiled.

The Inspector went on. "So, the dedication of the sonnets, Milord, the way it's so lovingly written and all, couldn't really be for Sir Wriothesley."

At that point the Constable decided to very casually spring the trap. "Some have suggested, Sir Thomas, that the way your name is often hyphenated, you know, 'Walsing-Ham', that the sonnets might have been dedicated to you. W.H.? Walsing-Ham? You know."

Walsingham signaled that he had had enough. "Why in Hades would William Shakespeare dedicate them to me? And there must be a thousand more possibilities for the initials W.H."

"Hmmm, I suppose so." Maunder looked unconvinced.

"And haven't I heard that your full name is Walter Henry Maunder?" That got a nod of agreement. "Walter Henry! By Jupiter, that's W.H.!"

Maunder decided to go along with the ruse. With mock surprise, he said, "Well, now, that would really have been nice. Do you actually think Mr. Shakespeare --"

"No." Thomas ended the subject. "Now, was there anything else, Inspector?"

Maunder acted as if he hadn't finished the conversation about the Sonnets yet. He wandered about the study and stopped in front of the large stone fireplace. "And some of those sonnets just don't make sense if written by such a successful playwright like Mr. Shakespeare. They seem to be written by someone ... in despair. Someone hurting ...and desolate. Listen to this."

He unfolded a long sheet of paper and read, quite beautifully and quite meaningfully.

> *When in disgrace with fortune and men's eyes,*
>
> > *I all alone beweep my outcast state,*
> >
> > *And trouble deaf heaven with my bootless cries,*
> >
> > *And look upon myself, and curse my fate.*

Thomas was listening, very touched by this. But Maunder had more.

"But then the writer goes on to add:

> *Then haply I think on thee,*
>
> > *For such sweet love remembered*
> >
> > *Such wealth brings,*
> >
> > *That I scorn to change my state with kings."*

No one spoke. Thomas, obviously very moved, turned away from the Inspector and said seriously, "Definitely written by a man in love."

There was a long period of emptiness as Thomas's thoughts pleasantly digested the words: "*for such sweet love remembered -- such wealth brings -- that I scorn to change my state with kings.*" Slowly his mind began to seep back to the events going on in the study. Maunder had quietly been watching the reverie envelope his rival, and then slowly dissolve. Finally, Walsingham asked, "But you said you had a question?"

"Oh, yes, Sir Thomas," Maunder said, returning to the subject. "Here we have two writers, with so many identical lines. It's uncanny."

"Yes, it is, isn't it?" Thomas conceded.

"But, Sir Thomas, there is one line that really causes me concern."

"And that is …."

"In *As You Like It* Shakespeare writes this very mystifying line," Maunder took a few seconds to take a slip of paper from his pocket and slowly unfold it. Walsingham couldn't help but think all this was being done to add to the theatricality of the occasion. Finally, he read, "Shakespeare wrote '*When a man's verses cannot be understood, it strikes a man more dead than a great reckoning in a little room.*'"

Neither man said anything. The Constable slowly nodded as if thinking as he stared at the slip of paper. Thomas knew immediately. Christopher had slipped into a play attributed to Shakespeare a personal reference to the murder scene at Deptford -- over that supposed reckoning of the bill. This was the event that Christopher felt made him "more dead" and at the same time choked off all his "verses."

"Odd, don't you think, Sir Thomas? Once again, it sounds more like Mr. Marlowe, don't you think?"

Thomas, stunned, had no answer. Finally Maunder broke the silence. "So I was wondering…" he began.

"Yes?"

"So I was wondering – since this line really seems to apply more to Mr. Marlowe…."

"Yes?" Thomas repeated, trying to give no clues.

"… did Mr. Marlowe and Mr. Shakespeare … ever … meet?"

Walsingham was caught, not knowing which way to answer. There was no time to think of all the possible pitfalls of either a yes or a no.

The Inspector just waited, like a hound at the fox's hole.

Finally, Thomas said, "No."

"Oh," the Constable said. "I was just wondering." He gave the slightest of bows acknowledging he was about to leave and headed for the door.

"By the way, Constable, did you ask that question of Shakespeare?"

No one was playing games any more.

Maunder stopped and turned to Walsingham. "Yes." After a suspenseful pause, he said, "It was that rare question he couldn't refer to Sir Wriothesley."

"And he said?"

"Shakespeare?" Maunder's pause made Thomas squirm. At last he responded. "He said the same thing. They never met."

With that, the Constable was gone.

CHAPTER 25

# RELATIVES COME CALLING

The Grand Dining Hall at Scadbury Manor was more for show than eating. The room was long with the wall on one side curved to accommodate a series of tables for food, water, knives, and finger bowls.

The heavy draperies seemed to muffle every sound. And no matter how many candles the servants lit, at night the room always seemed gloomy.

The opposite wall held portraits of the Walsingham ancestors from three centuries back. There was none of Thomas yet. He thought the pictures were pompous. He planned to have his done when his hair had turned to gray and he had lines in his face to emphasize the wisdom he had gained.

There was one long table, designed to seat twenty-eight guests, with three candelabra down the middle. Meals were seldom taken there. It was easier to dine in the cozy breakfast room that was smaller but close to the kitchen.

That night, however, Thomas had an important subject to discuss. And, also, since Henry was visiting at the manor, it was enough of an excuse to ask the kitchen help to carry everything up another half-flight of steps.

But Thomas wasn't going to place the three diners down the full length of the table. So he sat in his usual seat at the head with Christopher immediately on one side and Henry on the other. The three of them sitting in this cavernous room at one end of the table made the diners appear almost like three children at a birthday celebration.

"Look, Christopher. Line after line. All the same," Thomas was scolding as he handed over sheet after sheet.

"Thomas, I just write. And naturally, sometimes I word things the same way I did before."

Henry reached across the table for the bowl of salt in front of Christopher. "Really? Christopher, I always assumed you poised the pen and the words just floated out of your arse."

Marlowe took back the salt and said sweetly, "Henry, may your next pair of underbritches be handmade – one size too small -- by the Queen's Royal Blacksmith."

Thomas was determined to put his warning across. "Kit, Constable Maunder has been here three times questioning the duplicate lines. He now has more than a hundred examples – each almost identical."

"Thomas, I can't remember every line I've written – and exactly how I phrased it. I will try to avoid repeating something I've written before, but it really is quite difficult."

"There is nothing we can do about the identical lines the Constable has already found. But the important thing, Kit, is that from now on …." He was interrupted by a servant handing him a note.

Without the least bit of concern or panic, he continued. "How charming. Cousin Francis's carriage has just arrived at the front gate. He must really be in a loving, family mood since he usually summons *us* to *his* chambers."

Christopher stood, placed his chair back and went out the servants' entrance, chanting, "By the pricking of my thumbs, something wicked this way comes."

Without being told, a servant cleared away all of Christopher's plates and food. He forgot to take the wine glass.

"Thomas, Thomas, where are you?" The voice of Sir Francis echoed through the halls.

Thomas sat quietly, not bothering to answer. "It's always nice when relatives come to visit, isn't it, Henry?"

Sir Francis kept shouting.

Entering into the dining hall, Sir Francis was saying, "Thomas, are you in the – oh, here you are. I looked over half the estate."

Sir Francis and Wriothesley exchanged glances. There was no warmth traveling either way.

"Sir Henry."

"Sir Francis."

"Thomas, there's something we have to discuss."

"Of course."

Sitting down, Sir Francis noticed the extra glass of wine that the servant had forgotten to clear. "A third glass?"

Not the least bit flustered, Thomas moved the glass closer to Sir Francis. "The servant said you were coming. For you. Your favorite Grigio."

Sir Francis looked as if he were not thoroughly convinced. He sipped the wine. It was Grigio. "Wriothesley, I have some family business to attend to with my cousin."

Not having finished his dinner, Henry didn't know what to do and just looked at Sir Francis, who said more firmly, "Wriothesley, it's *family* business."

One could almost feel the indignation emanating from Henry. "Of course, of course," he said. "Then I take my leave." He stood, took one more morsel from his plate, indicating he was not done dining, and walked to the door, chewing.

As he left, he nodded his farewells first to one and then to the other. "Thomas. Sir 'Alsingham."

Sir Francis answered with the ease of a parent putting off a child, "Henry, you know my name's not 'Alsingham.' It's <u>W</u>alsingham."

Henry stopped at the door but didn't turn. "Oh. I just assumed the 'W' was silent – as in 'whore.'"

Thomas squirmed at the remark. He'll regret that someday, he thought. Henry, why do you do that? But he said nothing, thinking, Cousin, it's your move.

"Thomas, Constable Maunder has come to see me. He suspects that all the plays being written by Wriothesley's new ward are really the work of Marlowe. He's checked line after line, page after page."

"How could that be?"

Sir Francis's voice had an ominous tone. "Well, for a second, Thomas, let's just suppose you didn't really kill him."

"Francis, he's dead. And all of Maunder's wild ideas will not bring my world back to me." Thomas sounded very sincere. The glisten in his eyes almost looked like the beginning of a small tear.

Sir Francis nearly believed him. And then he remembered how clever his cousin could be. "You know what will happen if I find out he's still alive."

Thomas's voice lost all friendliness. He was tired of all these threats. "I can only guess that once again the bonds of blood will get me special privilege."

Sir Francis squinted at him and threatened, "And those bonds can be very tight."

Thomas stared back in defiance.

"I regret doing this to you, Cousin," Sir Francis began, not too convincingly, "but a troop of my men will be here in the morning. I feel I have to verify that the charges made by Constable Maunder are not actually true."

Thomas turned away. (Did his cousin really think anyone would believe it was really Constable Maunder's idea?)

Francis went on. "Every room will be inspected. Every corner will be carefully checked. Every blade of grass will be thoroughly scrutinized. And don't forget: I *know* Scadbury Manor including every hiding place you and I …. If he's not here: no problem. But if he is…." He let the words hang there, letting Thomas know he believed full well that Marlowe was at Scadbury. "Just a warning," he added as he downed the rest of his wine. Without another word, he walked out of the hall and slammed the door.

Slowly and seriously, Christopher and Henry returned to the table and stood.

"I leave tonight," Christopher said finally. "I'll get to Spain."

Henry grabbed a quill from the side table and began to write. "They'll expect you to go to Spain. I've got friends in Venice. Go there." And he handed Christopher the note. "Here."

Thomas was still stunned. "Stop it. Both of you! Cousin Francis would never have mentioned the search tomorrow unless he's got every road out here guarded already. Why search for someone when you can smoke him out?"

"And why wait for the hangman when you can try to outrun him?" Christopher shouted as he grabbed the note from Henry and dashed up the stairs.

Thomas ran after him. "Kit, Kit, don't be a fool."

But Christopher was already far ahead.

# CHAPTER 26

# JOSHUA

**M**inutes later, not far from the manor house a large barn door flew open just as Joshua, the fastest steed in the Scadbury stables, raced through the dark, down a side path, almost throwing his rider as he made the first turn. The steed jumped over a fallen fence, and charged down the middle of a field of vegetables.

Scadbury had many wonderful horses. But Joshua was different. He was not only the manor's fastest steed but he was also the smartest.

Joshua knew every path, every field, every road, and every pothole on the manor – even at night. Scadbury had more than a thousand acres and, everyone said, Joshua was the only living soul who knew each of them. If you had to get somewhere in a hurry, Joshua was the horse.

So when the steed raced across that field of vegetables in the moonlight, there was no chance he would stumble on a row of young crops or run into an apple tree or fence.

And there was no way the two riders, sitting astride dark horses, waiting in the shadows, would be able to follow him through that field. They couldn't take the chance. So they took a side road to try to catch him at the next turn.

At the end of the field was a road that connected to the bridge over the dry moat at the far end of the estate. Joshua knew every inch of the road, and even in the dim moonlight, easily headed down the left fork, cutting the turn smoothly. Joshua was now far ahead of the two pursuing riders.

Almost at the bridge, a third rider heard the sound of approaching hoofs and moved into the middle of the road.

As Joshua reached the intersection, both horses reared. The other rider lost control of his horse and Joshua raced past him down the road to the bridge. Just a few meters to go and they were free.

But two more riders stood their horses in the middle of the old drawbridge, blocking man or beast from going past.

As the chase reached the bridge, all three of the horses began to rear almost throwing each of the riders.

One of the pursuers grabbed Joshua's bridal and the other pulled back the cloak of its rider .

It was Thomas Walsingham.

"My god, you gentlemen scared me," Thomas said, trying to calm Joshua. "I thought I was being ambushed." The prize steed was still unsettled. "Easy there, boy," he said patting him.

"Sir Thomas?" one of the riders seemed surprised.

"Yes?" Thomas asked, wide-eyed, still working to control Joshua.

"We -- well -- we thought you were someone else."

"Oh! Who?" Thomas asked innocently.

"Just ... just someone else."

\* \* \* \* \*

Hours later a small boat sailed out into the channel. It was foggy and the boat was traveling slowly.

Christopher stood on the front deck, leaning on a pile of crates, a canvas bag in his hand. It had been so easy to ride out of Scadbury once the chase drew everyone else to the drawbridge.

Christopher watched as his beloved England – and his partner slowly slipped further and further away.

Soon it was so foggy he could no longer see land.

A fog horn sounded.

Christopher Marlowe was on his way to Italy.

PART 3

# The Chase
# Across Italy

## CHAPTER 27

# LOVE LETTERS

Thomas sat at the table in the gazebo in the small rose garden outside the west tower. It had been only a few days since Christopher had sailed and yet everything was different. There was no one with whom to talk. (Poley? Frizer? Oh, no.) And every meal had to be eaten alone now.

There was no one to whom he could slip an unseen glance whenever one of the servants said or did something stupid. No one with whom to share the little inside jokes that made them laugh almost like two small children. No one to try to get the first grab at the food in the picnic baskets out in the south meadow -- even when it was too cold to be eating outside. ("Who cares? It keeps the wine cold. And besides we've got a blanket to share in case.")

And there was no one else to *coincidentally* stand up, ready to go to bed, whenever Thomas stood to retire for the night. They knew it was morbid to joke about Thomas Kyd's remark, but Thomas would usually ask, "Do you think anyone has got the 'bed warmer' ready?"

Christopher would stifle a smile and say something like "Oh, I'm sure the 'bed warmer' is *definitely* ready."

"You can tell?"

"Oh, I can tell."

But then, after Christopher left for Italy, everything suddenly changed. There was no reason for Thomas to look forward to the day. Except for the letters. True, writing made him feel as if he were talking to Christopher. But it wasn't the same.

Thomas sat in the gazebo, knowing this was one of Christopher's favorite places. The morning air was a quite chilly but the cool, fresh wind felt so good. And he had a scarf, in case he got cold.

He took a deep breath and enjoyed the smells of all the new growth around him. Even sitting down to write made him happier.

He adjusted the chair, took out a sheet of paper embossed with his family crest and put it on the table. He gently fingered the white quill with the bright red tip that Christopher always used. It was a small reminder of the tall, thin poet with the inane smile who, by then, had been gone four days. (Only days?) He dipped the quill into the small ink pot.

He thought for a moment and then scrawled:

*21 March 1605*
*A lonely Scadbury, England*

*My dear Kit,*

> *How long has it been? The calendar says only days. But already it feels like years. I wake in the mornings and fill my hours with these letters to you.*

He stopped writing and smiled.

> *Each month Robert Poley will arrive in Venice with my letters and funds for your livelihood. Of course he has specific instructions to stop at many places before meeting you — you know: letters to friends, shopping for me, delivery of documents and such. That's just in case Cousin Francis or the Constable may have guessed that you might be in Italy. But I really have no reason to think that.*

> *And I have always used Poley as my courier, so I suspect we should have no concern now.*

*On the fifteenth day of each month at midday, be in St. Mark's Square to meet him. He will have my letters – maybe more than you will have time to read – and more than enough funds.*

*Please, please have a large supply of letters for me. I want to know everything about Venice – and you.*

*If there is anything else you need, just ask. Filling your every request makes me feel as if you are here.*

*Your exile will end soon. I promise. Once Cousin Francis accepts that you are no longer here, it will be safe for you to return.*

*As always,*

*Thomas*

The letter arrived suspiciously just days after Christopher got really settled in his new home. He could not understand how – but there it was. Thomas had worked his usual magic.

He lovingly folded it and placed it into an inlaid cypress box he had bought just to preserve the letters from his partner.

The chambers in the home of *Senatore* Spinelli were small but more than adequate. ("Thank you for your note to him, Henry.") The only thing Christopher had to do each day was to write. Lately, however, he started wandering about Venice. Small compared to London.

Amazing, he thought. More than one hundred little islands clustered three miles out in the Adriatic Sea off the coast of Italy. With majesty beyond compare. England's formal and archaic architecture did not approach the beauty of the stately palazzos, the maze of canals and walkways that seemed to go nowhere, and art, art, art – everywhere. And the colors throughout the city, not the restricted grays and browns of England, were vibrant and daring. Many days he "postponed" his writing until the more humid afternoons and spent the mornings just wandering. Getting lost among the canals and *calles* was the most enjoyable. No horses. No carriages. Only people strolling over bridge after bridge, going from one small island to the next. Or residents winding their boats down the narrow, twisting canals. And then the occasional ornate *gondola* belonging to some nobleman or Duke. He missed London and Thomas, but this was nevertheless exciting.

*Signorina* Spinelli, the *Senatore's* teen-age daughter, was an excellent cook and Christopher was often invited to dine with the family. *Signora* Spinelli, her mother, pretended she was teaching her daughter to cook as a prelude to the girl becoming a fine wife. But in reality, she realized that her daughter was already the better cook and so most of the preparations were left to the daughter (except, of course, the delicate *risotto*, "Mamma's *specialito*"). That arrangement assured there would be no comparisons of the *cucina* between mother and daughter, and freed the *Signora* for important things, like sewing and gossiping with neighbors.

On the fifteenth of the following month Christopher stood in St. Mark's Square, just below the *Campanile*, the high tower in the center of the square. Around him were a myriad of merchants and Venetians crowding into bakeries or poking around the outdoor vegetable and meat stands.

He didn't see Poley and wondered what he would do if he failed to find him. Wait there all day? Come back the next day?

Suddenly he felt a large package being shoved into his hands from behind him. It was wrapped in brown burlap and tied with thin rope.

He turned and there was Poley wearing the striped shirt of a gondolier and a very, *very* fake moustache, which could easily have been the tail of a dead cat. Poley wasn't smiling.

Christopher, of course, almost doubled in laughter. But either because of fear of being exposed or the embarrassment at being laughed at, Poley grabbed the package that Marlowe held and seemed to disappear into the fog.

Christopher tried to follow but the "gondolier" was magically gone.

\* \* \* \* \*

A few months later Christopher sat in his upstairs room looking out at the Grand Canal.

*18 September 1605*
*Faraway Venice, Italy*

*My Dear Thomas,*

*I never seem to be able to recognize Poley each month. Where does he get those disguises? And does he think he really needs them? His best was probably the archbishop outfit he wore last month. I almost knelt and kissed the ring. And the two old nuns next to me kept trying to catch his attention. He finally "blessed" them with a poorly executed sign of the cross and then disappeared. (Just like the "the holy miracle of the ascension," maybe? Or would that be the "assumption?") He certainly makes a better courier than a murderer.*

Christopher gazed at the boats paddling silently up the canal. A small vessel piled high with bolts of elegant fabric passed his window. Venice definitely *was* different.

*I have given Poley my two latest scripts, "The Merchant of Venice" and "Othello." Both of them embolden the wonderful world of Venice – its vibrant life – its color and beauty.*

Then he added excitedly:

*And they've invented a thing called forks here.*

But then he couldn't resist including, so emotionally,

*I so much wish you were here. You would love Italy. I've learned that in this country – as well as in Spain and France – women are allowed to appear on stage. They don't use young boys to play the female roles.*

Women had never been permitted to act in Elizabethan theatre. By tradition the female roles were taken by young boys -- their higher pitched voice and delicate size making it easier for the audience to believe that the character was female. This arrangement always seemed to work a little better in the lighter comedies than in the heavier roles of Lady Macbeth or Othello's wife, Desdemona. In the more pliable comedies it was easier to accept the pretence. And Marlowe, once he

The Shakespeare Conspiracy:
*A Novel About the Greatest Literary Deception of All Time*

began writing as Shakespeare, found a device that helped both actor and audience. After a scene or two, the women in the play would find some reason (or excuse) to disguise themselves as men. That made it easier to accept: it was a *man* playing a *woman* playing a *man*. This façade went on until the last scene when the *young man* would remove the disguise and astoundingly become the female love interest again.

> *I was as amazed at seeing women on stage here, probably as much as Italians would be seeing boys playing the roles in England.*

> *Maybe Thomas Kyd's line from "The Spanish Tragedy" was more meaningful than we thought. Remember? He wrote "What's a play without a woman in it?"*

> *Italy is different. If you would come to visit, it would really be paradise.*

> *Yours always,*

> *Kit*

He folded the letter and placed it on the pile of others he had awaiting Poley. In a way, it was pleasant knowing Thomas would soon be holding this same paper.

# CHAPTER 28

# REMEMBRANCES

It was almost dusk two months later. The evening was breezy but very humid.

Thomas sat by a window at Scadbury and looked at the afternoon sunset.

He wondered what Christopher was doing at that exact moment.

He had read Christopher's last letter many, many times but he unfolded it gently and read again.

> *13 November 1605*
> *Venice, Italy – A Million Miles Away*
> *My Dear Thomas,*
>
> *Remember our poem "The Passionate Shepherd to His Love?" It was the last poem written by Christopher Marlowe before he "died /was murdered /disappeared."*

Thomas liked it when Christopher referred to that poem as "our poem." In a way it was. In a way it had really been written by both of them.

> *That whole love song erupted after just one phrase from you. Do you remember, Thomas? You wrote, "Come live with me and be my love."*

Did Thomas remember? When they first met, Thomas had been recruited into doing a little more spying at the request of his Cousin Francis. The mission was to help ferret out the instigators of a plot to overthrow and kill the Queen, a plot commonly known as the Babington Conspiracy. Christopher, Sir Francis's newest recruit, was assigned to help Thomas, more as a chaser of details than as full espionage assistant.

They had worked together for a few months, both greatly enjoying the conversation of the other. Christopher liked the way they laughed a lot – frequently laughing at someone else without the person suspecting that he was the butt of the humor. Marlowe would roll his eyes or give a smirk and Thomas would have a difficult time, struggling valiantly to keep a sober face, pursing his lips into wild distortions to remain sedate. And the more Thomas strained *not* to giggle like a schoolgirl, the more Christopher would get a glassy stare or cross his eyes, as Thomas tried desperately *not* to glance toward Kit. And that devilish Marlowe loved the thought that he could destroy the formal decorum of the stately Sir Thomas Walsingham with only a glance, a cough, or slight clearing of the throat. It was such a sacred inside joke.

One day Christopher was assigned to ride to Scadbury to deliver some papers to Thomas. When he arrived, he found Walsingham riding Joshua. Thomas thought it best to review the papers in the silence away from the manor, so he suggested they ride to the small caretaker cottage near the east fence. The cottage was the ideal place for privacy since all the staff had been moved to live in the manor house years before.

And, though he didn't quite know why, Thomas thought it might be nice to be there alone with his young companion.

The small wooden building had a musty smell as Thomas opened doors and shutters to let in the fall air. Surprisingly the inside was inviting, hardly disturbed from the days when the caretaker everyone called old Louie lived there.

The sun filtering through the dusty air quickly warmed the room. Thomas sat on the small cot that Louie had used for a bed and read. Christopher sat beside him and waited as document after document was analyzed and evaluated. But the ride had been exhausting for the young poet and he put his head on the small pillow at one end of the couch.

It wasn't long before he was in a state of half-sleep. He could hear the sounds outside the cottage but he was savoring the few minutes of rest, and hoping Thomas would keep reading and let him nap just a bit longer.

Thomas finished reading, put down the papers and smilingly observed his young assistant. For the past few weeks he had been enjoying Christopher's quick wit and clever banter. But now he just let his gaze savor the attractive young spy beside him. He was thin but quite muscular. His hair was a bit too long but full and almost packed with natural waves. Interesting that he had never noticed the long eye lashes, quite lengthy for a man. Obviously, the crystal-green eyes must have distracted him.

The mustache need trimming. Maybe, Thomas thought, he could offer to do that for him. All at once, he realized he was concocting wild fantasies like the young female servants in the mansion. How adolescent, he thought. But he was savoring every moment of watching Christopher sleep.

After many long minutes, without thinking he reached down and ran the tip of his hand gently across the arm of the friend at his side. Christopher, who was by then breathing heavily, didn't react. Thomas leaned back and waited for him to slowly start to stir.

Thomas had not noticed Christopher slightly open his eyes at the gentle touch but pretend to continue sleeping.

After that they met only two or three times. But Thomas could never quite get the young poet off his mind. He had intended to write an informal invitation suggesting they meet again – possibly at Scadbury Manor. But as he started to write, his note evolved into a simple, blatant, one-line love song: "Come live with me and be my love."

Of course, he realized Marlowe might take offense at the forwardness of his suggestion. Or maybe laugh at the ridiculousness of it. He never thought it would result in a reply. But Christopher had written back a beautiful, romantic, classical poem which he called "The Passionate Shepherd to His Love." Nothing was the same after that.

Thomas took quill and wrote:

> *Do I remember? That poem? Oh, yes. And your reply began, "And we will all life's pleasures prove ...."*

> *Christopher, if only it could have lasted forever!*

But just as he was about to put down the quill, a new thought crossed his mind.

He dashed the line:

> *Kit, what are forks?*

## CHAPTER 29

# A DANGEROUS MISFORTUNE

*18 November 1605*
*From A Frightened Scadbury, England*

*Kit,*

*Bad news. Very bad.*

*Our friend, printer Edward Blount, rode out here to Scadbury today with what he excitedly said was "wonderful news."*

*It was not.*

*Sir Walter Ralegh has written a poem that replies to your poem -- or what we call <u>our</u> poem — "The Passionate Shepherd to His Love." He's entitled it "The Nymph's Reply to the Shepherd."*

*All of a sudden everyone in London is talking about Sir Walter and you. We don't need this attention — especially since Cousin Francis and the Constable are still burning with questions and suspicions.*

*Blount says that last year he printed a few copies of Ralegh's poem but didn't expect it to become popular. But then, as if by storm, it has begun to generate great demand of late. And, he tells me, it appears that for every order for Sir Walter's new poem, he gets an order for a copy of yours. The entire country has decided that they are "companion poems" that should be read together. Suddenly this puts your name on everyone's lips and again entangles you with Ralegh. That's bad. Bad. <u>Bad</u>. And it's the reason for this special letter I'm dispatching with Poley today.*

*Blount, of course, didn't know you were still alive and was excited to tell me about the popularity of the two poems. (He realized word of this phenomenon could not have reached Scadbury and so he was thrilled to ride out here to give me his "great news.") He believes that Sir Walter wrote this as a tribute to you, his late, great friend. "This will be an enormous boost for the memory of Christopher," Blount told me.*

*Unfortunately, it will. And once again, it will call attention to all the inconsistencies connected with your "death" at Deptford.*

*It does, however, explain a few odd things that have happened lately. Cousin Francis has abruptly become suspicious of Poley's trips and has arranged for one of his men to be aboard the same ship each month, supposedly to deliver things for him. My guess is that my pudgy little cousin thinks Ralegh knows if you're still alive. So now he and that cunning Constable must be back trying to learn "if yes -- then where?".*

*I'm worried.*

Christopher's poem "The Passionate Shepherd to his Love" had become instantly popular shortly after he wrote it. It was *romantic, idealistic, youthful and naive* – all the things that one would use to describe Marlowe at the time he met Thomas.

Sir Walter Ralegh's companion piece, a reply to the shepherd, was cloaked in a format of a lover's *realistic* response to an impassioned, youthful writer. The Ralegh poem countered each of Christopher's idyllic, innocent images with a similar one seen in a different, very pragmatic, light. He tells the shepherd that – *in real life* -- flowers do fade, youth doesn't last, and winter comes.

Sir Walter wrote:

> *If all the world and love were young*
>
> *And truth in every shepherd's tongue,*
>
> *These pretty pleasures might me move*
>
> *To live with thee and be thy love.*

Ralegh's poem went on to expose the myth in each of the loving reasons that Christopher's poem gives for living together.

In the last verse, however, Ralegh *did* give his poem a slightly encouraging, wistful thought:

> *But could youth last and love still breed,*
>
> *Had joys no date nor age no need,*
>
> *Then these delights my mind might move*
>
> *To live with thee and be thy love.*

Of course, few noticed that Marlowe, *the supposedly hardened member of the spy network,* had lavished his piece with love and naivety while *the purportedly romantic, supposed-lover of the Queen* (yes, the one who had named new provinces in her honor and even gallantly thrown down his cape to keep her shoes dry) had offered the more sobering view.

Naturally, Ralegh's poem did not help Marlowe's covert efforts. Once again, Christopher was a topic of popular conversation and his ties to Sir Walter were once more foremost in the minds of the Constable and Sir Francis.

Sir Walter's poem did just what was *not* needed, Thomas thought. Once again it called attention to all the inconsistencies connected with Marlowe's death.

*Kit, this will give Francis and Maunder new energy to start putting fact to fact. So please, be careful to whom you talk and take care of every word you say.*

*I'm afraid we're back in that same pot of hot porridge of months ago. Remember: <u>careful.</u>*

*Thomas*

# CHAPTER 30

# OMINOUS WARNINGS

A few months later, Christopher was rereading some of the letters from Thomas.

The day was ending. And sunsets were always spectacular in Venice. Christopher sat in a gondola. He could almost hear the voice of Thomas as he read his most recent reply.

> *18 February 1606*
> *A Worried Scadbury, England*
>
> *My Dear Kit,*
>
> *You really must be more careful. Two new plays <u>both</u> taking place in Venice. Constable Maunder could catch that. He knows Shakespeare's never been <u>near</u> Italy.*
>
> *Cousin Francis's troops searched this estate for ten days in terrible heat after you left. He'll get you for that.*
>
> *And Skeres came by looking for more money. He's obviously decided that my bribe to him was "the gift that will keep giving forever."*
>
> *He told me Cousin Francis was furious at Maunder. He overheard Francis scream at him, "Two plays — <u>both taking place in Venice</u>! Maybe Marlowe's next play will list the specific*

*canal where he lives. Would that make it any easier for your idiots to find him?"*

*I love it when Francis gets angry.*

*And if he ever learns that the source material for both "Othello" and "The Merchant of Venice" were written only in Italian – and never translated into English – both you and your buddy Shakespeare may face the executioner.*

*Be careful, Kit. And think. Please think!*

Christopher sat in the gondola and put the letter down. He loved getting any correspondence from Thomas, but he much preferred the joyful, romantic ones over the practical ones with dire warnings. He picked up the quill, dipped it into the small ink pot riding precariously on the bottom of the boat and began to write:

*31 March 1606*
*Lovely Venice, Italy*

*Thomas,*

*I will be more careful. Yes, both plays do take place in Venice. I just got wrapped up in the beauty of the city. I forget sometimes how clever Maunder can be.*

*To quote from one of the works of the immortal Will – no, William – Shakespeare, "This fellow is wise enough to play the fool."*

*Almost a year. Will it ever be safe to return to London?*

*Every sight, every moment here is stunning. But how much more wonderful it would be if I weren't alone. Forget about Poley and bring the next letter yourself. Hurry before my missing you begins to discolour all the splendor of this country.*

*As I wrote in my sonnets: "Make but my name thy love."*

*Kit*

Christopher lay back in the gondola and thought of Thomas and England. He let the boat float on its own.

He realized how different their lives must be. Though both were lonely, Thomas was living a boring life while Christopher's days were filled with wonder and excitement.

Thomas was seeing the same fields and sights of Scadbury while Christopher was experiencing spectacles that had dazzled the world for centuries.

Every day Thomas saw the same staff and servants while Christopher was meeting interesting and stimulating people.

It certainly was not fair. Definitely not fair to Thomas.

# CHAPTER 31

# PADUA

Thomas lay on his back in a field of wild flowers at the far corner of Scadbury, looking at cloud patterns above. Somehow, in some way, the manor seemed to become less and less attractive as each day went on. He realized the problem was not Scadbury.

The companionship, Christopher's voice, the euphoria when they were together – all gone. What was worse is that Thomas had no idea when this nightmarish existence would end. Sometimes he became frightened when he had trouble even conjuring up what Christopher looked like. Had it really been that long?

He didn't want his letters to sound too maudlin. Things had to be difficult for Christopher also, who by then had hurriedly moved to Padua.

He wrote:

> *26 April 1606*
> *A Grey, Grey Scadbury, England*
>
> *Kit,*
>
> > *Is it possible it's been only a year? The longest year of my life.*
> >
> > *I'm glad you moved to Padua. Poley was getting some peculiar questions from the captain of the ship, wondering why*

*he always spends so much time in Venice. And that ship also carries materials for Cousin Francis, so we didn't know how much information is relayed to him.*

*Poley delivered your most recent script, "The Taming of the Shrew." I noticed it was set in Padua.*

*I'm sure when Constable Maunder and my dear Cousin Francis see that play, they will <u>never</u> surmise that their shrewd ex-spy has moved a mere eleven miles away from Venice. So clever of you. How could they possibly <u>guess</u> you're in Padua now?*

*Kit, you didn't even travel the distance that Scadbury is from London. I read the script. Cousin Francis is certainly going to realize you'd have to be in Padua to be so familiar with that town. <u>He knows Padua. He lived there for four years doing his graduate studies at the university</u>.*

*Oh, god, be careful!*

*I regret to relate this but it may make you a little more cautious: Francis was finally able to get Sir Walter Ralegh into prison. The charge was treason. He's in the Tower of London and can certainly be thankful he's not in Bridewell; but it looks like he's there for ever.*

*Again, be cautious.*

*You can't imagine how much I miss you. Sometimes I just imagine you're here with me. But you're not.*

*Thomas*

* * * * *

Months later Christopher sat alone, reading Thomas's letter at the formal dining table of Count Gian-Franco Marinelli. The palazzo was spectacular, and Padua almost rivaled the food and art in Venice.

Christopher picked up his quill and wrote.

*1 September 1606*
*Wonderful Padua, Italy*

*Thomas,*

> *When Poley told me I was to leave Venice, I had to scramble to find a city and a home. Luckily Senatore Spinelli had a close friend in Padua, Count Gian-Franco Marinelli. I haven't quite figured out what's he's a count of. But so long as I can stay here in the huge, huge palazzo, he's a count. And I think he's given me half of the whole place as my own. He seems to be really impressed that I'm writing plays, but says he's never heard of anything written by Thomas Shelton. (Do you like my new name? It's the "nom de plume" I'm using here in Italy. It's the one I used when I let Edward Blount publish my translation of "Don Quixote.")*

Years previously Marlowe had translated Miguel de Cervantes lengthy novel *Don Quixote* from Spanish to English. He picked a pseudonym for two reasons – first as a rather daring lark (so consistent with Marlowe's untamed existence) and secondly because he wanted to develop his reputation as a budding playwright, not a translator of literary masterpieces.

A close friend of Walsingham, a printer named Edward Blount, had the work published under the name Thomas Shelton. Marlowe liked that name. Thomas Shelton. Yes.

> *Though the Count is a good friend of Senatore Spinelli, he has never heard of Henry Wriothesley. If you met Count Marinelli, you would think he and Henry could be very close. Two horses from the same stable. Believe me.*

> *There was no way I could have set "Taming of the Shrew" anywhere but here. The city is a center of art and culture. And it cried out to be the setting for "Shrew." Padua was the home of Dante and Donatello. And there's a young astronomer at the university named Galileo who seems to be making some wonderful, wonderful discoveries.*

*The Cathedral here has the body of St. Anthony, most of it not decomposed -- even after 500 years -- they say. And the tongue is supposedly like new. I'm not sure I want to visit the church. All I would need is for that tongue to start moving and questioning me about all my sins — most of them with you. I'm not big on tongues.*

*If the tongue does start criticizing me, I'm going to tell him: those sins were all <u>your</u> fault.*

*Remember, "The fault, dear Thomas, lies not in our stars but in ourselves." Right?*

*Kit*

## CHAPTER 32

# DANGEROUS THREAT

Christopher didn't know it but his days in Padua were also numbered.

Even though Thomas had no sign that anyone suspected Marlowe's exact whereabouts, extensive precautions were always a way of life to Walsingham.

In stark contrast, Poley *always* felt he was about to be apprehended. So, he was continuously scared. But even *he* hadn't noticed anything different lately.

And Christopher, of course, was only concerned with letters from Thomas, the sleepy beauty of Padua, or any new scenes he was able to finish writing.

So the incident came as a shock to everyone.

It was the fifteenth of the month and Poley would be arriving in Padua that day with letters from Thomas, more money than Christopher could ever need, and the usual bag of Christopher's favorite foods, special treats and supplies.

Marlowe's latest letter to Thomas was ready for Poley. He penned a missive filled with loving appreciation.

*3 May 1607*
*Padua*

*Thomas*

*Thank you for sending the pots of ink, the heavier paper, and my other good quill pen. There is something else you can send, however. In the next package, please include one Thomas Walsingham. You can find Walsinghams just outside of London at Scadbury Manor. One would be enough.*

*But the supplies need not include any cheese. The Italians have quite mastered that art far better than England ever will.*

*Kit*

Why bother Walsingham with his one complaint. The blue cheese that the Italians called "gorgonzola" was drippy — they called it "weeping" — while good English stilton had a nice, firm feel. But, Christopher realized, he could live with weepy blue cheese.

Just as midday arrived, Christopher decided to meet Poley on the street outside Count Marinelli's palazzo. Poley always arrived from the south, so Marlowe left by the side entrance and walked carelessly south on the *Via Avagoria*.

When Christopher was a few steps onto the road, he could see Poley coming from the other way. He had long ago given up wearing the disguises. Anyone who would follow him would certainly know what he looked like.

As Christopher walked down the narrow street, he did *not* notice the two tall men just steps behind him — noticeably tall for Italians. *But Poley could see them.* And he could see how close they were.

Without warning, Poley turned into the walk leading up to the nearest *palazzo* and began banging at the door. Confused, Christopher just stopped, trying to determine what Poley could possibly be doing.

The two men behind him walked past Marlowe toward Poley — obviously for a better view of what was happening. That was when Christopher realized that he was standing inches behind spies trying to learn where he was hiding.

The neighbor's door suddenly opened and a very surprised *Signora* Frisella was almost blown back by Poley's screaming and shaking. "Sir Walsingham wants his fifty million *lire* now," he shouted — not a word of his English making any sense to this Italian woman. "Sir Walsingham says I'm to get the money today or the demons of hell will descend on you," he yelled.

*Signora* Frisella, of course, matched him volume for volume, her swearing in Italian in almost perfect counterpoint to his screams. Seconds later, her husband appeared in the doorway and added his *basso profundo*.

As the tall men stared in bewilderment, Christopher, by then only a few steps behind them, cautiously backed into the side entrance of Count Marinelli's home. The two men were too fascinated by Poley's spectacle to notice Marlowe leaving.

Finally, in a burst of anxiety, the husband ran out into the street and began shouting "*Carabinieri...Polizia...Carabinieri...*"

Hearing the call for police quickly sent the two men scurrying up the road. And they were gone.

*Signora* Frisella and Poley continued to yell at each other until a uniformed officer arrived minutes later.

Then, just as suddenly, Poley became the epitome of dignity, smiling but looking bewildered.

As the officer approached, Poley questioned, oh, so sweetly, "Count Marinelli?" while gesturing first to the Frisella home and then to the Marinelli home next door.

The Frisella couple was dumbfounded. Utterly mystified, they both pointed at the same time: next door.

Poley smiled angelically, gave *Signora* Frisella a wet kiss on the cheek and beamed "*Grazie*" as he headed down the street, innocently handing Marlowe the two large parcels as he passed.

Christopher lowered his head and laughed.

And because of that, Marlowe realized he had to find a new home: this time he again moved just a few miles away -- to Verona.

## CHAPTER 33

# VERONA

The recent incident in Padua made Poley even more nervous every time the captain of the ship made a casual remark about his courier stops. Actually that should have caused no serious concern. After all, the ship was a courier-delivery ship and the captain made his stops to accommodate the appointments of the passengers. But Poley would get paranoid and Thomas would play it safe by suggesting Christopher move on. Naturally, he had to leave it to Marlowe to decide where he would locate next.

But the move did solve one problem. It concerned Shakespeare and the word "Padua."

William Shakespeare had by then pretty much mastered the ability to send any questions or comments about the plays to his "wonderful sponsor who is my muse, my inspiration, my repository of facts, ideas, and background."

"Oh, yes, Sir Wriothesley and I have meticulously discussed that subject" (or question or historical detail or whatever), he would expound auspiciously, "but I think *he* is so much better able to encapsulate our thinking that you really must discuss it with him."

No one seemed to notice that William used the *exact same phrasing*, word for word, no matter what was asked.

But "Padua" was a problem. The Globe Theatre had decided to stage *The Taming of the Shrew*. Ordinarily that should have caused no problems. But for some unknown reason, Shakespeare would have this confused look whenever anyone (actor, playgoer – *anyone*) mentioned the name of that town. ("Mr. Shakespeare, when Petrucio leaves Padua...") His lack of familiarity with the name (or even worse the Italian pronunciation, *Padova*) would elicit an alarming state of confusion.

It never occurred to him to go into his rehearsed speech whenever he was befuddled by *any* question.

Or maybe that wouldn't have been such a good idea. ("How are you feeling today, Mr. Shakespeare?" "Oh, Sir Wriothesley and I have meticulously discussed that subject but I think he is so much better able to encapsulate our thinking. You really must discuss it with him.")

Nevertheless, it was a relief to everyone (Christopher, Thomas, Wriothesley, and Poley) when Marlowe finally left Padua.

By the beginning of the next month, Christopher had finally settled in Verona. A fortnight later, he read the latest missive from Thomas.

> *9 December 1608*
> *Forlorn and Dismal Scadbury, England*
>
> Kit,
>
> > *Soon the New Year will be here. Has it really been three years, Kit? But I am glad to hear you like Verona. I know it's difficult to keep moving but.... Skeres came by again today, with more tales about Cousin Francis and the Constable.*

Then Thomas added, with light sarcasm,

> > *Isn't it amazing what they can sense simply by reading two plays that <u>both</u> take place in the same Italian town: "Two Gentlemen of Verona" and "Romeo and Juliet?"*
>
> > *"I know you're tired of hearing this," Skeres heard Francis telling Maunder, " but, don't you wonder why Mr. Shakespeare seems to be giving us a guided tour of Italy when he's never even been there. And now, Constable, <u>two</u> plays – both about <u>Verona</u>."*

*Really, Kit, why couldn't it have been "Two Gentlemen of Nottingham?"*

*Or why couldn't Romeo and Juliet be Dutch kids? A suicide's a suicide, Kit -- <u>anywhere</u>.*

*And what would have been wrong with "The Merchant of Liverpool?"*

# CHAPTER 34

# REVENGE

Sir Francis was accustomed to soft, apprehensive raps on the high oak doors to his inner office.

So, he flinched at the sudden pounding.

"Yes?"

Sir Henry Wriothesley, just two steps ahead of the guard at the office door, charged into the room and up to the desk. "You sent this note, Sir Francis, saying you wanted to see me – *here* – in your office?" he asked, waving the note in the face of Sir Francis as if it were a smelly dead animal – before dropping it clinically on the desk.

Sir Francis nodded to the guard who left and silently closed the doors.

The only reply from Sir Francis was, "Yes, Sir Henry."

The two of them looked at each other and said nothing – almost as if they had never met before.

"You wanted…?" Wriothesley asked, sitting, without invitation, in a large, red-velvet 15$^{th}$ century settee.

Sir Francis waited the obligatory few seconds before answering. This showed who was in charge of the interview. "Yes, Sir Henry. I have a few questions about your young ward, William Shakespeare."

Once again, there was the stalemate of silence.

"Could you be a bit more specific?" Henry ventured.

Each stared at the other with a metallic glint.

"Certainly, Sir Henry." Sir Francis put down his quill and folded his hands on the desk. "There seems to be a multitude of questions concerning the obvious discrepancy between Mr. Shakespeare's background and Mr. Shakespeare's writings."

"Really? Like what?"

"Well, to begin with, he's been writing all those plays but he's had hardly any education."

"And why would he need that to write the bawdy fare that goes on at those vulgar playhouses, *Francis?*"

Sir Francis was aware of Henry addressing him on a first-name basis, there in the office of England's Secretary of State. Wriothesley smiled, knowing full well that he was taking perilous chances.

"Then, where does he get the material for all his plays, *Henry?*" Two could play this first-name game.

"Where? *Where?* I have a library second to none and *you ask where he gets his material?*"

"And his knowledge of court manners? And his familiarity with so much of Italy? He's never been to court and never been out of the country."

"This may surprise you, Francis, but *I* have. *I* have been to court and *I* have spent time in Italy. Those are *my* stories that he tells. *I* am his muse." Wriothesley smiled demurely and seemed to be almost striking a classical pose on the velvet settee.

"His last two plays were both set in Verona. Henry, he's never left England."

"Verona? Why? Because I happen to love Verona and suggested William use that as a setting for his two new plays. Did you notice that Romeo's family name is 'Montague?' That's my grandfather's name, remember? I thought that touch would be cute." Henry rode this treatise to the fullest, thankful that Christopher had told him of the tribute that he had included: a reference to Wriothesley's grandfather's name.

"And, remember, Francis, for years I taught the Italian language to local aristocrats. I *do* know Italy *and* Italian. These are *my* stories he tells. If I weren't his sponsor, I'd be expecting half of all his payments from the Globe Theatre." Henry looked almost insulted.

"But my friends tell me...."

"Your *spies* tell you, Francis...."

Sir Francis smiled. "They tell me he spends more time with the Widow Vautrollier and Mistress Davenant and some local...." Sir Francis paused, searching for the proper euphemism.

"*Professional female friends?*" Henry suggested smiling.

"Yes. He spends more time with his *friends* than he does with you."

"Really, Francis," Henry scoffed, shifting to a more elegant pose. "You, above all, should be aware of the difference between the quantity of time," he paused to add an intellectual tone, "and the *quality* of time."

Sir Francis was losing his calm, "Henry, let me put it very bluntly: either someone else is writing his works or *somebody's* helping him."

"*Helping him?* Yes," Henry put on his most modest air, "and it's me." His delicate pose made it look as if he were throwing a gentle kiss across the room.

Sir Francis was getting nowhere and tiring of this vulgar display. "Well, then, thank you, Henry. You've been much help."

"Of course," was the simple answer as Wriothesley pompously walked to the desk, grabbed his note and paraded out. The performance really needed an orchestral fanfare.

A door at the back of the room quietly opened and Constable Maunder walked to the desk.

"Did you hear?"

"All of it," Maunder replied, not wanting to offer any evaluation.

"Tomorrow I will sign an order to have Sir Henry Wriothesley taken to the tower of London for a while in an effort to... how shall I put it? … give him time to think if there could be some other way – or person -- that Shakespeare could be using for his information. Decide on some charge. But Henry will know why he's there."

"And you'll also arrest Shakespeare?" Maunder asked.

"Oh, *no*, Constable. We'll just leave Shakespeare here without his '*muse.*' That should prove that Henry Wriothesley is really *not* the inspiration for the plots and tales attributed to William Shakespeare. Shouldn't it?"

Maunder looked at his superior and could almost hear his thoughts. Sir Francis had to be thinking "What a coincidence, Henry Wriothesley. You have a name that actually *does* begin with a silent 'W'. But this time, it's not a 'W' as in 'whore' … but as in 'whom'. Yes, as in 'whom' … whom shall we put into prison now?"

# CHAPTER 35

# SHAKESPEARE PANICS

*5 October 1609*
*Desolate Scadbury, England*

*Kit.*

*Well, Cousin Francis finally got him. Though the charge was treason, he told Henry that his assignment to prison was actually to loosen his tongue and get some truth about Shakespeare. Myself, I think it was that remark that Henry made in our dining room when he called Francis a whore. Wriothesley told me he defended himself to Constable Maunder when he was presented with the summons. "As I've explained before, Constable, I spend endless hours with Will discussing all those esoteric subjects and all the fine points about Italian towns, court manners, and ... It's really <u>my</u> stories he tells."*

*Of course, the arguments did no good. And so now Henry enjoys free living quarters in the Tower of London. And, he insisted on taking his new cat — no-- not cat -- feline, to jail with him. To kill the mice in his cell, he said.*

*I can almost see it now. Henry walking down those dark, dingy halls cradling "Chanteuse" in his arms and then placing a few pieces of dirty cloth on the floor before putting down the damn cat.*

Oh, well, Christopher thought as he read the missive in Verona. Why have a few mice running around your cell when you can have a never-ending supply of dead ones lying around?

Thomas must have read his mind, because he added:

*Half-eaten dead ones.*

Christopher sat reading by the window of his room, high on the top floor of the small room in Verona. His new host there was Augusto Rizzo, another friend of *Senatore* Spinelli. No one seemed to question these requests from the senator but instead hospitably opened doors to this "Thomas Shelton," an unknown English author.

The Rizzo home was large but certainly not palatial. Nevertheless, Christopher's two small rooms in an upstairs garret gave him a wonderful view of the rooftops and sights of all of Verona. How Thomas would love this city, he thought. Christopher gazed out over the rooftops and could see the *Duomo* and all the little food stalls on the *Via San Barnaba* below his window. How much more enjoyable all this would be if Thomas were here with him in his snug room at that moment.

He sat by a large, arched window, reading. Outside, the light rain gave the small room a comfortable feel.

Occasionally, the wind would blow a spray of rain onto him, but Christopher didn't mind. He was in the middle of a letter from Thomas.

*10 February 1611*
*Dismal Scadbury, England*

*Kit,*

*Lately our friend Will – excuse me, William – has been petrified. All I said to him was, "Why are you so upset?"*

*That opened the floodgates. "Why am I so upset? Why am I so upset? One day I have a famous and powerful nobleman as a protector – and poof – the next day he's gone to prison. That's why I'm so upset. And I keep encountering that Privy Council Inspector every time I turn a corner. Coincidence? I think not. I have now used every excuse possible to keep from talking to him."*

*So, Christopher, no one has seen Will in the last three weeks.*

*Before he left he came to see me and said, "Thomas, with Sir Henry in prison, I cannot even <u>chance</u> meeting Constable Maunder. I'm going to leave London and go where no one can find me. If anyone asks, tell them I'm in Brighton finishing a play."*

*Can you imagine that? He's reading a play.*

Christopher was laughing. He didn't know his companion even *had* such a sense of humor.

*But I can see why William got so frightened. Constable Maunder is really trying to tie the "dead" poet Marlowe to the not-too-articulate Shakespeare.*

*So please, please, be careful.*

## CHAPTER 36

# QUESTIONS, QUESTIONS

It had been months since Constable Maunder had visited Scadbury. So, it was an unexpected shock when Thomas noticed him standing in the doorway of the barn. How long, Thomas wondered, had he been just *standing* there, watching him grooming Joshua.

"Good morning, Sir Thomas," the Constable said once he realized his presence was apparent.

"Constable Maunder," Walsingham replied. "I didn't see you standing there."

"Admiring that wonderful steed. Joshua, isn't it?"

"Is there anything about Scadbury you *don't* know?"

"There are a few things I don't -- but would *like* to," Maunder added impishly, the double meaning tossed into the air like a playful ball.

"*Anything*. Anything you'd like," Thomas replied with a gentle lilt in his voice, matching the Constable's clever response. "Just ask."

The two of them smiled at one another, each enjoying the excitement of the game they both had been missing of late. Thomas returned to the long, hard brushing of the horse's coat. "I told you. Just ask," he repeated mischievously.

When he got no reply for a few minutes, he stopped grooming the beautiful chestnut prize, and turned. "Well?"

Finally, the Constable played his first card. "Well … don't you think it's odd," he asked so naively, "that there are so many similarities *and connections* between Mr. Shakespeare and Poet Marlowe – and they never even *met* each other?"

"Constable, haven't you already asked all the questions possible about those two people?"

"Some mysteries just get more interesting the more you study them," he answered honestly. "Don't you think so?"

"*Mysteries?*" Thomas asked a bit too innocently? "What mysteries?"

"Well, Sir Thomas, here's one. Thomas Kyd wrote a play about Hamlet, the Prince of Denmark, when he was living with Poet Marlowe. And now, almost a decade later – Shakespeare has written one about the same person."

"You're asking about Shakespeare's *Hamlet?*" Thomas sounded actually puzzled. "The stories are there in Hollingshed's *Chronicles* for anyone to pluck and use." (Walsingham felt rather proud of his beguiling phrase "pluck and use.")

Maunder chuckled. "But, Sir Thomas, isn't that '*plucking*' one more case of something Shakespeare does that seems more like something Poet Marlowe would do. After all, it was Poet Marlowe who was *living* with Thomas Kyd when Kyd wrote his *Hamlet*. And Mr. Kyd died before Shakespeare could even meet him."

Thomas went back to grooming Joshua, pretending he was trying to grasp what the Constable was alluding to. "And…so…?" he asked.

"So…that made me notice another odd coincidence. Don't you find an unusual connection between Marlowe's play *The Jew of Malta* and Shakespeare's *The Merchant of Venice?*" They're *both* plays about a Jewish man's plights on an island off the coast of Italy."

"And *that* makes you assume there's a connection between my former ward and William Shakespeare? I'm not sure I see any connection."

"Well, how about this, Sir Thomas." Maunder had thrown in the first two situations as a casual first course, saving his strongest assault for last. "I'm sure you know about the incident with Marlowe and a fellow poet friend named Thomas Watson. They were involved in the death of a man."

"I have heard about that. The murdered man was named Bradley. Christopher had mentioned it to me. But his friend, Watson, was cleared of the murder and released."

"If I understand it correctly," Maunder went on, "it was Poet Marlowe and this Mr. Bradley who were having an argument that grew into the prospect of a deadly duel. Then, Marlowe's friend, Watson, who was living with Mr. Marlowe at the time, intervened. Watson supposedly grabbed Bradley's sword and ran him through."

"And, so?"

"Well, Sir Thomas, that was more than seven years ago but two similar situations have arisen just recently."

Walsingham waited, knowing full well that Maunder was going to go on.

"Can't you spot them?" Maunder finally asked.

"No, Constable. I can't."

"Well, that incident was a case of *one person*, like Marlowe, being in a fight when *a friend* intervenes, grabs the knife and kills the *opponent*.

"And the two recent similar situations?" Thomas asked, sincerely baffled.

Maunder took a few seconds to take a deep breath of the country air, adding to the drama of the moment. "Well," he finally went on, "The first one is the fight in the new play at the Globe Theatre. What happened between Watson and Bradley is exactly identical to the fight that Juliet's cousin has with Romeo. Her cousin and Romeo are fighting when Romeo's friend Mercutio steps in, grabs the cousin's knife and kills him."

Walsingham was trying to look interested when Maunder went on. "Odd that *Shakespeare* would model a stage fight so close to an incident in *Marlowe's* life. They never met, remember?"

Christopher had mentioned to Thomas that he used the fight between Watson and Bradley as his model for the scene in *Romeo and Juliet*, but he never expected anyone to notice the similarity. How could anyone even *know* about that fight with Bradley? Thomas suddenly realized that this simpleton was no fool.

And Maunder waited patiently for Walsingham to take the bait. "And the other incident?" Thomas finally asked.

"The time Mr. Frizer killed Mr. Marlowe," the Constable fired back quickly. Then slowly, he added, "That *too* was identical, wasn't it?" His unsmiling façade seemed as if he had just scored a check-mate. "Right?" he finally asked.

At that moment the line from *Henry VIII* seemed to be ringing in Walsingham's ears: "This man is exceedingly wise, fair-spoken and persuasive." Yes, Maunder was putting piece to piece and coming up with some menacing conclusions.

Thomas was going to have to warn Christopher.

## CHAPTER 37

# RETURN TO STRATFORD

Once Wriothesley had been arrested, Shakespeare was nowhere to be found.

He made only one visit to London and that was to tell Thomas Walsingham he was going to leave the city for ever. There was no way he could chance meeting Constable Maunder now that his patron – and his protection -- was in prison. One specific question from the Constable about *any* of the plays and he would be up before the Privy Council.

And, he knew full well that the cell next to Wriothesley might as well have his own name on the door.

Oh, no. Shakespeare had to disappear.

And yet he was afraid to go back to Stratford. That, he reasoned, would be the first place Maunder would look.

But in desperation, he decided to venture home just once to observe the mood there. Just in case he *had* to hide in Stratford.

But "home" proved to be worse than a world with Maunder and Sir Francis and Beelzebub combined.

"You want to do *what?* she screamed.

"Well, I just thought that maybe I could...."

"You want to come back *home*? *HOME?*" Anne Shakespeare could be heard up and down Chapel Street, the main thoroughfare in Stratford where their new home was located. "My loving husband hasn't been in this house for years and now you want to come *home*? You call it *home*?"

"I've been sending money regularly, haven't I?"

Anne turned her head slowly and shot a look that actually propelled William to sit down on one of the hard wooden chairs beside the kitchen table. "Oh, yes. *Yes*," she began in deep rumbling voice that built in volume and pitch with every syllable. "You did send funds. *You sent them with the new husband of the Widow Vautrollier. Just to get him out of the house for a few days. Out of the house -- so you could have your way with his...*" At this point she paused, out of breath and searching for the vilest term she should find. "*... his wife.*" She spit out the word with the volume and screeches she usually reserved for calling the dogs in the evening.

"Anne, I don't know where you're getting those stories ...."

"From *Oxford*!" she bellowed.

"Oxford?"

"*Oxford*," she yelled like a judge condemning a prisoner to death. "*Does the name 'Mistress Davenant' ring your bells?*" Shakespeare was silent. "Yes, Mistress Davenant?" she went on with poisonous sweetness. "And that little bastard named William she has tearing around the tavern? Remember him?"

"I don't know what ..." Shakespeare began.

"Don't lie," she roared. "Vautrollier's own husband had to be the one to tell *me* what *you* were doing." She slammed a jug onto the table with a deafening crash. "And every one of our neighbors here in Stratford has told me about tales they've heard from friends in Oxford." When her husband tried to look as if he didn't quite understand, she exploded. "Mistress Davenant! *Mistress Davenant!* Think!" And then, lifting her breasts with her fists, she spit out "You must remember – *them?*" She sat across the table from him, glaring.

Shakespeare said nothing.

"Would you like to hear more?"

William looked down and finally said, "No. No, I think not."

Anne Shakespeare was eight years older than her husband and noticeably bigger than William, outweighing him by almost five kilos. And she looked more formidable. The moment had a tension that seemed to be developing into a theatrical scene where the wife tears off one of the husband's limbs. Maybe two.

Shakespeare had played in this scene with her before and knew enough to remain silent until he could tell she was breathing more evenly.

"I bought you this house," he ventured at last.

She grunted.

"And now we have a family crest."

She shifted her weight.

Parlaying his new-found status, William had been able to get a crest for the Shakespeare family, something of which he was rightly proud. And a few years earlier, in 1596, with his new riches he had purchased New Place, the second-largest home in Stratford. And the only one made of brick in the whole town. This, he reasoned, would placate his "loving wife" while he was in London, "performing."

It did not.

So when Shakespeare decided he had to become "undetectable," Stratford, he reasoned, was probably not the spot. It should be avoided since it would be the first place Maunder would look for him. And besides, his wife's reaction could hardly be called *receptive* or *gracious*. So, he reasoned, he could forget about going back home.

He decided he would divide his time from that point on, moving surreptitiously, among four or five places: Widow Vautrollier's (whenever he could get her husband out of London); the Tavern of Mistress Davenant in Oxford (where no one would think of looking); Lord Wriothesley's estate (where he had a quarters, though he did not want to remain there permanently lest he be easy to locate); and a few of his female friends in and around London (where he was unquestionably one of their best customers).

It would be necessary to visit Scadbury occasionally to collect funds from Sir Thomas; but for the most part he had to keep moving.

Maybe go back to Stratford later.

Yes, maybe later.

## CHAPTER 38

# CHRISTMAS IN MILAN

By the following Christmas Marlowe had moved again, this time to his fourth city in Italy.

It was safer in Milan. A bigger town, dating back three centuries before Christ. There was much more traffic and Poley could come by horseback from the port in Genoa which was miles away. But that made it more difficult for anyone to learn where Poley was going.

Poley had been given the location of the place where Christopher was staying -- a huge home belonging to Widow Inga, another friend of the *Senatore* from Venice. Marlowe lived alone in one of the houses she owned – a whole house to himself.

Christopher wanted to meet in the *piazza*, in front of Milan's *Duomo*, the huge cathedral. The church was, as the Italians worded it, "not quite finished yet." They had been building it for more than 250 years but history would show they still had a few more centuries to go before completion.

Poley was concerned but agreed to meet in public. He had noticed some odd travelers in Milan that looked like those he had seen in Genoa when the boat landed.

Christopher waited in the *piazza*, relaxed, knowing Poley would be coming soon. The day was chilly but the sun was warm. The crowd seemed to be richly dressed, perhaps a carryover from the holiday season. Christmas bunting and decorations were still up awaiting the Epiphany celebrations. And the almost life-size Nativity scene filled the center of the square. But all this elation was crowned by the satisfaction of knowing he had finished writing three new scenes that very morning.

Marlowe sat high up on the front steps of the *Duomo*, lost in thought. Then he noticed the quick movements of a man in the crowded square. Could that be Poley?

He watched carefully as the man made his way between merchants and shoppers in a pattern that was noticeably puzzling. And then he saw *them*. Two other men in dark, heavy cloaks following the exact same path.

It *was* Poley. And he was being followed.

Poley snaked his way through the crowded *piazza*, closer and closer until Christopher felt he had to slide across the church step where he was sitting to be behind a pair of loud merchants shouting with both their voices and their hands. He wasn't sure if he could be seen.

Then all at once he caught Poley's eye. There was an instant of recognition and movement toward Christopher. Paralyzed with fear, Christopher saw the cloaked figures nearly overtake Poley. Worse, he noticed, they each carried a length of rope.

When Poley was within a few meters of Christopher, he suddenly stopped and thrust his pack of letters into the hands of a bewildered shopper, who was loaded with bundles of bread and pork. When the befuddled man almost dropped everything, Poley placed the letters directly on top of a leg of pork that had its foot over the shopper's shoulder. The baffled bystander could do nothing but watch Poley disappear into the maze of people.

Immediately, the two followers grabbed the bewildered man by both arms and securely tied ropes to each wrist. All the food and the bundle of letters went bouncing onto the cobblestone *piazza*. He argued and struggled but to no avail as he was dragged down a narrow street nearby.

A commotion erupted -- voices, people pointing, others grabbing his packages from the ground, and some following the prisoner down the passageway.

Christopher was too shocked to move. Then he noticed Poley on the church step behind him. Poley inconspicuously laid down the package of envelopes he had originally slapped onto the unsuspecting man in the piazza. He gave a look of warning to Marlowe, and was gone.

Christopher picked up the bundle, stuffed it under his tunic, and left – with a far greater appreciation for his cohort than ever before.

## CHAPTER 39

# THE FAITHFUL COURIER

After that close call in Milan, Christopher found notes from Poley indicating it was too risky to meet in public.

"Best for me to go to your home," he wrote. This was a safer method of delivering letters from Walsingham. It would appear far less suspicious if someone were following him. And, even more importantly, it meant that Christopher would be safely inside the house in case there was any trouble.

Marlowe designed the code. Poley's signal would be to pull the bell chain three times, wait, and then pull it two times. Three plus two. (In spite of his newfound respect for his friend, he couldn't help designing a system that Poley would find irritating and confusing.) Three and two. Christopher laughed, hoping those were two numbers that Poley couldn't get mixed up.

It was raining hard and Poley was getting soaked. He rang three times, waited, then two times, and waited. And waited -- getting soggier and soggier by the minute.

Finally, the delivery opening was unlocked. This small door was used in the finer areas of *Milano* to deliver things without the trouble (and risk) of opening the entire kitchen door.

Poley quickly thrust his hand into the opening with a stack of letters, wrapped in rabbit hide to keep them from getting wet.

Unfortunately, *he* was not wrapped in rabbit hide and *was* getting wet. Very wet.

Christopher took the package. Poley waited patiently to receive letters, scripts, anything. When there was nothing, he started to feel around inside. Maybe he could reach whatever was supposed to be taken.

Christopher fleetingly flicked Poley's fingers with the letters, teasingly holding the new script away. Poley felt from side to side. Finally, Christopher grabbed Poley's hand and began to shake it vigorously.

"Hello. My name is Christopher," he said. "What's yours?"

This, of course, seemed a lot funnier to Marlowe than to his sopping-wet courier.

Finally, Christopher gave him the package containing script and letters. Through the delivery opening he watched Poley rushing away, probably inventing never-heard-before profanities.

Christopher walked upstairs. The small room was strewn with sheets of paper – but it was cozy and warm. He decided not to light any candles but instead read his new mail at the window by the light of the storm.

> *13 March 1612*
> *A Gloomy and Solitary Scadbury, England*
>
> *Kit,*
>
> *You asked how I get your scripts performed now that Shakespeare has gone back to Stratford.*
>
> *I take them to the scrivener and say they're from Shakespeare and the scrivener takes them to the Globe Theatre. What fools these mortals be.*
>
> *Skeres keeps coming around to trade information for money. It's become steady income for him but I'm satisfied with it too. For a few coins I get to know everything going on with Cousin Francis. Ah, how we contaminate our fingers with base bribes!*

*Skeres has been boasting to me how he's learned exactly where to hide in order to hear everything said whenever there's a meeting with Maunder. He says he's got this system down to an art (and he seems to get bizarre pleasure from being able to eavesdrop on the head of England's spy service.)*

*But lately, he tells me, Francis has been more furious. Skeres heard him ask "One of your men goes every month on the same ship with Poley, right, Constable?"*

*"Yes, Sir Francis, to Italy."*

*"Where in Italy?"*

*"Well, lately Poley gets off at Genoa and then rides to various towns. He seems to be spending a lot of time in Milan every trip."*

Christopher closed his eyes for a moment and tried to think. This was not good. He continued to read:

*So, you see, Christopher, it's time to move again. T h i s time, go south, instead, don't you think?*

*I have friends in Naples and I've asked Poley to   d e l i v e r my request to them after he visits you. I'm sure         t h e y will gladly welcome Thomas Shelton, writer.*

*Remember:*

*"Tomorrow and tomorrow and tomorrow…*

*Creeps in this petty pace from day to day."*

*It has been so many years. But it will end, Christopher.*

*I pray: it will.*

*Am I being foolish to ask if you think about me as much as I think about you? Yes, I am being foolish.*

*Your Thomas*

# CHAPTER 40

# SICILY

arlowe was in his seventh city in seven years, moving next to Naples and then to Messina and finally to Sicily. Every time he felt he was safely hidden, the Constable's spies would discover some bit of information, or talk to someone who had seen Poley leaving the ship.

Moving from city to city was never easy. Christopher had, by that time, exhausted all the recommendations that *Senatori* Spinelli had given him. And Marlowe always had to trust his former landlords to tell Poley how to find his new location.

Christopher was tired. He was tired of living in other people's homes or smelly inns. He was tired of food that had originally seemed to be so delicious but now tasted like it was swimming in olive oil and garlic. And he missed England.

Not as much as he missed Thomas. He wanted to go home. He wanted to feel Thomas's hands on his shoulders the way he always held him when he wanted Christopher to listen carefully. He wanted to just *look* at Thomas, the smile in his dark brown eyes even when he was pretending to be angry. He wanted to be relaxed and not worry about who might discover his whereabouts. He wanted to spend endless hours with Thomas talking about absolutely nothing. He wanted to see that silly grin when Thomas would try to trick him and then realize Christopher was wise to him all the time. He wanted the hidden sidelong glances as they secretly chuckled whenever someone said something stupid. But most of all he missed relaxing completely, knowing that Thomas was handling everything.

But he knew he couldn't go back. Not yet. And his newest excursion was to Sicily. How much farther south could he go? This was it.

He tried Palermo, the island capital. It was big and confusing enough to hide any spy. But he didn't like the place. It was dirty and loud and crowded.

So, he was living in a small inn in *Syracusa*, the town the English called Syracuse. It was actually a village that was situated on another island -- a few meters off the island of Sicily.

It was beautiful. It was quiet. And he really didn't care any more. He was tired of running – and hiding.

The only thing that could lift his spirits was the occasional visit from Poley. Not that they spoke much, but Christopher did enjoy irritating "his beloved courier," as he called him.

The door of his small room had a mail opening which Marlowe unlocked when he heard the code knock: three knocks and then two.

Poley's hand appeared with envelopes. Christopher took the envelopes and began to lick the hand.

Poley began to panic.

Christopher held Poley's arm so he couldn't pull away and began to suck his thumb sensuously.

Poley kept struggling. Oh, god, what is going on inside that room?

Finally, Christopher gave the palm one long, last tonguing and put the new script and letters into his hand.

He could hear Poley running down the steps.

Inside Christopher opened the first envelope. Thomas had written:

> *26 June 1612*
> *An Uneasy Scadbury, England*
>
> *Kit,*
>
> > *You asked if I liked "Winter's Tale."*

*You know you're not <u>helping</u> the situation.*

*Your last three plays were each set in the towns where you were living: "The Tempest" in Milan and Naples; then "Much Ado About Nothing" in Messina; and finally, "Winter's Tale" in Sicily.*

*I suggested you go south. But, Kit, even people who have never been to Italy could plot your travels – if they had a crude map and a list of your plays.*

*Maybe Francis was right. If you have a death wish to be arrested, just include a street address in your next play.*

*I got a note from Henry in prison. He's been moved to new quarters in the Tower of London. He said his mother <u>pleaded</u> with Lord Burghley to have him moved. Can you believe it? His <u>mother</u> pleaded for him. The man has no shame! But, happily he now has a suite that costs his mother nine pounds a week. He suspects they are the same quarters where they kept Mary, Queen of Scots, for so many years. Yes, Henry got fine quarters and the prison captain gets nine pounds a week. Ill blows the wind that profits nobody.*

*Henry said he asked for the change only because Jacques seemed so unhappy. I have to assume that Jacques is his new French cat. (But who knows what he's got in there with him.) His last note also mentioned that with the exception of your historical works he noticed that none of your plays take place in England. If <u>Wriothesley</u> notices that, imagine what <u>Cousin Francis</u> must be thinking.*

*I know you're tired. And I know you want to come home. But please, please, <u>please</u> be careful.*

*And do not – I repeat: do <u>not</u> -- send me the script for some idiotic play like "Hamlet, the Prince of Palermo."*

# CHAPTER 41

# "HE'S ALIVE"

"He's alive."

Sir Francis was speaking evenly, as if talking to a child.

"Yes, Sir Francis." Cecil Parker, one of his best spies, stood uncomfortably across from the desk. He was nervous as he always was when he could tell Sir Francis was in a very bad mood. A gentle, cool tone was always a warning. And usually the prelude to an explosion.

How Parker wished he had been asked to sit. His nervousness would not be so obvious.

But Sir Francis had not merely forgotten a social courtesy. He was very familiar with that tactic and used it often. Parker uneasily fingered the edge of his tunic.

"He's still alive."

"Yes, Sir Francis, but every time --"

"And, unfortunately, *everyone* seems to know he's still alive, Parker."

"Yes, Sir Francis." Parker realized it was best not to argue.

"Parker, how many times has the constable sent you on the same boat as Poley?"

An embarrassing pause. "Eight, sir."

"Eight?"

"But, Sir Francis, Constable Maunder sends a different spy on that ship every month and so I --"

And then the explosion came. Sir Francis' face suddenly turned red. "And you still can't find him?" he screamed. "All these years, you've known *where* he was, *what he's been doing* and even the towns where he meets that stupid messenger. *And none of you can find Marlowe!*"

Parker tried to speak but got hastily interrupted. "I know Marlowe's a very clever spy. But he's making a mockery of *me* and the King's entire *judicial system* -- while these plays he's written tell us exactly where he's living."

Sir Francis took a breath and went on calmly, sweetly, as if once again talking to a child. "Not one play is set in present day France ... or Spain ... or even England," he said, then adding a minor concession, "except for a few historical pieces about English kings that would make no sense in Italy. *But*, the plays go from Venice to Verona to Naples to Sicily to *everywhere* in Italy like directions for a treasure hunt." He gave Parker a sarcastic smile.

"Sir Francis," Parker began his list of excuses. "Shakespeare's disappeared. Sir Wriothesley keeps insisting that *he's* the one who gives Shakespeare all those stories. Italy is a big country and courier Poley makes twenty stops every time the ship anchors. And no one's actually *seen* Marlowe in Italy. We really only suspect that...."

Sir Francis went back to his writing. "Well, you will not be on that ship with Poley tonight." Ignoring Parker's quizzical glance, he went on. "I've arranged for a special boat to take you directly to Syracuse. This time *we find him*. I promise."

Explaining, quite proud of himself, he went on "And, I've arranged for a second boat to take another of my best informants there also. You'll both stay there until he's found. If you don't find him, he will." Then he played his winning card. "Kind of a little challenge. You know ... see who wins."

Parker knew his boss's ways and a myriad of concerns raced through his mind. "How will I know who this other spy is?" he asked.

169

"You won't. You won't know him and he won't know you. One of you will make sure Marlowe is dead ..." he looked up sweetly, "...and the other *spy will not return alive.* That should prove effective. "

Parker fought desperately to see the whole picture.

"Don't look confused, Parker. Each of you will have the same assignment. Find Marlowe and then kill both him and the other spy. People will ignore it as merely a local duel. Think we'll succeed this time?"

Parker got the frightening picture. "How will I even know who to kill?"

"Well, that's the game, Parker. But here's a hint. When you see someone coming at you with a knife and the head of Marlowe -- kill him." Sir Francis smiled sweetly.

He loved these vicious games.

\* \* \* \* \*

Miles away at Scadbury, it was dark already and Poley was excitedly trying to tell something to Thomas.

"How do you know he's not going on the ship tonight?" Thomas asked nervously.

"The captain told me. Parker's not on this trip. Sir Francis got a special boat to take just him directly to Sicily. He knows he's in *Syracusa.* "

Thomas dropped into a chair. "Oh, god. All right. All right. Just go, Poley. Get on that boat. See what you can do."

Then Poley added, "And he's learned where Christopher is living."

"Go," Thomas said, almost in a daze. "Let me think. Just let me think."

CHAPTER 42

# STRANGERS IN A STORM

There was thunder, lightning, gusts of wind, and a downpour of rain.

The door opened to Marlowe's bedsit, his small room in *Syracusa*. A soaked, dripping-wet Christopher Marlowe entered carrying one end of a large trunk which had handles on each end – the handle on his side broken.

The other end was carried by James Burnell, an attractive young man of about twenty-five with reddish-blond hair and green eyes who was also completely drenched from the rain. Outside they could hear more thunder and lightning.

Christopher put down his end of the trunk. "I could never have made it alone." Where he stood, puddles of water accumulated on the floor.

Burnell wiped his hand across the top of his head, squeezing out a handful of rain. He shook his head to try to flip off some of the water. "The rain – and that broken trunk – how could I *not* help?"

Christopher dropped his coat on a chair and quickly picked up some cloth to mop up the puddles. Then, he went over to the stove. "I'll light a fire. You better get out of those clothes. Let me drape them around the stove."

Burnell looked a little surprised. "No, I shouldn't stay. And besides they wouldn't dry in this weather anyway."

Christopher busied himself lighting the stove, not looking at his guest. "Then you can stay the night. The bed's small but it's the least I can do." There was no answer from Burnell. "You can't go out into that storm again."

Christopher stood up and went over to remove Burnell's coat. "If you stay, they'll be dry by morning." His guest let him take the coat.

Burnell hesitated. By morning? That was unexpected. Finally, he said softly, "Alright." He started to remove his clothes, handing each item to Christopher who draped them strategically around the stove. When he was almost nude, Christopher tossed him a bedcover as he handed over the last of his clothes. He draped the cover as best he could, rather revealingly, around himself.

"Give it a few minutes. This stove heats very quickly." Christopher said, starting to remove his own clothes. He grabbed a small hand towel to hold in front of himself as he reached for a pan which Burnell passed to him.

"Some hot brandywine will help," Christopher said, pouring wine into the pan and placing it atop the stove. He went to the old cabinet against the wall and got two tankards. "What were you doing there on the *Via Lunga*?"

Burnell paused but didn't seem the least bit uncomfortable. "Leaving a friend's house," he said.

Christopher got out some bread sticks and put them by the side table near the stove. "Well, I certainly was lucky you were passing." Then, he asked, "but your accent? You must be from London. South of London, I would guess?"

Burnell just nodded. Christopher reached for the hot metal pan on the stove. With a cry, he dropped it, spilling the wine onto the floor. He dropped the towel and grabbed two of his fingers. He had the look of terrible pain as he weaved from side to side in agony.

Burnell grabbed his hand and plunged the burnt fingers into his own mouth. "Just relax," he said. "This will help."

Christopher was shaking his head and moaning for a few minutes and then seemed to recover a bit. "Oh, that does help," he said. "Where'd you learn that?"

The answer was a bit mumbled; trying to speak with fingers in his mouth, "Grandma Burnell."

"Well, someday I must meet Grandma Burnell and thank her. Oh, that's really much better."

There were a few moments of poignant silence – the two of them standing there, naked, Christopher with his fingers in Burnell's mouth.

Finally, after quite a long time, out of nowhere, Christopher asked, "How long have you been working for Sir Francis?" Burnell just stared at Marlowe incredulously and said nothing. "I've been watching you following me for four days." Still no response.

"So, I was wondering when you'd make your first move."

With that Burnell grabbed for his coat on the back of the chair, letting Marlowe's fingers slip from his mouth.

"Don't bother," Christopher said. "I took out the knife when you handed me the coat. Besides, every good spy knows the curse: kill someone during a thunderstorm and you'll be killed during the next one."

Burnell looked at him for a long moment and slowly reached over and put Marlowe's fingers back into his mouth.

"When you've been working for Sir Francis as long as I have," Christopher went on, "you learn not only to spy but to expect to be spied on." There was nothing from his guest except a vague stare. "But you're good," Christopher said, moving in noticeably closer and looking directly into Burnell's flecked green eyes, "and twice you had the chance to knife me and you didn't."

Burnell took the fingers from his mouth but didn't let go of Christopher's hand. "You just seemed …a bit too attractive to kill."

Christopher reached over and wiped away the wet hair from Burnell's face. Then he said, "Maybe … we could hold off playing spies till the morning?"

Burnell just kept staring at Marlowe. Then slowly there was the hint of a slight smile and the tilt of his head. "Well, why not," he said, "then … till the morning."

# CHAPTER 43

# MORNING

The morning was dark because it was still raining heavily. Christopher kept trying desperately to wake up. He could hear someone banging at the door. And it sounded like the person was saying "Kit ... Kit ... Open the door."

He got up from the bed and staggered to the next room, still naked. When he opened the door, there stood Thomas, wildly talking, but Christopher was too shocked at seeing him to understand what he was saying..

"Thomas – what are you doing here?"

There was no time for greetings or explanations. Thomas grabbed Christopher's trousers from the floor and threw them to him. "Get dressed. Quick."

Nothing made sense to Christopher, and he was still not awake. "Thomas, how did you get to Italy? Why are we ...?"

"Francis found out where you live," he almost screamed, picking up the shirt from the floor. "He's got people on their way here to kill you."

Christopher took his trousers and started to put them on.

"Get dressed," Thomas repeated. "We have to run. *Now*!"

But the frantic pace stopped as Burnell, wrapped in only a bed cover, walked out of the bedroom and stood next to Marlowe. "Christopher, who is this?"

Walsingham stood stunned, still holding the shirt. He squinted as the reality hit him. He took a deep breath.

"Who? Nobody," Thomas whispered. "Nobody, really." With that, he walked out of the bedsit and started down the steps.

Christopher hastily tied his trouser waistband and ran through the rain after Thomas -- barefoot and shirtless.

"Thomas, wait – wait," he kept calling. Christopher finally caught up and grabbed Walsingham by the arm to stop him.

"Kit, I traveled all the way from London to warn you and try to personally stop this. But …" and here he tried to speak but couldn't. After a painfully long time, Thomas said, chokingly, "So easily you wield the unkindest cut of all." He shook his head and then handed the shirt to Christopher. He put an envelope into the pocket of the drenched shirt. "This was for you – from someone who obviously loved not wisely but too well."

There followed an agonizing moment while Christopher could think of nothing to say. Then Thomas turned and walked down the street through the rain and rounded a corner out of sight.

Bystanders watched as Christopher opened the envelope, bulging with money and a frantically written letter. He stood there stunned, watching the ink on the note beginning to run in the rain. After a few minutes, in a daze, he headed back to his room.

The door to the bedsit was still open. Through the doorway Christopher could see the naked body of his guest lying on the floor floating in his own blood, Burnell's knife sticking out of the back of his neck.

He dropped the money and walked to the open window. He looked out across the rooftops toward the harbor and then put his face into his hands and slumped onto the window seat. He knew he should run for his life; but he just couldn't.

* * * * *

That night a small boat started out from the harbor, almost in silhouette against the reflective water.

Thomas sat on a trunk near the back of the boat clutching a small canvas bag.

*Syracusa* – and Christopher -- got farther and farther and farther away.

# PART 4

# The Arrest

## CHAPTER 44

# THE DESPERATE VISITOR

Thomas sat at the small table in the gazebo, staring out into the direction of the long, narrow stone path through the rose garden. He wondered if the wilted bushes and dead stems were really just reflections of his own feelings.

It had been two months since he had sailed from *Syracusa*. For weeks he seemed to be obsessed with thoughts about that morning in Sicily -- sometimes thoughts dominated with burning hate and other times drenched in hurt.

Thomas wanted so badly to be able to overturn time and return to the days before *Syracusa*. True, he had been lonely and worried about Christopher then. But this was worse. Now his world was terribly nightmarish with no possibility of waking up – or ever improving.

Gradually, week after week, he made a conscious effort to avoid thinking about Christopher. But no matter hard how he tried to occupy his mind, his thoughts somehow always returned to that morning in Sicily. And then he would find it was so hard to bring these thoughts to a halt.

Think about something else, he would tell himself – anything else.

But instead of his mind centering on something else, it seemed to be empty, keeping him almost in a hypnotic state. He went about the days putting off even the simplest of tasks, and, whenever he could, avoiding contact with any of the staff.

Henry Wriothesley was still in prison and Shakespeare was nowhere to be found, so there was no chance of any of those welcome interruptions.

But, day by day his mood slowly changed – he seemed to become more numb.

And, so he stared, at nothing really. And then he heard someone approaching from behind. He was not in the mood to talk to Poley or anyone else about some unimportant detail concerning the grounds, or the manor, or the horses, or --

Maybe, if he just stood still, the person would think him deep in thought about some serious situation and go away. But soon he could tell the person would not.

"Poley," he asked, not bothering to even move. "Problems?"

"Yes."

"What?" When no answer came he turned. It was Christopher. "What are you doing here?"

"Thomas, I have to explain."

"Explain?" The word came out a little more explosively than he had intended. "The way it looked to me there was no explanation necessary."

Then he added sarcastically, "Or possible." A long silence followed as thousands of thoughts, questions, and possible remarks crossed Thomas's mind. Finally, he said, "I think you'd better go." He sat and stared at some invisible nothing on his hands.

"Go? Go where?"

"Maybe back to that bedfellow in Sicily."

"I have nowhere I can go, Thomas. I barely made it here -- to apologize." Thomas turned to him with a look of incredulity and Christopher realized that any attempt at an apology was ludicrous. When Thomas didn't answer, he said, "Then as a favor, I'm asking if I may stay -- just a few days -- maybe until ...."

Thomas's voice was desperate. "Kit, you expect me to live here, day after day, knowing you're around?"

"Thomas, I was alone, locked in that country for seven long years. I was so lonely."

"Were your seven years any longer than mine? Or any lonelier?"

Then Thomas looked at him directly and his voice changed. "And now Poley tells me, this wasn't the first one."

Christopher took a deep breath. "No, it wasn't," he said quietly. He searched for something to say – anything to rid them of the uncomfortable, empty stillness. "Maybe I should go to Constable Maunder."

"And then we both die?" Thomas asked.

"I'll tell him I went to Italy against your will and when I returned to England, you shut me out."

"If you wrote plays the way you tell lies, you'd be holding horses for the gentry outside the Globe Theatre."

"Thomas, I have nowhere to go."

Walsingham drummed his fingers on the table wondering what would happen if he simply said no.

"Nowhere, Thomas." Christopher waited. Finally, Thomas spoke.

"Just go." Walsingham's voice was devoid of meaning. It was as if he were giving a passerby a simple direction.

When Christopher made no movement to leave, Thomas repeated, "I said '*Go*'."

Christopher stood there in disbelief. Then he turned walked to the gate.

Walsingham turned to see Marlowe slowly leaving the garden just as Robert Poley entered with a look of confusion as to what was happening.

Poley watched as Marlowe left and Walsingham turned back to scrutinizing his own hands. "Is Poet Marlowe staying?" Poley asked.

Walsingham shook his head.

"Sir ... uh," Poley didn't know what to say. "The ... uh ... servants have lunch ready in small dining room. Would you like to ..." he trailed off, knowing Sir Thomas could not hear him.

Poley couldn't tell how long he stood there, watching Thomas disappearing before his very eyes. Finally, he said "Sir, lunch is served." But there was, of course, no answer. "Perhaps, Sir, if you don't intend to dine, I should wrap the food in a cloth and take it to Mr. Marlowe. He seems to be starting the rather long journey to London town. Is that all right with you?"

When there was no answer, Poley quietly turned and left.

Thomas sat and once again tried not to think. He wasn't sure how long he had been there when he heard footsteps behind him again.

"Sir, I did as you told me," he heard Poley saying. "I rode to stop Mr. Marlowe and told him to return as you asked."

Surprised, Thomas turned to see Christopher and an innocent-looking Robert Poley both standing there, just looking at him, Marlowe obviously just as confused as Thomas.

With the respectful servant-like voice that he always used, Poley went on, "I did as you told me and set up sleeping quarters in the West Tower for Poet Marlowe. I think everything is sufficient."

Poley continued to stand there as if waiting for more instructions and merely following orders.

Finally, Walsingham realized there was really nothing he could do. The easiest way to end this situation was to give in to this soft-hearted peacemaker.

He spoke without turning back to them. "You can stay for a while in the West Tower. I'll have Frizer take you food. But you've got to agree to stay away from me. I don't want to see you. I don't want to talk to you. I don't want to be near you." Thomas got up and headed for the manor. "At least do that much." And he was gone.

Christopher walked to the table, sat, and quietly said, "Thank you," to no one in particular.

Unimplicated, uninvolved, and completely unflustered, Robert Poley turned and left – with just a hint of a soft smile on his face.

## CHAPTER 45

# ONLY THINKING
# MAKES IT SO

Christopher sat in the small room at the top of the West Tower with papers strewn everywhere and the small bed in the corner covered with notes, clothes and two precious books from the library below. Hollingshed's *Chronicles* was open, face down, on a page about Julius Caesar.

He picked up his signature swan quill, white with the bright red tip, and wrote a few lines and then crossed them out. Again, he tried with no luck. He hated it when he blocked. He started to write again but stopped before even the first word was on the paper, shaking his head.

Unnoticed, Walsingham entered and put down a tray of food. He waited. This was the first time Thomas had ventured up to Marlowe's secluded quarters and he had an uncomfortable feeling. Then he picked up a sheet and read some of the dialogue.

"Just leave it, Frizer," Christopher muttered, definitely not expecting it might be Thomas.

Thomas waited and then finally broke the silence. "Still trying to decide what Brutus says as he stabs him?"

Christopher put down the quill and rubbed his fingers, now sore from hours of writing and scratching out lines. "I really don't care any more what Brutus says…or Anthony …or even what *you* say."

Thomas carried the tray covered with bread, cheese and a light wine over to Christopher and placed it next to him. "Kit, I'm trying. I really am. I just can't…."

Finally, Thomas headed for the stairs.

"I know you feel deceived," Christopher's words stopped Thomas at the top of the long spiral staircase.

"Yes, I do."

"Thomas, you were the one who once told me: nothing is either good or bad, but only thinking makes it so."

Walsingham didn't turn. He thought for a long time, just standing there on the landing, fingering the metal glove of an old suit of armor, hanging there at the top of the staircase for more than a century. Finally, he said "Kit, if you want, you can start taking your meals in the dining room." And then he added softly, "But only for meals."

Marlowe nodded and reluctantly went back to work, trying to write. But his mind was not on Brutus.

## CHAPTER 46

# DINNERS AT SCADBURY

𝕿he first meals together were tense, especially for Christopher, who felt he was somehow on a trial or conditional basis. Thomas, on the other hand, felt very comfortable and really enjoyed seeing Christopher sitting across from him at the long dinner table. He tried not to let it show -- but it was like old times.

One night in the second week of meals together, the two of them reached for a basket of bread at the same time, colliding hands. Christopher looked uncomfortable but Thomas just smiled, picked up the basket and held it for Marlowe to help himself. Slowly Christopher took the bread and nodded. Walsingham smiled and continued to watch Marlowe for a long time.

\* \* \* \* \*

It was barely a week later when Christopher was heading to the stairway to the West Tower late one night. As he passed Walsingham, he saw Thomas offering him a book. Christopher took it as Thomas held a single burning taper so Marlowe could read.

Christopher examined a few of the pages about Anthony and Cleopatra. Without a word he took his candle and started up the long staircase to his room at the top of the tower. Walsingham silently watched him ascend the long spiral staircase to the top of the tower –

and then waited there for endless minutes – long after the stairway was completely dark.

* * * * *

Day by day, dinners were becoming more casual and relaxed. Frequently Marlowe would read as they dined, happy to have access to the fortune of books in the Walsingham library. One evening as Christopher read during dinner, Thomas quietly stood up, picked up a dish of lamb and went unnoticed to where Marlowe sat, adding a bit more meat to the young poet's plate. Pretending not to notice, Christopher smiled but kept his eyes down and continued reading.

* * * * *

A few weeks later Thomas and Christopher were having breakfast one bright morning in the small upstairs dining room. Marlowe was trying to edit a sheaf of papers while Walsingham sat and dotingly watched him. A servant entered with a note.          "The proverbial carriage approaches," Thomas read. Christopher grabbed his papers and a last piece of fruit and disappeared into the small alcove by the window chanting, "Cauldron, cauldron, double trouble. Cauldron boil and cauldron bubble."

As the servant picked up all of the extra table items, Thomas said, "Show the guest in," and waited with the casualness of someone thinking about the plans for the day ahead. He didn't look up when he heard the servant open the door. It had to be Maunder, he realized.

"Queen Henry is here." Wriothesley stood posed in the doorway – resplendent – *avec un chat nouveau*. The new cat, a symphony in white with small black touches, was languidly draped over his right shoulder like expensive ermine. His left hand cradled his own golden locks and his right hand was in a far extension holding one of Raleigh's new tobacco concoctions -- unlit, of course. His face was tilted upward and to the left, with a wry, enigmatic smile. He must have worked for hours in front of a mirror on that pose.

The room exploded in a cacophony of excitement as Christopher returned. "Henry, why are you...?" "How did you ...?" "Henry, what the ...."

Henry said nothing. Just smiled. And then he held up his hands like a monarch silencing his loving audience. Christopher and Thomas knew to be silent and waited.

"I checked the foyer. Where's my bloody portrait?" One could tell from the devilish grin that he had rehearsed the line. The other two knew better than to ask questions. Henry, of course, had his remarks prepared.

"First things first. Are you two speaking yet?" This got looks of uncomfortable glances. But no answer. "Well, then, maybe more than..." (a broad wink) "...just speaking? Well?" Again, nervous shifting and fleeting looks, but no definitive replies.

"Oh, *really*, you two," he went on. "You know the course of true love never did run smooth." Henry turned to Christopher. "Write that down. It's a good line."

Well, Christopher thought, maybe – 'never did run smooth*ly*.'

"Henry," Thomas began, "the prison...?"

Wriothesley picked up Thomas's glass and toasted: "To James the First and his wonderful sense of justice in pardoning all the innocent babes that your bloody cousin put into prison. King Jimmy pardoned us all. Well, almost all. Ralegh and a few stalwarts are still in." The cat began to gently nuzzle Henry's cheek. "Oh, isn't that sweet of you, Pierre?"

"Henry, the prison!"

"Well, I can't say I would necessarily change it for a cottage by the sea in Brighton. But ... I got along all right," he smiled broadly, "mainly because of a very *fine guard* in my tower. Of course, no visitors were allowed. But when he was on duty – three times a week – he just wouldn't bother to notice if one of my servants who *happened* to be visiting someone *else* in the prison, dropped by to make sure I was doing well. Wonderful food and necessities *for me*. And for *this sweet guard*: some decent food, some precious baubles, and ... well, he was

taken care of very fittingly. And my life? Let's call it," (he smiled) …"
tolerable."

"A little better than tolerable, wasn't it, Henry? Didn't your mother…?"

"Oh, *that*. After all, what are mothers *for*?" Then he looked from side to side, pretending to check that no one was listening, and whispered, "The cell? *All…in…purple. The whole bloody thing…in purple… velvet!* And the food?" He kissed his fingers. "If one *must* serve time for transgressions against the crown, well…."

"Maybe we can get the new King to absolve the punishment deemed for the late Poet Marlowe," Christopher suggested.

"Sweetheart," Henry said pinching Marlowe's cheek, "all you have to do is stay on the good side of Thomas, and you'll have no worries – ever. So long as he's your patron…."

And then abruptly he remembered his *real* news. "Oh, and I'm now the patron for *another* new ward: a writer – in the … how shall I put it … in the *early stages* of learning to write." He blushed. "A very attractive young man named Charlton. I'm…" he went into his dreadful French accent, "…*comment dit-on*? … 'keeping him' … for the new King, of course." He smiled wickedly.

"Now where's my portrait?"

## CHAPTER 47

# BACK HOME

Once Sir Wriothesley had been released from prison, Shakespeare felt that he was able at last to sleep at nights.

Though he still had to be concerned that *any* questions about his writings were referred to Wriothesley, Shakespeare knew that his protector was back and he could breathe more easily. Someone else would have to answer to Constable Maunder and that fart Sir Francis.

Sometimes Shakespeare wondered why *Henry Wriothesley* had been taken to prison – but *he* had never been arrested. Sir Francis had manipulated the original indictment against Henry to be some vague charge of treason.

But it *was* a close call. At his trial Henry Wriothesley had been initially condemned to death; but Sir Cecil Burghley, president of the Privy Council, must have realized just how fabricated the charge was and commuted the sentence to life imprisonment. Everyone in England knew that was always a lucky break since there were countless incidents that could trigger a prisoner's release. Thus, Henry felt he had been spared. At that point all he had to do was wait.

And wait he did, until that day the new king, James I, in an effort to manifest his magnanimous nature issued an edict to release almost all prisoners. The few exceptions were those who were still on the enemies lists of Privy Council members – prisoners like Sir Walter Ralegh.

So, Henry Wriothesley was free and Shakespeare was once again seen on the streets of London (though not too frequently and definitely not too conspicuously). One couldn't be too careful, he felt.

Consequently, Shakespeare reasoned, *now* it was time to chance a return to Stratford.

"I am the one who paid for this house, Anne."

She sat at the kitchen table in granite silence.

"And so now I am returning to live here."

She snapped her head to stare at him. Before she could say anything, however, Shakespeare went on. "Yes, I am leaving London for all time. This is my home and this is where I am going to live. From this day forward."

Shakespeare's wife stared at him. Where had he gotten this new sense of dominance? In a way she found it rather attractive. And he had been gone so long that it was almost like meeting a new person. Besides, she thought, what could she do? It *was* his house -- in his name.

"You're not planning to settle in *my* bed?" she finally said, rather threateningly.

"I'm taking Susanna's old room upstairs," he said with quite an authoritative air. He left no room for discussion or compromise.

Susanna Shakespeare, their oldest daughter, had married John Hall, a local physician, in 1607. Only Judith, the youngest, still remained at home with her mother.

"And don't be getting any fanatical ideas that you'll be welcome in my bed occasionally," Anne decreed. "Only God can guess what disease and disorders you carry from all those wonderful lady friends of yours in London."

"They don't have any diseases."

"Mistress Davenant has lice."

"She does not."

"Oh, really. And how would *you* know that?"

William fumed. It really irritated him when Anne was able to trick him like that.

"And I hear that Widow Vautrollier has scabies."

William was not going to fall into the same trap twice. "What makes you think so?" he asked innocently.

"Her husband told me that much when *you* sent *him* with the money," Anne shrugged as she watched the look of panic slowly build in her husband. The widow's husband, of course, had never said such a thing, but it did make her happy to watch the great William Shakespeare squirm. What diseases, he was wondering, might be lurking in his system at that moment.

"And," she went on, "if I hear a single breath about you making vile overtures to any of the neighbors here in Stratford...." She had to stop for a moment to think. "...you'll find this home to be a mite worse than Dante's seventh ring of hell."

Where did she ever learn about Dante, he wondered. And what in Hades was the seventh ring?

Anne didn't bother to move or busy herself around the kitchen. The granite sovereign just sat and stared.

William picked up his small canvas bag and started up the stairs. Susanna's room was just as she had left it, cluttered, disorganized and chaotic. And there was a thick coat of dust everywhere.

But he didn't care. He was, at last, away from London. Away from probing questions from other actors asking how certain scenes should be played, scenes he had *not* written and probably had never even *read*; away from Maunder and Sir Francis and the possibility of seeing either of them on the street one day; and away from the noise, the smell and the rotten London weather. Yes, he was here in Stratford to stay. He didn't care if he ever returned to the big city.

Stratford was small, quiet, and provincial. He knew most of the residents and would soon meet the new arrivals. Surprisingly, although the residents of this township knew that William Shakespeare had been away in London acting on the big stage, they had no inkling that he had been writing. Or that he was credited with very successful plays.

The *titles* and the subjects of productions were the focus at the local theatres. The authors were not. For the most part, few patrons knew who had written each work at that time. In many cases it was revealed, only years later, who had penned a particular play. And in some cases the script was done by a team of writers or written by one author and revised by another. No, people were seldom aware of the author. As it was worded: the play's the thing.

So, Stratford was going to be relaxing and quiet, at last. Shakespeare had had enough excitement for a while. And, besides, he wondered, there *must* be a few lonely women right here in this small village. The Lepford woman three doors down had that fat husband of hers who worked two days a week in Manchester. And he couldn't help but notice that new young thing by the church. She must have moved in there after he left town. His mouth watered just remembering the fleeting look he got through her window as he rode into town. And over by the well there was Missus Colebar, who had such large breasts that they always seemed to be almost bursting from her too-small dresses. That, of course, was especially odd, he thought, since she sews her own clothes.

And there was also....

# CHAPTER 48

# REGRETS

W eek by week, Marlowe became more comfortable at Scadbury. It became obvious that he was no longer limited to leaving the tower only for meals. Often he would spend a good part of the day in the library, checking details about the lives of kings or little known facts about their countries. More and more he began to stay there to write. Walsingham would come in, take a book from a shelf and lean on a bookcase, pretending to be reading while he really just stared at Christopher. On one occasion Marlowe finished a page and reached for a new sheet of paper. As he prepared to write on it, he noticed it already had writing from someone else. It read:

**"What wound did ever heal but by degrees?"**

Christopher smiled but didn't look up, knowing that Thomas was smiling too.

Late one night Walsingham sat reading in the study as Marlowe approached, a candle harshly lighting his face.

"Thomas, the door to the West Tower is locked."

Walsingham looked up from his writing. "Impossible. The key?"

"Not in the lock."

Thomas thought for a while. Why would the servants do that? "Well, why don't you sleep down here tonight in the south bedchamber?"

Christopher nodded and headed down the hall. Within a few minutes he was back in the study.

"It's locked also." As Walsingham started to speak, he added, "And that key is gone too."

Thomas sounded exhausted. "Then use one of the guest chambers."

"I checked them also. Actually, all the bedchambers are locked. And, for some reason all the keys seem to be missing." Christopher registered a bit of a smile. "The only room open is yours." He waited and then added innocently, "Maybe we'll just have to share that tonight?"

Walsingham put down the quill and rested his chin on one hand. After serious consideration he stood and headed down the hall. "I can unlock the guest chambers."

Arriving at the door, he unlocked it. Marlowe looked at him and hesitated. Walsingham just stared at the floor. Finally, Marlowe entered and closed the door.

Slowly Thomas walked back to the study.

In the guest room, Marlowe waited a few minutes and then decided to leave. Walking to the door to the West Tower, he reached into his pocket, got the key, and unlocked the door. Slowly he climbed the spiral staircase to his small room at the top.

Thomas waited a few minutes in the study and then suddenly turned and went to the guest chambers, stopping outside the door. Making up his mind, he opened the door and went inside.

Marlowe, of course, was gone.

Silently, he headed down the long hall to his own room -- alone.

## CHAPTER 49

# THE TRUTH

icolas Skeres was always uneasy whenever Sir Francis sent a message saying he wanted to see him. For the life of him, he could not think of a single good thing that could come out of such a meeting. And his mind was swarming with the myriad of troubles that *could* result.

He waited outside the heavy, carved wooden door of the inner chamber, going over in his mind the possible reasons for the meeting. He could think of many.

He knocked.

"Come in, Skeres," he heard from within. That frightened him – the fact that Sir Francis knew who was knocking.

Skeres opened the door slowly but confidently, closing it silently behind him, and walked to the desk that was so large it made his master seem more formidable behind it.

"You asked to see me, Sir Francis?" He made sure his voice was even and confident.

"Yes, Skeres. Have a seat." That made matters even worse. From experience he knew that when Sir Francis was considerate, you were in trouble.

Skeres sat and looked across the desk trying to appear casual and unconcerned.

Sir Francis waited. It always helped to raise the tension with a lengthy period of silence. Then slowly he got up from the desk and strolled to the straight-backed seat where Skeres sat. There were no arms on the chair to make it more comfortable and the rigid back made it feel like an inquisitor's bench. This was not a good sign.

Skeres wondered if somehow Sir Francis had discovered his hiding place where he could go to secretly eavesdrop on all the conversations with Constable Maunder. No – that was impossible.

Sir Francis stopped at the corner of the desk and sat on the edge of it, fingering the metal stamp he used to fix his wax seal onto letters.

"How long have you worked for me, Nicolas?" (Why is he calling me by my first name?)

"Well, I don't know, Sir Francis. Many years. Maybe twenty?"

"Yes, about twenty. And in all that time you've always been a faithful and devoted employee." Skeres said nothing and tried to look casually interested.

There was a long pause before Sir Francis continued. "So if there was a single indiscretion, it should, of course, be overlooked in view of the years of loyal work. Right?"

Skeres knew the risks connected with either agreeing or not. He tried to look puzzled, hoping to convey wonderment at what Sir Francis could possibly be talking about.

"To get to the point, Skeres, there have been so many questions about the death of Poet Marlowe that we've now pretty much established that he's still alive. So, I thought, 'Why not just call in my friend Nicolas Skeres and ask once again about that day so many years ago?' If there *was* anything he had been afraid to mention at the time, we could easily discuss it now – after all these years of working together."

Skeres suddenly knew where the conversation was going and it was the one he feared most.

Sir Francis spoke thoughtfully as he leisurely encircled the chair where his victim sat. "I was hoping perhaps you could help clear up the situation. You know, such as, exactly what did happen that day at Widow Bull's place in Deptford. I wondered if time may have helped clear up some of the details." Sir Francis stopped pacing but didn't look at Skeres, as if his mind were still putting together the fine points of the question.

Then to Skeres's surprise, Sir Francis turned and said, "Of course, there would be no repercussions against you. The two of us have been through too much together to let any one incident cause problems between us. But it really might help to explain some of the contradictions we keep finding after all these years." Sir Francis raised his eyebrows in a questioning glance and said no more.

Skeres realized he had one brief moment to decide what to do, but he knew that there had arisen too many episodes, all indicating that Marlowe *was* still alive. It was useless to keep lying. "Well, Sir Francis, there *was* a little problem that I regret I didn't relate to you sooner," Skeres began. "Sir Thomas told me that if I went with those men that day, Poet Marlowe would be suspicious and not want to join us. So he said the best thing would be if I waited at Scadbury Manor while Frizer and Poley did the work."

Skeres checked to see how this was registering with Sir Francis but there seemed to be no reaction. He added quickly, "I didn't get no money or anything, you understand. But Sir Thomas said this would be the only way they could handle it. Well, late that day the other two returned, all bloodied and told me what happened. When they showed me the coroner's report and all, I realized that everything had gone good enough."

Still no reaction from Sir Francis.

"So I jist left, knowin' that the job had been takun care of. I guess I shouldda told you, but I thought you might be really angry with me."

"I understand, Skeres. You felt that this was the only way to get the job done and you had accomplished what I wanted." Sir Francis walked back behind the desk and sat. "Thank you for your honesty, Nicolas."

Skeres waited, his heart beating wildly. "Is that all, Sir?"

"Yes, Skeres. Thank you."

Skeres took a deep breath, stood and headed for the door.

"Oh, and Skeres -- don't mention any of this to anyone, would you?"

"Course not, Sir Francis." That last request for confidence, he felt, certainly allayed much of his fear. "Thank you, Sir Francis." He left, eased the door shut silently, leaned on the door, closed his eyes and breathed a deep sigh. It was going to be all right.

But, just to be safe, he decided to leave the building from the back entrance and walk along the street next to the river. It was getting dark already and he didn't see the three men standing by the corner of the building.

He did, however, hear them call his name.

The next day Sir Francis was notified that, unfortunately, one of his employees had been the victim of what must have been a robbery and his brutalized body was found on the near bank of the Thames.

# CHAPTER 50

# AGONY

He just couldn't find Christopher anywhere. It was almost noon and lunch was waiting in the sunny breakfast room: a buffet of cheese, cooked eggs, bread and fruit tartar.

Thomas hadn't seen Christopher all day. He had checked the West Tower. There was neither the writer nor any new pages. But Thomas did notice one peculiarity. The stone had been moved over the small crawl space in the floor – the stone covering the little "dungeon" where Thomas and Cousin Francis would hide when they were children. That, Thomas reasoned, meant Christopher had not been working but rather squandering the hours as he did when he got restless – doing anything to keep from writing.

And none of the servants had seen him all morning. Frizer, who was chopping up a fallen tree near the stables, said he hadn't noticed Marlowe anywhere.

And Poley was off on some courier trip so there was no need trying to find him.

Walsingham combed the manor, floor by floor, room by room. He was looking, but never shouting Christopher's name out loud. (In spite of his rather unconventional life style, shouting was the kind of thing English lords just *did not do*.)

He began to search the grounds near the manor. There are so many places a person could be on a thousand-acre estate. But he knew there were only a few that Christopher frequented.

Then he saw him – sitting on the wall by the old bridge that spanned what once was a moat. More than a hundred years ago, the Walsinghams lived in a fortified structure, not quite a castle, but rather a fortified mansion, right at the edge of the old moat.

Little, except some old walls, now remained of the structure. And the moat was now merely a deep, circular ditch, dry for years. It always amazed Thomas how the whole family and all the servants existed in a single structure within that little circle no more than a hundred meters across.

But where the main path to the manor crossed the dry moat where the drawbridge has once stood, the family had built a wooden overpass with low walls on either side.

And Christopher sat there on one of the walls in deep thought.

"Kit, lunch is ready."

The reply was anything but pleasant. "I don't feel like eating."

Thomas immediately realized things were amiss and decided to tread lightly. "Something wrong, Kit?"

The question didn't seem to rate a reply. Maybe Christopher felt there was no need to affirm the obvious. Thomas crossed to the bridge and sat next to his partner and said nothing.

After a long time Christopher spoke as if talking only to himself. "I want to go into London."

Walsingham gave the remark plenty of time and then said softly, "Why?"

"My life is over, Thomas." There was a lengthy pause. "I spend day after day here at Scadbury doing nothing."

"You're writing."

"Writing? For whom? For what? So that some imbecile who has fled to Stratford can get all the credit, all the satisfaction, all the praise? For *that* I keep writing?"

Thomas gave the remark plenty of time, perhaps adding some credence to the idea that he understood. Then he asked, "What would you do in London?"

"I don't know. I just know it would be something different in my life. Maybe I could go to the Globe and see a performance of *Midsummer Night's Dream* and bask in the applause at the end and maybe hear some remarks from the audience as they left the theatre. Maybe I could get myself caught and hanged. Anything would be a change."

Walsingham understood these occasional moods that Christopher got into. How could he blame him? Marlowe had remained on the estate since his return from Italy. And, since no one except those at Scadbury knew he was there, he had to hide whenever visitors or friends came by. Wriothesley and Shakespeare were the only outsiders who knew about the situation.

Wriothesley's new "*ward*" seemed to be keeping him very busy and consequently he visited Scadbury less and less frequently. And the only thing Thomas knew about Shakespeare was that he had gone into hiding to avoid any questions about his writings. No one seemed to have any information --- or even any rumors – about him anymore. Thomas never thought he'd long for the day when Shakespeare might come to the mansion and enliven Christopher's life. At least the parade of insults going back and forth between the two of them would be helpful in easing this current depression.

Though the fits of melancholy had surfaced before, lately they seemed to be more frequent. And far deeper.

"We'll go to Paris for a few days," Thomas ventured, knowing full well the idea could not compete with seeing a staging of one of Christopher's own productions.

Finally, Christopher said, "What am I waiting for Thomas? I'll never see my works produced. I'll never hear the applause. I'll never know why I'm writing."

Thomas knew better than to say anything.

"Life is a tale, told by an idiot, full of sound and fury, signifying nothing." Thomas waited. Almost choking, Christopher went haltingly on. "This path, Thomas, leads but to the grave."

---

(Two centuries later, the poet Thomas Gray would write an insightful poem entitled "Elegy Written in a Country Churchyard." It would contain haunting words that might have been inspired by Marlowe himself at that moment.

*The boast of heraldry,*

*the pomp of power,*

*and all that beauty, all that wealth e'er gave –*

*await alike the inevitable hour.*

*The paths of glory lead but to the grave.*)

---

The two of them said nothing. Then, Thomas gently pulled Christopher's head to his shoulder. He could feel his young friend trying to suppress the sobbing.

## CHAPTER 51

# THE WILL

C onstable Maunder knew that Sir Francis Walsingham was expecting him. But, in spite of that, he knocked timidly at the door.

"Enter, Constable."

"Sir Francis," Maunder began as he approached the desk, "they had the reading of the will today."

"When did he die?"

"I believe it was two weeks ago tomorrow, Sir. Yes, it was two weeks ago. It was a coincidence, but he died on his birthday."

Sir Francis looked bothered. "In two weeks why have there been no eulogies? Lesser playwrights have died and garnered myriads of tributes. Shakespeare dies and not a word is written about him."

"I know, Sir Francis. No one can explain it."

"Weren't there a multitude of accolades penned when Marlowe ...?"

"Died?"

"Disappeared," Francis added with scorn.

"For Marlowe? Yes, sir. Very many."

"Anything written by Shakespeare?"

"No, Sir Francis. Shakespeare's works didn't start appearing until about four months after Marlowe's ...."

They exchanged painful glances.

"When did plays start appearing under Shakespeare's name?"

"Well," the Constable was thinking this through, "the first play to appear with his name on it was in 1598, I believe. Five years after Marlowe's death. But others before that were credited to him."

Sir Francis gave him a meaningful look. An angry meaningful look.

"But the first legal record of a payment to Shakespeare from the Lord Chamberlain's Men was for a script in 1594. That was only one year after ...."

"My dear cousin and his young love are making public fools of us, aren't they? And they know how idiotic we would look trying to arrest my own cousin for *not* killing someone. So, until we find Marlowe ...."

Maunder decided it best to send the conversation down a different path. "But you are right," Maunder went on, "that no eulogies have appeared about Shakespeare. It's almost as if the rest of the literary world has separated the *writings* from the *writer*. Nothing from a fellow poet, or an actor, a friend, a publisher. Not a single remembrance. It's odd. Very odd."

"Maybe because he returned to Stratford?"

"No, Sir Francis. The language is the language of all of England."

"It's because the whole world can see that the imbecile from Stratford hasn't been writing all that ...." Sir Francis stopped. "And the funeral services?"

Maunder hesitated, trying to decide how to answer that diplomatically. "Only family and neighbors."

"But no writers, fellow actors, or theatre people at the funeral?" Maunder shook his head. "More peculiarities," Francis concluded. "No one at Shakespeare's final services? When Ben Johnson died all the nobility and gentry were there. What happened this time?"

The Constable's eyes searched the room trying to decide how to reply. "Well," he began, "it appears we are correct: the literary world seems to separate the writer from the works in this case." The answer, though very true, didn't satisfy Maunder any more than it did Sir Francis. Both men mulled over this thought, but knew something was wrong. "As a matter of fact, Sir Francis, most of his neighbors knew he had gone to London to be an actor but I don't think any of them knew of his writing accomplishments."

That absolutely baffled Sir Francis. "How old was he?"

"He was 52."

"And he died of...?"

"He died of -- a venereal disease, Sir," Maunder answered clinically.

"Constable, you're smiling. Maybe a *variety* of venereal diseases?"

"From what I've learned, sir, yes." Then to embellish the thought, the Constable added, "And he left small sums of money to his children as well as to his godson?"

"What godson?"

"Well, Sir Francis, it's always been pretty well accepted that the son of Widow Davanant was Shakespeare's child. When he was living in London, Shakespeare seldom made the two-day journey back to Stratford. But when he did, he would always stop for the night on the way there and on the way back at a place called "The Tavern" in Oxford. It wasn't an inn ... just a ..." the Constable searched for a suitable term, "just a ... 'tavern'. But each time Widow Davanant seemed to be able to accommodate William for the night. Well, when she had a son she proceeded to call him 'William.' As the boy grew up he always claimed that Shakespeare was his father and everyone in Oxford seemed to accept it."

"And?"

"And this boy, referred to in the will as his 'godson,' was bequeathed a sum of money along with Shakespeare's two daughters."

"One has to be impressed by his dedication to the cause of procreation," Sir Francis said sarcastically. "I don't suppose my dear cousin Thomas knows about the death yet."

"I'm sure he does not, Sir. I can't imagine that anyone would ride all the way out to Scadbury just to tell Sir Thomas that Shakespeare has died."

"Then, Constable, I think you may want to pay Sir Thomas a courtesy visit and inform him. His reaction may be interesting. Perhaps very revealing too."

"Yes, Sir Francis," Maunder said, bowing slightly and heading for the door. He fully understood his assignment.

## CHAPTER 52

# IMPOSSIBLE PARADOX

"*A*h, come in, Constable," Walsingham's voice was warm and familiar. "I'm in the library." By that time Maunder was familiar with Scadbury Manor and headed directly for the library.

"Well, Sir Thomas, I was in the neighborhood and I thought I might --"

"Might drop by?" Walsingham finished for him. Both smiled at the absurdity of that oft-used opening comment.

It had been two days since the Constable had received his "assignment" from Sir Francis to see what he could learn from Thomas's reactions to Shakespeare's death.

High above, in one of the two small alcoves, Marlowe stood listening. The manor library had been built with one side a single story in height and the outside wall vaulted two stories up with a high window and two small rooms at the top, originally designed as reading areas. These made it convenient for anyone to eavesdrop on people in the library.

"And...?" Walsingham asked.

"I came because I have some news for you. They had the reading of the will a few days ago," Maunder began.

Thomas pretended he had deduced it. Pointing at the Constable, he announced, "-- of Henry the Eighth, I'll bet?!"

"Of Gentleman William Shakespeare."

"Why didn't I guess," Walsingham let the ruse drop.

"Longest will I've ever seen."

"Well, you know those writers."

"He wrote it only two months before he died," Maunder added.

"Meaning?"

Maunder answered this as if it were very obvious. "That it was current – and obviously *very* relevant."

"*Well.*" Thomas added, revealing that he was greatly underwhelmed.

Maunder pretended not to notice the subtle jab. "Very detailed too. He listed every one of his possessions and household goods – everything – a bowl, a sword, plates, jewelry – everything. He even willed all of his clothes – to his daughter Joan. Though heaven knows what she'll do with them." As he spoke the Constable casually took a book from the shelf, as if by random. "Ovid?" he asked.

"Yes, the poet Ovid," Walsingham acknowledged. "At the time he wrote it, most of England considered his writings to be quite pornographic. And he *was* big on men sleeping with boys, you know."

"The source for Shakespeare's poem 'Venus and Adonis,' wasn't it?"

"I believe that's well accepted," Walsingham conceded.

Maunder continued as if thinking out loud. "And parts of *A Midsummer Night's Dream...*" seeing Walsingham nod, "and, if I remember correctly, didn't I read that Christopher Marlowe was also a fan of Ovid? Didn't he translate all of Ovid's 'Amores' while still a student at Cambridge?" Thomas looked surprised at the Constable knowing that. "And didn't I hear that Poet Marlowe's translation was banned and copies of it were publicly burned as part of the Archbishop's crackdown on offensive material?" The Constable smiled.

Thomas gracefully took the book from him and returned it to the shelf, asking, "How did you ever learn all of that?"

210

The Constable's shrug answered the question. Then, referring to the book, he asked, "Expensive?"

"Constable, you know what books cost. Yes, very expensive. In a few years the new printing press may make it possible for everyone to own books. But not now."

"No books," Maunder said cryptically.

"No books?" Thomas asked, raising his hands to indicate "meaning...?"

"In his will. Shakespeare listed no books. Not a one."

Walsingham sat, put his elbow on the desk and his chin in his hand and looked puzzled. Maunder went on, "Because he obviously owned none. Books are some of a man's most expensive possessions. If you own them, you bequeath them -- to *somebody.* Shakespeare seemed to will even his smallest possessions. But -- no books."

"Well, obviously he was a writer and not much of a reader," Thomas suggested, not too convincingly.

"Not even a copy of 'Holingshed's *Chronicles*'," Maunder added with the tone of a chess player announcing *checkmate.* "Didn't Will..."

"William," Walsingham corrected automatically and then said "Ohhh," trying to shake off the habit.

"...use Holingshed as the base for a great many of his historical plays?"

"I wonder whose copy he kept borrowing." Thomas asked lamely.

Maunder feigned a look of sudden coincidental insight. "And wasn't that also the source of many of Marlowe's works?"

Walsingham pretended to think this through. "Coincidentally, yes."

"And there were no copies of Ovid or Plutarch or any of the 200 other books Shakespeare used for his writings."

"Well, we have to assume that he was ravishing Sir Wriothesley's library for every volume he needed."

"Sir Thomas," Maunder began slowly. "Shakespeare's been gone from the Wriothesley estate for ten years. And there *have been* quite a few plays written in that period."

Thomas seemed to be silently mulling this over.

The Constable allowed a long pause to bait the hook. "And --" he said, and then paused again.

"And?" Thomas asked suspiciously.

Maunder decided to end the cat-and-mouse game and added seriously, "And no mention of even a single printed copy of any of his plays." Thomas said nothing, realizing the bantering was over. "You would think any writer would have at least one copy of each work of his that had been commissioned into print. And at least have a copy of the most recent quarto, don't you think?" Maunder asked.

Thomas answered seriously. "Well, there were so few copies printed ...."

"Five hundred, weren't there?" Maunder asked innocently, scanning the covers of the books lined meticulously on the shelves. "And that friend of yours who helped you finance some of the printings, Mr...."

"Blount," Walsingham gave in -- realizing the Constable knew anyway.

"Right. Edward Blount, who has the local print shop here. I heard that Blount said he had no way to get written versions of all the plays, except – as he told his friends – 'Luckily, Sir Thomas happened to have copies...,'" Maunder smiled, "'...of all the plays.'"

The Constable picked up a printed quarto of Shakespeare's works from the shelf he was scanning – trying to make it look like an accident that he had found that particular edition. He took the publication and opened it. "The title page states 'Printed According to the True Original Copies.'" He stopped and stared at Thomas.

"Of course," Thomas said, standing up. "I had been collecting them for Sir Wriothesley – while he was in prison." Gently taking the book, he added, "My goodness, Constable, you have fathomed out a store of trivial facts."

"I try, Sir Walsingham. I try."

There wasn't much room for pacing in the small alcove where Marlowe was listening, but he moved anxiously from one side to the other. It had *not* been a good day, or as Thomas worded it, "It's a day when all your problems line up against you, Christopher."

And now to hear Maunder talking about all the writings and glory being attributed to Shakespeare, Marlowe was pacing frantically. How can they be so stupid, Christopher wondered. Can't they see? Idiots who hold horses don't write plays.

The Constable looked up as the gentle sounds of floorboards squeaking came from the room above. Walsingham's soft smile and even gaze seems to indicate that he had heard nothing.

The Constable fingered the spine of another small volume on a shelf and gazed thoughtfully around the library. "And no mention of any of his plays," he added. Thomas gave him a puzzled look. "In the will, I mean. He didn't will his plays to anyone."

Walsingham tried to give this a noble bent. "Well, see that? Modeling his own will to the will of Caesar – just the way Shakespeare wrote about it – leaving everything to the people."

Maunder quickly countered, "Please, Sir Walsingham. Thirty-seven plays, two long narrative poems, 154 sonnets --"

"I get the picture, Constable," Thomas cut him off. "He didn't bequeath any of his plays or his poems or --"

"Should have been his most valuable possessions – his writings. Why would a person list every little pot and plate in his will and never mention his writings?"

"It does seem odd, doesn't it?"

"Yes," Maunder went on, "there has always been *so much* about the man that seemed odd."

Walsingham looked for anything that could ease the discussion onto a tangent. "Maybe he was a Catholic?" he asked, trying to sound sincere.

"Well, it's been pretty well established that he really did die a Papist. Everyone in Stratford seemed to know that. Born a Catholic and died a Catholic."

Walsingham tried to sound concerned. "Well, really? And I suppose it's too late to try to arrest him for that now?"

Maunder gave a smile that said, "Don't play with me," and headed for the door. "Then I take my leave, Sir Thomas." He stopped in the doorway when he and Thomas were startled by Christopher's voice.

"But, Constable, at least his life included receiving the praise for writing all those wonderful plays," Marlowe said boldly with a flair of sarcasm as he slowly descended the spiral staircase to the library.

For a second the Constable didn't recognize the gentleman he

had met in that same room at Scadbury years before. But then, he recalled the chance meeting on the day he had "accidentally" gone into the library, finding this person and Shakespeare.

"Ah, Cousin Richard," Maunder greeted.

"*Winston*," Thomas corrected, knowing full well that Maunder was once again playing the fool.

"Yes, Winston," Maunder corrected himself. "How is everything in Cambridge?"

"*Warwick*," Thomas threw away the line.

"Warwick," Maunder corrected himself again, a little too smoothly to be sincere.

Even though Thomas was as surprised as the Constable with Christopher's unexpected entrance, his voice was firm and even – a signal to silence Marlowe. "Cousin Winston, the Constable has learned that William Shakespeare -- who died recently -- was an acknowledged Papist."

As Marlowe took the last step from the stairway into the library, he was fuming but the Constable continued the charade in his same, calm tone. "To everyone's surprise," Maunder added.

As Marlowe started to speak, Thomas was quick to cut him off, "So the Constable really was quite correct about the man all along. I mean being so suspicious. Wasn't he?" When he got no answer from Marlowe, he added heavily, "I said 'Wasn't he?'"

Christopher finally gave in. "Yes, he certainly was." He stared at the Constable, still wanting a confrontation. But, to Thomas's bewilderment, Maunder refused to take the bait.

"Well, very good work, Constable," Walsingham concluded as Maunder and Marlowe merely continued to stare at each other. "And, uh ... thank you for coming to tell us," signaling that the meeting was over.

"Oh, yes. Well, Sir Thomas, I can find my way out. Thank you." Maunder crossed to the door but did not look back. "And the word is that he died of a venereal disease."

Chuckling, Walsingham added, "Well, that's our Will...liam. "

Maunder left and Walsingham collapsed into a large, overstuffed chair by the desk. Neither he nor Christopher said anything, both of them knowing how dangerous the situation had been and the possible consequences of Marlowe's outburst. In the past the sparring, had been fun but this time it was simply perilous. And somehow the Constable *had* learned that Thomas worked with the printer Edward Blount to get the folio published. Dumb as a fox, wasn't he? But why had Maunder continued the charade about Cousin Winston when Christopher came down from the alcove? He couldn't possibly be *that* dense.

Marlowe spoke first, obviously trying to avoid the subject. "Well, at least now there are only three people who know."

"Christopher!" Thomas shouted. "You've got to realize –"

"I know! I know!" Marlowe stopped him. "I *realize* it was fire that I was playing with. But I can't do this any longer, Thomas." Christopher waited for some response. Thomas sat fuming afraid to say anything he would later regret. When there was no response, Marlowe went on. "And, the worst part is not being able to leave this -- this *prison*."

"Certainly better than Bridewell," Thomas sighed.

"Only bigger."

Thomas continued to sit silently in the large chair but felt it was time to try to sober his partner. "Kit -- I guess you should know – Ralegh was executed last week. Not hanged -- beheaded." Marlowe squinted in pain. "The charge was atheism. He was never released from the Tower of London." Thomas took plenty of time, letting the message sink in.

Finally, he went on. "His last words to the ax man were 'This is sharp medicine – but it is the physician for all diseases and miseries.'" Thomas waited but Marlowe said nothing. "I'm not sure I could be as philosophical at a moment like that." It was time for Thomas to drive the message home. "You see, Christopher -- Francis is *very* angry. And he knows you're back somewhere in London. He's just not sure *where*."

Marlowe sat at the desk and put his head down. "Thomas, I just don't care any more. I ...just... don't ... care."

Walsingham said nothing and did not go to him. He slowly stood, waited a moment and then walked out of the library, leaving Christopher to his personal demons.

Outside the manor, Maunder walked to his carriage and told the driver, "Just wait here. I'll be back in a few minutes."

## CHAPTER 53

# THE VALISE

**M**oments later Christopher sat quietly, staring at nothing in particular, when he heard the library door open again.

"Oh, excuse me. But I think I may have forgotten a small valise when I left," Maunder said with little conviction and without looking around the room.

"Perhaps you did," Marlowe added with even less sincerity.

The Constable had noticed that the man sitting before him seemed noticeably older than when they had met years before. He was thinner and his hair was as thick and disheveled as before -- but the black was matched almost strand for strand with wiry gray. And that thin moustache was so feint that it had almost disappeared.

And he looked tired.

"I didn't mean to bother you," Maunder began. "You ... you looked concerned about something." When Marlowe said nothing, he added "Certainly not about Shakespeare's death, I assume."

"Definitely not that," Christopher smiled. "Just a day when all the muses seem to line up against you."

The Constable didn't try to keep the conversation going. Quietly he took a seat right next to Marlowe on a long bench embroidered with rich textures of purple and gold.

Marlowe found it hard to believe that the person sitting so close was the fiend that had been pursuing him for so long. There was no air of pretext or deception – no aura of the hunter about to pounce upon the hunted. (What is he *doing* here?)

"Ah, yes, the torment when the muses are against you, " Maunder intoned, mostly to himself. "Be they the muse of fortune -- or happiness – or…." The Constable could almost feel the pain in the person next to him. And the sensitivity. "Maybe even the muse of love."

"Don't we all suffer at the hands of the muse of love?" Christopher asked rhetorically.

"Yes." It was Henry Maunder's whispered response. "But some of us seem to suffer the slings more achingly."

For some reason the silence wasn't uncomfortable. The two men merely sat next to each other, each listening to his own thoughts.

"You seem to be a victim of the muses yourself today," Christopher ventured cautiously

"Just … just pondering a question. No -- not a question. A problem."

"Concerning?"

"Duty," Maunder answered simply, not bothering to elaborate.

"Duty? An odd concern for a Constable of the law, isn't it? One would imagine duty to be the clearest of all assignments."

Maunder took a deep breath. "Therein lies the problem."

"Which is?"

"The hazy divide – between duty -- and assignment."

Marlowe looked confused. "Yes," Maunder added, "that hazy divide. Which is it? Duty or just assignment?"

Marlowe's glance at Maunder seemed to say he understood.

"And," the Constable went on, "there is always the question of…," here he paused trying to dislodge the more accurate words, "…the *consequences* following duty – or assignment – whichever it be."

The two men sat beside each other, each pondering the question. Each in utter silence. Even the usual sounds of the manor seemed to be stilled in deference to their thoughts.

After long moments, Marlowe broke the spell. "Then, I suppose it actually depends on the consequences, doesn't it?" Christopher seemed to be putting the pieces together in his own mind.

"Yes," Maunder was thinking, "I suppose it does."

Christopher seemed to be almost able to sense what the Constable was thinking – and feeling.

Maunder sat quietly for a few moments, running his fingers through his hair. "Those consequences," he began slowly, haltingly, as if he were carefully sifting the thoughts. "They can sometimes ... stifle a venture ... limit a human being ... or even silence a voice."

"But..." Marlowe began, and then his words trailed off. "But," he began again, "*...once an idea has been caged* ...." He paused, thinking. "*Once a voice has been silenced ... the world is never the same, is it?*"_

The Constable's head did not move but his eyes appeared to be nodding in agreement. "Beautiful thought," he mused. "*... 'Once an idea has been caged ... once a voice has been silenced – the world can never be the same.'* You should be a poet."

"What a pity that both Shakespeare and Marlowe are dead," Christopher said smiling at Maunder. "Maybe I could have passed the thought to one of them."

When Marlowe didn't go on, Maunder stood and just looked at him. Gently he brushed aside two errant strands of hair on the young poet's forehead. Marlowe looked up in surprise.

As the Constable headed for the door to leave, Marlowe followed him with his eyes, and then asked, "Might that be your valise on the floor by the desk?"

Maunder didn't turn to look back. "No, I don't think it is."

There was nothing on the floor by the desk.

# CHAPTER 54

# SILENCE

"And what did you learn?" Sir Francis asked, continuing to scan the sheets of paper in front of him.

Maunder stood by the desk and finally said, "It appears that Sir Thomas knew nothing about Shakespeare's death. And he had no knowledge about the details of the will."

"And there was nothing unusual? Nothing suspicious?" Sir Francis seemed skeptical.

Maunder played back in his mind the meeting when he returned to the library. He rationalized that until he was sure there was some significance, it was best to overlook the matter. But a voice, way in the back of his mind, kept asking if that was the real reason he was not mentioning it. Maybe it was.

"Nothing, Sir Francis."

# CHAPTER 55

# MANUSCRIPTS FROM THE GRAVE

ir Francis never let daily complications keep him from pursuing major projects. But the years following the death of Shakespeare in 1616 proved to be a turbulent time for him. Even though each year added very few new responsibilities for him as Secretary of State, many things seemed to fall onto his plate as England's spy chief.

The war with Spain took some ugly turns and the clashes between the two religions seemed to flare up every few months. Spain was still seething from the execution of Mary Queen of Scots and the defeat of their precious Armada. But the real salt for the wound was the ascension of Catholic Mary's own son, James (now a devout Protestant) to be the head of the Church of England. Sir Francis found himself dispatching spies and wondering which ones might really be selling more information than they were gathering.

And worse, the plague, which was virtually always present, would mysteriously flare up every few years. Whenever the death toll in the city reached forty, all public gatherings except for church services were banned within seven miles of London. Policing those periods always seemed to drain all the hours of his day.

On top of that, the new King decided to produce his own translation of the bible that had been, until then, the sole canon of the Catholic Church. The new version, which was to be called "The Authorized King James Bible," was designed to become the official version of the gospels for Protestant England. Someone had to oversee the book's translation, final approval, production, and installation within the Church. But who?

Since the new Bible would bear the king's own name, he wanted to be assured that there would be no problems with its introduction to the world. So he handpicked his reliable Secretary of State to oversee the project. He felt this would keep the production in competent hands – hands over which he would have direct and complete control.

(The king probably showed good judgment in insisting on such oversight. History has shown that the *second* edition of the new Bible had one startling typographical error. It read "Thou *Shalt* Commit Adultery.")

So, Sir Francis plowed his way through commitment after commitment. But days became weeks, and weeks turned to months, and before he realized it, years had passed since William Shakespeare had died.

And then, suddenly the ugly situation bubbled to the surface once again.

"Constable, do you believe in the hereafter?" he asked as he sat at the large desk comparing the notice in his left hand with details on the one to his right. They were announcements for two plays, both by Shakespeare – both at the new Globe Theatre -- one opening the following week (*Loves Labours Lost*) and one from a few months before (*Coriolanus.*)

"The hereafter?" Maunder asked, realizing this question was not designed to be answered.

"Because our friend Shakespeare has been dead for years now and he's written a dozen more plays from beyond the grave."

"Sir Francis, I too have been bothered by this," Maunder tried to be conciliatory.

"Twelve plays! *Twelve plays!* And he's been dead for years. Some playwrights don't write that many in a whole lifetime ... and certainly not after they've died."

"At the Globe Theatre they tell me they keep finding old scripts." That was true. The Constable had checked at the theatre and this was the best answer anyone there could give. The Globe had burned down in 1613 when an errant cannon ball started a fire during a production of Shakespeare's *Henry VIII*. It was rebuilt the next year but everything was still not back to normal. The place seemed to be more disorganized than ever. According to the harried management, people kept discovering old scripts by Shakespeare; and since the audience wanted to see them, the Globe, of course, would keep producing them.

"And *you* believe they keep finding old scripts?" Sir Francis asked pointedly.

"No," Maunder replied. Sir Francis kept examining the promotional sheets in front of him and drumming his stubby fingers on the desk. "The plays are no longer set in Italy. So Marlowe must certainly be back in England," Maunder added.

Sir Francis just glared at the notices in his hands. "Something is amiss here. Like ... like trying to play chess with one of the pieces missing. Constable...," his thoughts overtook his tongue.

The Constable Maunder waited, once again playing over in his mind the dilemma he had been living with for such a long time. Then he decided to mention that very, *very* delicate subject. "Yes, Marlowe obviously is back," he said.

Then he decided to broach the subject he had avoided for so long and added cautiously, "As is your cousin Winston." Sir Francis looked up and just stared at him. "From Warwick?" Maunder added. "Winston Walsingham?"

Suddenly Constable Maunder understood. "You have no cousin Winston, do you?"

"And there are no Walsinghams in Warwick."

All of a sudden it was all very clear. "I wondered," Maunder added reluctantly.

"Are you telling me that there is someone else living with Thomas at Scadbury?" Sir Francis's voice was unbelieving. "And you said nothing?"

"Sir Thomas said it was his cousin."

"Sir *Thomas* said!" Francis screamed. "Sir *Thomas* said!" He was breathing hard through his nostrils. "And it never occurred to you that --"

"Sorry, Sir Francis, tomorrow I will --"

"Ah, but you won't," Sir Francis said very quietly. "I will handle it myself this time. *Tonight!*" Sir Francis slammed the playbills on the desk with a force to shake the building and headed for the door.

"And, tomorrow, Constable, you are going to have some very serious explaining -- *here* ... in this office -- at midday."

# CHAPTER 56

# COUSIN WINSTON

"**A** glass of Grigio, Francis?"

Sir Francis didn't answer. He hadn't said a word since he'd entered unexpectedly a few minutes before, interrupting Poley who was laying out some wine and hard bread in front of Thomas.

The two men, silently facing each other from opposite ends of the long dining table, was the cue for Poley to quietly exit.

The formal room was dimly lit -- by only two large candelabra atop the serving table on the far side of the room.

"I'll get you some wine," Thomas said as he walked to the side table and picked up a large decanter.

"How is Cousin Winston?"

Thomas showed no signs of panic but immediately knew what was happening. "Cousin Winston?" he asked, his back still to his cousin.

Sir Francis let the statement roll off his tongue with naïve innocence. "Yes, Winston Walsingham -- from Warwick."

Thomas took the glass and crossed to the table, placing the wine in front of Sir Francis, who waited in silence, enjoying the situation. Finally, he continued, "You must remember our dear cousin -- from Warwick. I hear he's visiting here now."

Thomas carried the bottle of wine back to his end of the long table and waited, ready to learn his fate.

Sir Francis was suddenly comforting. "Now, Thomas, you needn't be concerned. I'm not stupid enough to let the world learn what a fool you've made of me – *and the King*." He lifted the glass and examined the color of the wine, turning the glass slowly in his hand. "But," he added sympathetically, "I am afraid *this time* dear Cousin Winston is really going to secretly meet with a terrible accident -- a very painful one -- I would guess."

He smiled and went on. "But, you, Cousin Thomas, will live happily ever after. Now didn't I tell you blood had its privileges?"

Francis put the glass back onto the table. "You will be all right without Christopher, won't you?" Then his voice changed to a tone of menacing reality. "Won't you?"

With a swift change of manner, he headed for the side table and grabbed one of the candles from a candelabrum. "And this time we know where he is, so he won't be able to escape." He started for the dining room door.

"Where are you going, Francis?" Thomas yelled. "Francis!"

"Where?" Sir Francis yelled back over his shoulder. "Where else? The West Tower."

Thomas dropped the bottle of wine which fell to the stone floor with a splintering crash. "The West Tower? Why?" he called running after him.

In his room atop the tower Christopher heard the faraway crash of the bottle of wine and stopped writing. As he looked down from the top of the steps he heard Sir Francis yelling, "Why? You know why."

"Francis! Francis!" Thomas was yelling as he followed through room after room. Sir Francis started up the long spiral staircase with Thomas a few steps behind.

Christopher looked around the small room and decided on the only option left to him. He left papers strewn and candles burning and climbed down into a small crawl space below the floor. Then, with a great amount of effort, he pulled the heavy stone that usually covered the opening back into place, leaving just a small crack open for a sliver of light and some air.

Sir Francis charged into the empty room, and, with an air of pride, noticed the lit candles and pages of script lying everywhere. As Thomas entered, Francis held up a sheet of script and grinned, indicating he had guessed correctly.

Then Sir Francis stepped outside onto the parapet and slowly waived the candle back and forth as a sign to his carriage below.

"The West Tower. Where else? From here you can see the entire manor and all of Scadbury." He seemed to really be enjoying the snooping. He picked up another sheet of paper and said, "You know, he really should have left this speech in *Macbeth*," he whispered innocently.

In the crowded space below, Christopher listened to the muted voices and tried to see through the small crack at the edge of the opening.

"Remember, Thomas," Sir Francis went on, "how we used to play up here as children -- for hours? We'd hide from your mother in that small space hallowed out under the floor over there." He smiled. "We used to call it our own little dungeon. But she was always afraid the stone might fall back into place and we wouldn't be able to breathe in there." The two men stared at each other across the room.

Then with a fake nostalgic smile, Sir Francis walked over to the stone covering the opening and pushed it with his foot, locking it in place. "'You'll die in there,' she used to yell. 'You'll die in there.'"

There was absolute silence in the room: Thomas's face in a stony gaze, Sir Francis with a menacing smirk.

At that moment a guard with sword drawn entered the room. "You signaled, Sir Francis?"

"Yes, Milo. I want you to remain here all night. I and a few others will return in the morning." The guard nodded. "But you're to stay *here*. Especially make sure that no one moves this stone in the floor." The guard nodded again.

Marlowe gasped for a few quick breaths and realized there was no air in the small, dark cavity. In spite of the chance of getting caught he tried to shift his weight to lift the stone a little, but there was not enough room for that. And he could no longer hear the conversation of the two men. In an act of panic, he again tried to force the stone up, but that was useless.

Candle in hand Sir Francis left the room and slowly descended the staircase. Thomas scrutinized the armed guard and made the quick decision to follow his cousin.

Back in the dining room Francis was pushing around the pieces of broken wine bottle with his foot. "I'll return at daybreak. We'll have no trouble finding him this time, will we?" Sir Francis smiled. He could see Thomas shaking with fear and loathing. "Have a nice evening, Thomas." Francis headed for the door, stopped and turned to enjoy the scene. Then, returning to the table, he lifted the glass of wine and made a toast to Thomas. "Oh, and thank you for the Grigio," he said downing the wine in a single swallow. Nonchalantly he let the glass drop to the floor, shattering it. He looked around the room and then yelled in the direction of the West Tower, "And, good night, Christopher. Sleep well."

He smiled and walked to his carriage where he waved to the guard standing on the parapet. The guard waved his sword and Sir Francis stepped into his carriage.

But that was the last sight the guard saw because a moment later the heavy lance from the suit of armor at the top of the stairway came slicing down on him, splitting his head almost in two.

## CHAPTER 57

# CARRIAGE TO LONDON

Robert Poley was mesmerized and dropped the lance. The blood was everywhere – on the floor, all over him, on the walls. Everywhere. Then he remembered Christopher and dashed to the stone covering the opening, kicking aside the guard's mangled and bleeding body. Trying to get his blood-covered fingers into any crevice, he yelled to Marlowe, "Push. Push. Keep pushing. Now. Push. *Push*!"

In the yard below Thomas ran to the carriage and stopped Sir Francis from closing the door. "Francis, I have to talk to you."

"Talk? What is there to talk about, Thomas?"

"I have a plan."

"Oh, you have a plan!" Sir Francis mocked him, shaking his head, not even bothering to look out of the carriage.

Thomas looked up at the parapet on the West Tower and saw that Poley had gotten a gasping Christopher to the arched doorway. "Yes," Thomas said and got into the carriage.

"Get out of the carriage, Thomas."

"I have to talk to you."

"Get out of the carriage." Thomas didn't make any attempt to leave, "All right." Sir Francis banged the side door as a sign to the driver. The carriage took off.

"Now this plan of your?" Sir Francis was smirking.

Thomas said nothing. He had a sad, almost soulful appearance as he seemed to be lost in thought.

"You said you had a *plan*?" Sir Francis asked again. He got no response. "Thomas, why did you insist on riding back with me?"

Almost mechanically, Thomas heard himself saying "Because … because … when your carriage got to London, they would know it came from Scadbury."

"And so? They would know it came from Scadbury."

But Thomas seemed to be in a different world, his mind numb with bizarre thoughts.

"Such a dilemma, Thomas. And to think that you're doing all this for another man." Francis shook his head mystified. "You know you should have gotten out of the carriage, Thomas. You'll have no way back from London till the morning. And I certainly am not having my driver take you back tonight."

"I'm not going back to Scadbury, Francis." Then he added, speaking more to himself. "Ever."

"What are you saying, Thomas? You're not going back to Scadbury!? What does that mean?"

Thomas sat opposite Sir Francis and just waited, saying nothing. Slowly his forlorn look showed signs of a sad smile.

"What are you talking about that you're nev …" Sir Francis began. But then his face distorted into a tight grimace. He tried to speak. "Thomas!" he managed to whisper. "*Thomas*…."

Thomas Walsingham sat quietly as Sir Francis clawed at the seat of the carriage and tried to cry out. But no words left his lips. He kept gasping and slowly slid down onto the floor of the carriage.

Thomas looked down at his cousin who was then writhing, his mouth open trying to scream. Softly he said, "Francis, I wonder if that Grigio might have been a little…spoiled…?"

He felt his cousin grab his ankle and try to speak. In vain Thomas tried to pull his leg away. "Yes, I think maybe it was. I'm glad now I didn't join you in that drink."

Francis made guttural sounds, trying desperately to cry out, but nothing came out except gasps and bizarre choking sounds. Finger by finger Thomas removed the grip from his ankle and then pushed the clawing body with his foot to the far end of the carriage. After a few moments there were neither sounds nor movement.

Thomas Walsingham sat there in the silent stupor that followed an evening of fear and frenzy.

But now it was over.

The carriage jostled noisily to London. He waited, silently realizing what he had to do next, aware of the danger if the carriage arrived from Scadbury with the dead body of the Secretary of State.

Finally, he leaned out of the carriage door and yelled to the driver. "Driver, driver. Something has happened to Sir Francis."

The carriage stopped and before the driver could question what was wrong, Thomas had climbed up onto the seat next to him. "We've got to get to London right away." Without saying any more Thomas grabbed the reins and started the carriage going at full pace.

The driver sat stunned, not knowing really what was happening. "We'll take the shortcut at the top of the ridge," Thomas shouted as he maneuvered the carriage onto a sharp left turn.

"At night?" the driver cried. "There's no way we...."

The carriage raced along the curving road at the top of the ridge, almost a silhouette in the bright moonlight. Thomas pushed the horses, making them go faster and faster. "Worry no more, my love," he whispered so softly that the driver heard nothing above the deafening sounds of the carriage on the narrow, winding road. "Christopher, worry no...."

"Sir Thomas," the driver screamed, trying to grab the reins. "Sir Thomas, you know you can't.... "

Thomas Walsingham pushed the driver away and violently pulled the reins to the right. The carriage, horses, and riders seemed almost frozen in time as they sailed silently off the cliff into the darkness.

Moments later there was only the echo of a horse's forced breathing and the almost soundless spinning of a carriage wheel.

It was three days before anyone even noticed the broken bodies and fractured coach.

## CHAPTER 58

# THE ARREST

Someone kept banging at the door but Christopher did not move. He just sat, slumped at the desk in the small study and stared in a daze at the fire burning in front of him.

Although it was only dusk, the room seemed very dark, dimly lit by two candles on the desk and one on a small table by the door. The flames in the fireplace cast an array of shadows over the tapestries on the walls. The study was in disarray, some of the furniture covered with cloth.

A clock ticked loudly, intensifying the silence.

More banging on the door. Then *more* banging.

Marlowe heard the huge door at the front entrance opening and then footsteps coming slowly down the hall. He didn't bother to move.

The study door opened and Constable Maunder walked in carrying a tall candle that gave his face a misshapen, shadowy look. Unobtrusively he put a bundle of papers on the table by the door.

"I knocked repeatedly but no one came," he said irritably. When there was no reply from Marlowe, he added, "So I let myself in."

Christopher knew who was there and what he wanted. There was no need to turn around or say anything.

"Where are the servants," Maunder asked. When he got no reply, he added firmly and more officially, "I said 'Where are the servants'?"

"After the funeral I let them all go," Christopher said in a resigned monotone. "No reason to keep them."

Thomas Walsingham had been buried on 19 August 1630 – four days after the discovery of the broken carriage and just three weeks after his portrait had finally been added to the procession of Walsinghams on the vaulted wall of the grand dining room.

Maunder wandered aimlessly around the room, picking up a sheet of paper and lifting to read it by the candle in his hand. He looked at Christopher and noticed that the hair was still untamed but now completely white and beginning to thin. "They read his will today." He put the sheet down. "He left a goodly sum to some scrivener. The will said it was for him to buy a ring. It seemed like a gift, obviously to thank him, for some favor perhaps."

There was no reason to continue the charade. "Maybe for not wagging his tongue all these years about the plays he's been copying." Christopher's voice was tired. He could not have cared less.

"Why didn't you go to the funeral?"

"You're very funny. You know why I didn't go."

"Impressive. Very impressive. And the church was full. Not like the funeral for Sir Francis. It seemed hardly anyone made it for that one."

"I'm sure the King was there," Marlowe replied automatically.

"Well, no. A bit of a surprise since this *was* the country's first Secretary of State and all. James was 'away from London', we were told. He sent some representative that nobody knew."

The Constable blew out the candle he was holding and placed it on the desk. "What will you do now?"

Marlowe answered sarcastically, "You needn't worry. I won't be running."

"But what will you do?"

"Constable, no more niceties. You have a job to do and you've come today to do it. He's gone. And so is my protection."

"I asked: what will you do?"

"Well, I was thinking perhaps of taking up residence for a while at Bridewell Prison. Maybe spend a little time studying the techniques of Rackmaster Topcliffe – you know, maybe to use in a play someday." He thought for a moment and then added mockingly, "And, if memory serves me, disseminating views on atheism is still a crime. Punishable by death, right? So hanging's another option, isn't it?"

Maunder didn't answer and Christopher became testy and a little louder, "Isn't it?"

Marlowe got no response to his sarcasm. He waited and slowly the air of bravado began to escape. Finally, said, "He shouldn't have done that."

Maunder waited, and then replied. "He did it for you."

"And what did it gain for either of us?" When there was no answer, Christopher went on sarcastically. "Thomas Kyd was right. I sin and others suffer. And Thomas was the perfect target: one who loved not wisely but too well."

"It happens every day: doing foolish things for love."

"Like dying…?" Maunder sat opposite Marlowe and said nothing. "I've always wondered, Constable: you've must have known for years …. "

"Of course, I *suspected* for years. But it wasn't until Shakespeare's plays kept appearing long after he died. Thirteen or fourteen, right? And mystically from the grave."

Marlowe shook his head. "Plays that appeared mystically from the grave. So there's the rub."

But then reality struck and Christopher added sarcastically, "And so now, Constable, you are here today to do your duty and finally get the man who has made such a mockery of you, and the Privy Council, and the king, and …" Marlowe's voiced trailed off.

Henry Maunder saw before him a drained and worn out poet -- aged more by turmoil than by years. "Well, my friend, now there seems to be a different problem."

Marlowe was stunned by the words "my friend."

"You see File 13 seems to be missing now." When Christopher appeared to be confused, Maunder went on. "That's the file about the murder of Christopher Marlowe. Well, actually it includes more information about William Shakespeare, so maybe we should have renamed it a long time ago. Maybe ... 'File 13: The Murder of the real William Shakespeare.' Thickest and most complete collection of documents at the Conciliatory. Years of work on my part just so Sir Francis could go to the Privy Council and ...." His voiced faded.

Maunder stood and walked over to the table by the door and picked up the large bundle of papers he had brought in with him. "Anyway, file 13 seems to be missing now," he said, dropping the bundle on the desk in front of Christopher. "And without it, there's really nothing that anyone -- even the Privy Council – can do."

Marlowe slowly began to leaf through the pages in the file, and then, confused, stopped to look at Maunder questioningly.

Maunder thought for a minute and then realized it was time. Yes, it was time. "One day I became aware of more than just the identical lines and other similarities," he began. "I became aware of what I felt was – how do I put it -- the orchestral range of your verbal music."

Christopher was touched. "*Orchestral range of verbal music.* Beautiful line. Mind if I use it someday?" He smiled for the first time.

"But that's what it was. *Verbal music.* And there I was assembling a file that would put an end to all that. And so ... which was more important: to bring one more atheist to the gallows -- or to assure that the music continued?"

Christopher was impressed and felt very flattered. This was what he had been missing. Someone to appreciate what he had worked so hard to do.

"But, you know," Maunder went on, "there was one big clue we all missed. It could have saved us many years of work. Shakespeare had the marvelous reputation of never making corrections in his scripts. No cross outs. No altered drafts. It never occurred to us that some scrivener had to be copying the works before anyone ever saw them."

The Constable shook his head. "And *I* should have noticed that — because I think I've read almost every word you've written."

"Every word," Christopher echoed. "Now that's punishment that could liberate a man from the fires of hell."

Maunder picked up a sheet from the file and scrutinized it. "Was it worth it, Christopher?"

Marlowe realized the Constable had just called him by his first name.

"Was it worth it?" Christopher looked around the room and wondered. "Was it worth it? Risking my life just so I could write?" He gazed into the darkness of the room. "Maybe at first."

Marlowe continued to gaze around the darkened study as if he were expecting to find an explanation in some shadowy corner. Finally he spoke. "'What's in a name,' I once wrote. *What's in a name?*" His voice was becoming bitter and hateful. "I'll tell you what's in a name. Slowly I began to realize that *I was writing*, but my name was being stolen from every play that appeared on the London stage. And with my name went each of my works. They were no longer mine. But each was rather one gigantic sham. Each play was just…another…ruse …."

Christopher went on slowly, "And I was fueling the biggest deception of all time." Then with irony in his voice, he continued, "Yes, me! The man who once wrote 'He who steals my purse steals nothing. But he who steals my good name….'" He put his head in his hands and laughed. "And he didn't even have to steal it. We *gave* it to him."

The flames in the fireplace flared up for a second. "A sham? A deception?" Maunder honestly questioned, as he stared at the flames. Then he crossed over and put his hand on Christopher's shoulders -- so reminiscent, Marlowe thought, of the way Thomas always did. "You should read a play called *Hamlet* -- by a man named Shakespeare." Marlowe laughed quietly and tried to look up at the Constable, but Maunder's firm grip held him rigid and there seemed to be a slight catch in the Constable's voice. "In *Hamlet*, Polonius is saying goodbye — possibly for the last time — to his son Leartes, trying to sum up a lifetime of advice in a few lines."

Then with simple majesty, Maunder went on. Somehow, he seemed to stand taller. Slowly – beautifully – he recited. "Polonius tells him '*This above all, to thine own self be true and it must follow, as the night the day, thou canst not then be false to any man*'."

After a moment, he leaned down and whispered, "That verbal music? That was very true to yourself...." Marlowe reached up and grabbed the hand of Maunder. "...It was beautiful and it was truthful."

For a long time the two of them silently watched the flames slowly dying.

Finally Maunder released Christopher's shoulders. "And, I hate to disappoint you, but I'm afraid you're just going to have to forego Bridewell and learning any of those tricks of the Royal Rackmaster," the Constable said, picking up the file of papers from the desk and scattering them into the fireplace. The fire began to blaze brightly, lighting the room so they could actually see each other for the first time. There was a broad grin on Maunder's face as he said, "If Sir Francis could only see me now ...."

Christopher nodded and added, "...it would *kill* him ... again." They both laughed and Maunder sat and silently looked at Christopher.

"*Henry*," Marlowe began, realizing that he was calling Maunder by his first name, "Henry ... was it only the 'verbal music'?" He waited before asking, "Nothing else?"

"Nothing else?" Maunder repeated, and looked around the room trying to put together an answer. The study was now beginning to darken again as the last of the papers smoldered in the fireplace, giving the Constable the concealment of darkness he so longingly desired at that moment. "Sometimes – maybe -- the music might be enhanced." Then he corrected himself. "Especially if ...." He watched the fire slowly shrinking to a mass of hot coals, giving the room a more unnatural glow.

"Especially if...?" Kit asked.

Henry Maunder stared silently at Christopher Marlowe but did not go on. Then, with no warning, he slowly crossed the room and once again put his hands on the poet's shoulders. Then, silently he bent down and quietly kissed Christopher on the top of the head. For long moments there was no movement in the room.

Finally, regaining his control, the Constable asked nonchalantly, "If I were to guess what Shakespearean play would probably be discovered next, what would you guess it might be?"

Christopher sat there, still stunned and confused. As the countless thoughts flooded his mind, he heard his own voice -- devoid of any meaning -- almost mumble, "If you were a betting man, you might want to put a few shillings on something called *The Tempest*."

There was a long, awkward moment, and then the Constable slowly walked to the door and out of the study. He closed the door behind him and looked back, his hand still on the handle. Then he walked to the main entrance and left.

Christopher put his head down on the desk. This was too much, he was thinking. Thomas's death, the visit from Maunder, File 13 … the gentle kiss. What was going on?

"Thomas, Thomas, Thomas," he whispered.

He wasn't sure – but maybe he was crying.

## CHAPTER 59

# BURIAL

The cheap wooden coffin pitched from side to side as the old wagon was pulled through puddles of mud and uneven ground.

Heavy rain the day before made the field soggy. And the blue-grey clouds overhead gave everything a dark and ominous look. It was going to rain again.

The old horse, pulling the wagon through the mire, was having trouble with every step, his hoofs sinking deep into the mud.

A solitary figure in a long black cloak slowly followed. He didn't seem to be concerned how the ruts and holes almost toppled the casket from the flat wagon. Nor was he aware how the wheels, going through the dirty slush, splashed mud onto his meticulously pressed garment.

Two men with shovels silently watched the wagon approach the gravesite. Unceremoniously they pulled the casket from the wagon and struggled to carry it to the open grave.

It was getting darker and cold, torrential rain suddenly began to fall.

With heavy ropes the two workers lowered the rain-soaked coffin to the bottom of the grave. One of them snaked the muddy rope out from beneath the casket as the other began to shovel dirt and mud into the hole.

The icy wind blew more fiercely. But the solitary figure seemed in a trance, not hearing the splatter of each shovelful of dirt landing on the casket below.

The workers continued shoveling, nearly unable to see with the wind and rain scraping their faces. Streams of mud began to wash over the bottom of the man's cloak and into the deep hole.

The solitary figure just stared at the grave.

The solitary figure just stared at the grave, unaware that by then his clothes were completely soaked.

Finally, deciding they had as much dirt as possible on the casket, the two gravesmen ran to the wagon and carried back a simple, carved headstone, carefully tilting it into place. The heavy rain, running down the cheap marble, made it difficult to read.

# *XTOFER*

## *1564 – 1633*

*Hier Lies XTOFER*

*Poet and Lyar*

*A Life Full Of Turmoil*

*His World Full of Mire*

*Filled With Raptures Of Love*

*And Verses Of Fyer*

The two men looked at Maunder for some sign that they were done but the Constable's thoughts were elsewhere. Since there was no response, they picked up their shovels and began to run hurriedly across the field, toward the old barn where the horses were always kept, both of the men trying desperately to shield their faces from the piercing rain.

A very old and very pained Henry Maunder knelt down and stuck a white quill with a bright red tip into the mud covered grave.

"At last -- Christopher -- *requiescat in pace.*"

By then it was completely dark and a sudden strike of lightning starkly lit the field for a few seconds.

He didn't move. He just stayed there, kneeling in the mud, with rain and lightning all around. He was staring at the white quill in the muddy grave.

Three days prior, Henry Maunder had found Christopher in the small rose garden off the West Tower. He was sitting in his favorite chair in the gazebo, slumped on the table in front of him. In one hand was his hallmark white quill with the red tip. The other hand was tightly clutching a small scrap of paper.

Maunder was sure Marlowe had died that very morning. He and Richard Poley had agreed to come by the mansion as frequently as each could – just to check on him. Christopher seemed to be ailing more and more each day. In the three years since Thomas had died Marlowe hadn't written a page.

Furthermore, when he got word of Wriothesley's death from some unknown fever while Henry was visiting the Netherlands, Kit seemed to lose all interest in even talking with people.

And so the Constable, who hunted Christopher, and the courier, whom Christopher had tormented, made a pact to visit him – each trying to get to Scadbury on alternate days.

On his previous visit, Christopher had looked pale, Maunder thought – starkly pale. And he had said he was tired – "so very, very tired."

Consequently, when he found Christopher slumped in his chair in the gazebo that morning, he knew the moment had arrived. Maunder sat next to Christopher and slowly unclenched the tight fist. It held a short note -- maybe intended for Maunder -- maybe for Thomas -- or, who knows, maybe for Christopher himself. It read:

> *Sonnet 72*
> *By William Shakespeare*

The name of Shakespeare had a single swipe of the pen through it. Below it was shakily scrawled:

*By Christopher Marlowe.*

He had written these two lines from Sonnet 72.

*"Let my name be buried where my body is.*
*And live no more to shame me nor you."*

The fierce wind easily picked up the scrap of paper and bounced it wildly across the field. Henry Maunder knelt there at the gravesite, not realizing the note was no longer in his hand. The rivulets of rain ran from the top of his head down his face and onto his cloak.

The words of the sonnet echoed in his mind. *"Let my name be buried where my body is – and live no more to shame me nor you."*

"All that beautiful writing," he thought. "All that exquisite verbal music. In a few years the names of both of them -- Marlowe *and* Shakespeare – will be long forgotten."

"Yes, Christopher," he muttered in the darkness. "Once an idea has been caged ... once a voice has been silenced ... the world can never be the same."

Joshua, the old horse harnessed to the wagon, painfully swung his head from side to side trying to shield himself from the piercing rain.

Another bolt of lightning flashed in the dark and, for a few seconds, the scene was once again frozen in black and white.

# Supplements

## I - HISTORICAL NOTES

## II - HISTORICAL DATA

# HISTORICAL NOTES

There are a multitude of reasons why William Shakespeare, the actor, could not have written the plays attributed to him. However, these three are the most common:

- He did not have the education, travel experiences, or background to have written those plays and poems.

- He obviously did not own any books, including any of the more than 200 from which material was used for these plays. His will divided every inexpensive item he owned but listed no books – which were certainly required for his writing. Books were so precious at that time that they would most certainly be willed to someone. He obviously had none.

- Plays supposedly written by Shakespeare continued to appear for years after the actor died – fourteen in all.

There are likewise a multitude of reasons which corroborate the premise that Christopher Marlowe did not die in a knife fight in the bar at Deptford. These are the three most common:

- Marlowe was mysteriously and coincidentally "killed" just days before he was to appear before the Privy Council for treason, a crime punishable by death. Almost every detail of his death, including all records by the coroner, by the church officials and by the government, are contradictory -- and, at best, ludicrous. The fight in a faraway tavern supposedly concerned the paying of a bill for dinner.

- Marlowe, England's foremost poet was instantly and suspiciously buried in an unmarked grave – never found to this day -- with none of the tributes for someone of his stature.

- The man who supposedly murdered Marlowe was immediately absolved of the crime by the Queen and went back to work for Marlowe's patron, Sir Thomas Walsingham.

**There are many reasons to believe that it was really Christopher Marlowe penning the plays attributed to William Shakespeare.**

- There are more than a hundred duplicate, similar or identical lines in the works attributed to Shakespeare and those written by Marlowe. There are no matches with other poets or other writers of that period.

- At the end of the eighteenth century an American University professor, Dr. Thomas Corwin Mendenhall, developed a system whereby the author of a work could be scientifically detected by a variety of mechanical devices such as word length, structure, etc. He undertook to experiment with the works of twenty famous writers, including Keats, Shelley, Thackeray, Lord Byron, Ben Johnson and even Shakespeare and Marlowe. The study was done in an effort to prove that Francis Bacon was in reality the actual author of Shakespeare's works. There were no matches -- until they got to Christopher Marlowe and then, to quote Dr. Mendenhall, "something akin to a sensation was produced. In the characteristic curve of his plays. Christopher Marlowe agrees with Shakespeare as well as Shakespeare agrees with himself." But, since Dr. Mendenhall knew Marlowe had died before Shakespeare wrote his plays, the results were designated "inconclusive."

- As recently as 1994, a literary scholar named Thomas Merriam worked with a computer scientist by the name of Robert Matthews to analyze and determine who wrote the works attributed to Shakespeare. The computer analysis determined Christopher Marlowe had actually written them. And, once again, since the world knew that Marlowe was not alive at the time, the results were categorized "non-decisive."

# HISTORICAL DATA

## FACT OR FICTION

**NOTE: To make verification easier, facts that are in more than one chapter will be listed for *every chapter* in which they appear – always in their order within the chapter.**

**PREFACE PAGE**

*FACT*: As stated, all documents, persons, dates, Shakespearean quotes and *recorded* events named herein are historically accurate except for one date: that of the death of Sir Francis Walsingham. This was changed for dramatic reasons.

*Fiction*: As stated, dialogue and events for which there are *no* records had to be created.

**CHAPTER ONE**

*FACT:* Details for Chapter One are all listed in Chapter Fifty-Nine, which is the continuation of the first chapter.

**CHAPTER TWO**

*FACT*: Scadbury Manor, twelve miles outside London, *was* the estate of Sir Thomas Walsingham.

*Fiction*: Although Thomas Walsingham is referred to throughout this novel as "*Sir* Thomas Walsingham," he was not actually knighted until 1597, which is four years after the *beginning* of this novel. This consistent designation was done to eliminate any confusion since his knighthood is not referred to in this novel.

***FACT***: The word "*god*" is not capitalized since it is a generic exclamation and not referring to God himself.

***FACT***: Thomas Kyd *was* served with the edict to appear before the Privy Council in May, 1593. He *was* the author of *The Spanish Tragedy* as well as other acclaimed works and was the second most prominent playwright in England at that time.

***FACT***: Marlowe had been living with Thomas Kyd for two years and had recently moved in with Sir Thomas Walsingham. The common term for two men living together *was* "chamber fellows."

***FACT:*** Homosexual relationships were quietly accepted at that time so long as one's liaisons remained within one's own class.

***FACT***: There are historians who agree that there was a romantic relationship between Christopher Marlowe and Thomas Walsingham. There are, however, strong opinions on *both* sides of this issue.

***FACT***: The portion of the edict which appears in this novel *is exact.* "By order of the Privy Council Thomas Kyd is ordered to appear before the Councilors on 11 May 1593 to answer changes concerning the discovery of vile heretical concepts denying the deity of Jesus Christ our Savior. Under suspicion of blasphemy, he will…." The edict then continued. (The phrase "vile heretical concepts" was *not* underlined in the original edict.)

***FACT***: Atheism *was* a treasonous crime and was punishable by death.

***FACT***: The edict *was* a result of the searching of the living quarters of Thomas Kyd and Christopher Marlowe.

***FACT***: Marlowe *was* notorious for making *many heretical remarks* about Jesus including all the ones mentioned in this novel. Marlowe did like to spew that Christ had been just a magician and that St. John the Evangelist was merely a "bedfellow" of Christ and that Jesus *did* use him "as did the sinners of Sodom."

***FACT***: The edict as stated *is* accurate: "There will be a reward of 100 crowns to the person who supplies information about such libelers."

The statements about the searching of Kyd's quarters and the reward of 100 crowns *are* accurate. The authorities did find six pages of what was called "vile, heretical" writings.

**FACT**: The papers *did* actually belong to Marlowe. Though he claimed at the time that he did know where he had gotten them, in fact they were part of the discussion sessions with Sir Walter Ralegh at his School of Night.

**FACT:** "*Ralegh*" *was* the conventional spelling of Sir Walter's name at that time.

**FACT:** The edict *did* read "If Mr. Thomas Kyd refuses to afford the Privy Council proper information, officers shall put him to the torture in Bridewell Prison."

**FACT**: Richard Topcliffe *was* the Royal Rackmaster at Bridewell Prison.

**FACT**: The details of the plague are factual, including the deaths of approximately 100 people a day in London.

**FACT**: England was at war with Spain at that time. The details of the war between Protestant England and Catholic Spain are factual.

**FACT**: Sir Francis Walsingham was considered to be the cousin of Sir Thomas Walsingham. (See **Historical Data** – Chapter Nine -- for clarification.) The details of his heading the British spy network and his being the England's *first* Secretary of State *are* accurate.

**FACT**: The Privy Council did consider Sir Walter Ralegh to be a threat but too close to Queen Elizabeth I to attack directly.

**FACT**: Christopher Marlowe *was* a spy who had often worked for Sir Francis Walsingham.

**FACT**: Some wives of Henry VIII *had* been imprisoned.

**FACT**: On March 26, 1593, Queen Elizabeth created a new Royal Commission to hunt down and punish "Barrowists, Separatists, Catholics recusants, counterfeiters, vagrants all who secretly adhere to our most capital Enemy (sic), the Bishop of Rome" (the Pope).

**FACT**: As amazing as this may seem today, the Commission *did* incarcerate anyone who "refused to repair to the Church to hear Devine service."

*FACT*: Christopher Marlowe *had* previously lived with Thomas Bradley, Richard Baines, and Thomas Kyd, before moving in with Sir Thomas Walsingham.

## CHAPTER THREE

*FACT:* Marlowe was *the* foremost playwright in England at the time and *was* considered a loose cannon, making all kinds of dangerous statements.

*FACT*: Marlowe *was* a member of Sir Walter Ralegh's inner circle of friends and did belong to Ralegh's School of Night and Durham House groups.

*FACT*: Marlowe was notorious for saying all those heretical statements as listed, including that Christ was a bastard, that his mother was a whore, and that John the Evangelist always rested his head on the bosom of Jesus. He did reason that, therefore, Jesus loved John as did the sodomites in the bible.

*FACT*: Marlowe was known for frequently using the notorious remark that "*All they that love not boys and tobacco are fools.*"

*FACT*: Marlowe was twenty-nine years old at that time.

*FACT*: Marlowe *did* have a string of theatrical and poetic successes unmatched in England at the time. By that date these included *Dr. Faustus*, *The Jew of Malta*, and *Tamburlaine*, among other works.

*FACT*: Marlowe was one of the nearly 100 spies answering to Sir Francis Walsingham, the cousin of Sir Thomas Walsingham.

*FACT*: Marlowe *did* go to Corpus Christi College, Cambridge, on a scholarship for those of modest means.

*FACT*: It is true that Marlowe did *not* elect to take holy orders after graduation (but instead went into the theatre).

*FACT*: Theatre at that time *was* akin to prostitution, thievery, and vagrancy. Theatres were *required* to be built outside city walls along with brothels, prisons, and lunatic asylums. The theatres *were* considered to be disreputable and dens of iniquity.

*FACT*: Despite the dark reputation that theatre had at that time, Queen Elizabeth I *did* occasionally attend performances.

*FACT*: Marlowe was originally recruited for spying by Sir Francis Walsingham while Marlowe was still a second-year student at Cambridge. The details about withholding his master's degree in 1587 and then awarding it later are accurate. The charge was that he had defected to Rheims and gone into a Catholic seminary. The intervention later by Lord Cecil Burghley, president of the Privy Council, seemed to establish that Marlowe had obviously been a double spy sent to Rheims by Sir Francis Walsingham.

*FACT*: "Good service" *was* a common code expression for "spying".

*FACT:* Sir Thomas Walsingham had recently become Marlowe's patron and protector – an arrangement that was critically important to all playwrights at the time. Playwrights and actors needed patrons for financial reasons and because of the law. The various troops of actors wandering all over England were considered to be vagrants and thought to be the cause of many problems in the country. The Second Act of Congress of 1592 – the Vagrancy Act – *did* lay down the laws which read: "Unlicensed vagabonds, common players, and minstrels, not belonging to any baron or other personage of greater degree can, by law, be whipped, have their noses cut off or burned through the ear". As a result, most actors, playwrights and theatre companies searched out a patron, who afforded them a measure of protection. As a by-product of this arrangement, the lords who sponsored such companies got acknowledgements and what might be called "good public relations" throughout England for their patronage.

*FACT*: Thomas Kyd *did* attempt to run away but was captured.

## CHAPTER FOUR

*FACT:* A trip by boat from Dover, England, to the continent would have been an obvious escape route for Thomas Kyd.

*Fiction*: There is, however, *no* record that Thomas Kyd tried to escape in this manner or that he was captured in Dover, England.

## CHAPTER FIVE

*FACT:* Richard Topcliffe was the Crown's Royal Inquisitor at Bridewell Prison. His predecessor *was* a man named Thomas Norton, who – like Topcliffe – had the reputation of being fanatically anti-Catholic and who – like Topcliffe – relished torture and torment. Norton *did* die in 1584 and Topcliffe was named to replace him as royal inquisitor.

*Fiction:* There are *no* records of Richard Topcliffe growing up in Southeast London.

*FACT:* Sir Walter Ralegh had named the province Virginia in honor of Queen Elizabeth I, who was referred to as "the virgin Queen," though many doubted the validity of the title. The story has persisted to this day that he dropped his coat over the puddle of mud so that Elizabeth could walk over it and not get her slippers dirty. He *had* brought tobacco back from the New World and it was becoming very popular in England.

*FACT*: Sir Walter Ralegh *was* referred to as "Walt Stick the Tobacco Man."

*FACT:* Thomas Kyd was thirty-six years old at the time of his torture in Bridewell Prison. His plays *had been* produced at four different theatre companies in London.

*FACT:* Thomas Kyd *did* incriminate Christopher Marlowe as the owner of the heretical papers.

*FACT*: Thomas Kyd was the number-two writer in England, second only to Marlowe. His play *The Spanish Tragedy did* have twenty-nine different productions in London, a record at that time.

*FACT*: Thomas Kyd would have been considered a "celebrity" at Bridewell Prison.

## CHAPTER SIX

*FACT*: Scadbury is in Chislehurst, Kent, and had been the home of the Walsinghams, beginning in the year 1315, during the rein of King Edward III. Today the estate houses the *Scadbury Public Historical Preserve.*

*FACT*: Thomas's cousin Francis *did* live in Scadbury for a while as young boy after his father died when Sir Francis was only one year old.

*FACT*: Sir Thomas Walsingham *was* thirty-one years old in 1593, only two years older than Marlowe.

*FACT*: The details about Henry Wriothesley *are* accurate. He was the Third Titled Earl of Southampton and the Baron of Titchfield (and a favorite of the Queen.) He *was* openly and flamboyantly gay.

*FACT*: At that time, gay activity – or as it was referred to then: "unnatural love" -- was quite common and considered to be acceptable so long as one stayed within one's own social class. A common English term for two men living together was "chamber fellows." It *was* a fact that many of the British kings *had* openly preferred men and made no excuses for it, including King Edward II and King James I, the successor to Queen Elizabeth I.

*FACT*: The stories about Wriothesley's gay activities while in the military are *factual* – sharing quarters with a fellow officer with whom he would "hug and play wantonly". The officer's name *was* Captain Piers Edmuns. Sir Wriothesley *did* contend that he learned to love other men while serving in the military. Historians have described his military service record this way, "He spent his active duty in bed with Captain Edmuns."

*FACT*: The details about Lord Cecil Burghley pressuring Wriothesley to marry his granddaughter are accurate. Wriothesley *did* pay the penalty of five thousand pounds for backing out of the marriage. At that time that amount *was* equivalent to millions of pounds in English currency today.

*FACT*: A painting, as described in chapter six was discovered many years later and was accepted – *for almost seventy years* -- to be the rendering of a woman named Lady Norman.

*FACT*: Wriothesley *did* wear his hair very long and styled in a feminine way.

*FACT*: The name "Wriothesley" *is* pronounced "RIZ-lee."

*Fiction*: There is *no* evidence that Sir Wriothesley gave the above-mentioned painting to Thomas Walsingham.

*FACT*: It was common knowledge that the Queen's occasional lover, Sir Dudley, the Earl of Leicester, *did* indulge in gay activities.

*FACT*: Queen Elizabeth I *did* wear an orange-hued red wig.

*FACT*: The heretical remarks listed *were* frequently made by Marlowe – that "Christ was justly persecuted by the Jews because of his foolishness" and that "Moses was just a magician who spent forty years leading the Jews out of Egypt – a journey that could have been completed in a single year."

*FACT*: Many writers actually *did* become spies because they needed to supplement their income. They usually earned more money by spying than by writing.

*FACT*: At that time the plague *had* closed all the theatres in London.

*FACT*: To earn more money, it was a common tactic for spies to simply accuse another person of being a heretic or a Catholic. It was not uncommon that the person accused was another spy.

*FACT*: Marlowe *did* often state that he made the remarks against the Church to "free people from a corrupt Church." He would state that he made these remarks hoping someone would realize what a mockery the church was. He also would declare that the old testament, like the new, was "filthily written and filled mostly with sexual scandals – all designed to keep men in awe."

*FACT*: Catholics were responsible for the Spanish Inquisition, a witch-like hunt in which those accused of being Protestants were killed.

*FACT*: As mentioned earlier, Marlowe frequently used the expression that "*All they who love not tobacco and boys – are fools*.

*FACT*: Shakespearean quote: "Parting is such sweet sorrow." *Romeo and Juliet*, Act II, Scene 2.

*FACT*: It is true that spies *did* frequently accuse others – including fellow spies – of being a Catholic, just to receive the rewards for exposing heretics.

*FACT*: On March 26, 1593, Queen Elizabeth created a new Royal Commission to hunt down and punish "Barrowists, Separatists, Catholics recusants, counterfeiters, vagrants all who secretly adhere to our most capital Enemy (sic), the Bishop of Rome," as the Pope was known at that time in England.

*FACT*: The Commission *did* incarcerate anyone who "refused to repair to the Church to hear Devine service."

255

*FACT*: Obviously, heresy in England meant being a Catholic. Heresy in Catholic countries meant being a Protestant.

*FACT*: Heresy and treason were interchangeable terms at that time. Catholic priests who were caught preaching in England *were not* charged with heresy but instead with treason.

*FACT*: Constable Henry Maunder *was* the Queen's Royal Messenger as well as the Constable-Inspector for the Privy Council.

*Fiction*: There is *no* evidence that Maunder's first name was Walter. This was invented to make him a "candidate" for the dedication of the Sonnets in a later chapter to "W.H." ("*Walter Henry* Maunder.")

## CHAPTER SEVEN

*FACT:* As stated above, Henry Maunder *was* the "Royal Messenger of the Queen," which also gave him the responsibilities of delivering edicts and other official documents. He *was* the person who delivered to Thomas Kyd the warrant sending him to Bridewell Prison. He *also* delivered the edict to Christopher Marlowe.

*FACT*: The portion, which appears in this novel, of the writ from the Privy Council about Marlowe is *exact*. "To repair to the manor of Sir Thomas Walsingham in Scadbury where it is understood Christopher Marlowe to be remaining and to apprehend and to bring him to the Court for daily attendance to their Lordships." The writ then continued.

*FACT*: The terminology of the Treason Act of 1570 *did* state that the *accused* was to be "hanged, drawn, and quartered." The gory description of this process *is* accurate, including the part about the prisoner being hanged until almost (but not yet) dead, being "disemboweled and emasculated" before his own eyes, and then "quartered." The four body parts *were* then placed around London and the head *was* stuck on a pole at the south end of London Bridge.

*FACT*: Women accused of treason were *not* subject to the above. Instead they were burned at the stake.

*FACT*: It is correct that *if* Marlowe had been able to get the charges reduced to a minimum, it would most likely have included puncturing and then cutting off his ears. Thinking at the time, however, was that the irritants from Marlowe were not with his ears, but rather with his tongue. Therefore, death was the only viable solution to the "Christopher Marlowe problem."

*FACT*: It *is* true that, for all practical purposes, there were no acquittals in Elizabethan state courts.

## CHAPTER EIGHT

*FACT:* Shakespearean quote: "Present fears are less than horrible imaginings." *Macbeth*, Act I, Scene 3. (In this novel: *Present fears are never as bad as our horrible imaginings.)*

*FACT*: Cecil Burghley *was* the president of the Privy Council.

*Fiction*: Marlowe *did* actually appear before the Privy Council, but *not* in the Privy Council chambers. He appeared before the Council in the Star Chambers. This was changed to avoid confusion to the reader since Marlowe *was* actually appearing before the *Privy Council*, though not in their own chambers.

*FACT*: Christopher Marlowe *did* appear before the Privy Council on May 20, 1593, ten days before his murder.

*Fiction*: There is *no* record that Thomas Walsingham tried to accompany Marlowe at his appearance before the Privy Council.

*FACT*: The charge against Christopher Marlowe *was* "heresy."

*FACT*: The details of the battles between the forces of Elizabeth I in England and Mary Queen of Scots of Spain are factual. Elizabeth *did* imprison Mary; the Pope *did* excommunicate Elizabeth I; and she *did* take the safety measures listed in this chapter. Because of the threat of assassination, this including sleeping with an old sword beside her bed.

*FACT*: Marlowe was originally recruited for spying by Sir Francis Walsingham while Marlowe was still a second-year student at Cambridge. The details about withholding his master's degree in 1587 and then awarding it later *are* accurate. The charge was that he had defected to Rheims and had gone into a Catholic seminary. The intervention later by Lord Cecil Burghley, president of the Privy Council, seemed to establish that Marlowe had obviously been a double spy sent to Rheims, most likely by Sir Francis Walsingham.

*FACT*: "Good service" *was* a common code expression for "spying."

*FACT*: Consequently, Marlowe *did* receive his master's degree.

*FACT*: Catholics in France, Italy, and Spain did feel that Queen Elizabeth I was merely a bastard child of Henry VIII.

*FACT*: Elizabeth did have Mary, Queen of Scots, executed and, as a consequence, Spain sent an armada which was defeated by the English. This *was*, of course, a major trigger for the war between the two countries.

*FACT*: The fleet of ships that Spain sent to dethrone Elizabeth I was known as the "Spanish Armada" and was defeated by England in 1588.

*FACT:* The spying by and against both England and Spain *was* a flourishing industry at the time.

*FACT*: There was much confusion concerning Marlowe's spying. It would have been easy for the Privy Council to assume that he had been a counters-spy or counter-counter-spy, making him guilty of heresy by either – or even both – sides. He *did* have eighteen major accusations against him.

## CHAPTER NINE

*Fiction:* There is *no* historical record of Sir Thomas going to visit Sir Francis as Marlowe appeared before the Privy Council.

*FACT*: Sir Francis Walsingham was older than Sir Thomas and short of stature. Queen Elizabeth frequently referred to him as her "little Moor," although there appears to be no real reason for the Moorish reference.

*FACT*: When Sir Francis Walsingham was only one year old, his father *did* die and he *did* live at Scadbury for a while with Sir Thomas's family.

*FACT*: Most historians state that Sir Francis and Sir Thomas were actually second cousins even though they always referred to each other as "my cousin." However, some historians believe they were uncle and nephew, arguing that Sir Francis was the youngest brother of Sir Thomas's father. But, they were relatively close in age and, since Francis had lived at Scadbury with Thomas for years, they found the term "cousin" to be the most convenient.

*FACT*: Queen Elizabeth *did* name Sir Francis Walsingham to be England's first Secretary of State in 1573. Sir Francis *was* the head of the English spy network. Historians frequently name him as the architect of modern espionage.

*FACT*: Sir Francis's accusation about Marlowe (being convicted of brawling in the streets of London, being deported from the Netherlands for his part in a counterfeiting scheme, and even being jailed for being an accomplice to murder) *are all accurate.*

*FACT*: Marlowe *had* worked as a spy for Sir Francis for eight years.

*FACT*: Shakespearean quote: "It is certain that when he makes water his urine is congealed ice." *Measure for Measure*, Act III, Scene 2.

*FACT*: Heresy *was* the charge against Marlowe by Richard Baines. He *did* receive eighty crowns for the attack. Before moving in with Thomas Kyd, Marlowe had lived with Baines in the Netherlands for a while when they were both spying for Sir Francis Walsingham. There was a residue of animosity based mainly on a counterfeiting project in which they were both engaged while they were chamber fellows.

*FACT*: Richard Chomley *did* claim to have been converted to atheism by Marlowe and he *did* state that "Marlowe is able to show more sound reasons for atheism than any divine in England is able to give to prove divinity."

*FACT*: The charges made by people like Baines and Chomley were not the only accusations against Marlowe. There *actually were* eighteen such charges.

*FACT*: Marlowe had joined most of Sir Walter Ralegh's groups. One of them *was* rumored to be a coven for warlocks (male witches) and some did propose spelling the word "God" backwards. Some of these groups *did* promote devil worship or black Masses. But, it is also true that these groups had members of some of London's most respected citizens. It *is* true that the Queen herself had given Sir Walter Ralegh the Durham House, located in the Strand, in 1592. Later, however, the home did become synonymous with Ralegh's divergent groups.

*FACT*: There *were* more than 7,000 locations selling tobacco in London at that time.

*FACT*: The following quotes *were* attributed to Sir Francis: "You should ask, why should this gift [of Marlowe's] be so squandered that it not give glory to its Giver," and "London will say a wrathful God has taken His rightful revenge on a vile blasphemer."

*FACT*: Nicolas Skeres, an employee of Sir Francis, did attend the "murder" of Christopher Marlowe.

*Fiction*: In spite of speculation by a few historians, there is *no* actual proof that Sir Thomas was ordered to kill Marlowe.

*FACT*: Marlowe *was* "killed" within ten days after his hearing before the Privy Council.

## CHAPTER TEN

*Fiction*: There is *no* historical record of Marlowe and Walsingham having this exact conversation about staging Marlowe's murder.

*FACT*: Robert Poley and Ingram Frizer *were* two of the employees of Sir Thomas Walsingham.

*FACT*: Poley's name was pronounced "POOL-ee."

*FACT*: William Danby *was* the Queen's Royal Coroner at the time and *did* prepare the official report about the death of Christopher Marlowe.

*FACT:* Obtaining a body from the front steps of a residence during the plague would have been an easy task. The bodies of those who had died during the previous night were actually thrown onto the steps for the death carts to carry away the next morning.

*FACT*: Shakespearean quote: "Who is so firm that can not be seduced?" *Julius Caesar*, Act I, Scene 2.

*FACT*: Shakespearean quote: "We fail? But screw your courage to the sticking point and we'll not fail." *Macbeth*, Act I, Scene 7. (In this novel: *Then screw your courage to the sticking point and we'll not fail.*)

*FACT:* Shakespearean Quote: "Mischief, thou art afoot. Take what course thou wilt." *Julius Caesar*, Act III, Scene 1. (In this novel: "*Mischief, thou art afoot ... and may Zeus and Minerva be with us.*")

## CHAPTER ELEVEN

*FACT*: The death carts *did* go daily to pick up bodies of those who had died of the plague during the previous night.

*Fiction*: There is *no* record of how a body was obtained for the murder scene of Marlowe, or even if one *was* obtained.

*FACT*: The Marlowe "murder" *did* take place at the inn of Widow Eleanor Bull in Deptford. Those in attendance *were* Christopher Marlowe, Ingram Frizer, Robert Poley and Nicolas Skeres.

*FACT*: Widow Bull's inn at Deptford *was* on the Thames River. It *is actually* three miles outside of London.

*FACT*: Documents *did* state that Christopher Marlowe died of a stab wound to his right eye, two inches deep.

## CHAPTER TWELVE

*Fiction*: There is *no* record of a metal portfolio engraved with the name "XTOFER."

*FACT*: "XTOFER" *was* a common spelling at that time for the name "Christopher." It *was* pronounced "Christopher." This was similar to our present-day use of "Xmas" for "Christmas."

*FACT*: Christopher Marlowe *was* usually referred to as "Kit" by his close friends.

*FACT*: Sir Thomas Walsingham *was* Marlowe's patron.

*FACT*: It is true that Sir Thomas Walsingham was not present at the murder scene.

*FACT*: Since the theatres were closed because of the plague, many people tried to get away from London in order not to be contaminated. It is well accepted that Marlowe *used the excuse* that he was staying at Scadbury to avoid the threat of the plague. The more probable reason was his relationship with Sir Thomas Walsingham.

*FACT*: Frizer and Poley *were* employees of Thomas Walsingham. Poley *was* the courier for his employer and *had* returned that morning from an assignment in Holland. It was notable that Walsingham sent him immediately to Missus Bull's. Obviously, there was an important job for him to do that day.

*FACT:* The records *did* show that the four of them "had lunch, sat around talking, drinking, and smoking throughout the afternoon and then Widow Eleanor Bull served them dinner about six in the evening."

*FACT*: The coroner's report *did* actually state that after dinner, Marlowe and Frizer begin quarrelling "about the payment of the bill and the *reckoning* thereof." The term "reckoning" has become a key term in most descriptions of Marlowe's death. One of the highly regarded biographies about Marlowe, written by Charles Nicholl, is entitled *The Reckoning*.

*FACT*: The coroner's report, as written in this novel, *did* correctly state that "Marlowe grabbed Frizer's knife, gave him some small cuts on the arm. Then Mr. Frizer grabbed his knife back and stabbed Marlowe in the right eye, killing him instantly."

*FACT*: As mentioned previously, Deptford *is* three miles outside of London.

*FACT*: Sir Thomas Walsingham *did* use Poley as his courier and had sent him to the Netherlands. Poley had returned to London the morning of the "murder."

*FACT*: Both the coroner's report and the records at St. Nicolas Church were *identical in detail* and basically identical in wording, *including all the same errors.*

*FACT*: There has never been an explanation to why the killer was listed as Francis Archer instead of Ingram Frizer. No one knows how the error occurred which has led to even more questions of a conspiracy. The date *was* also *incorrectly* listed as 1 June instead of 30 May.

*FACT*: The person murdered *was* listed in the coroner's report as "Morley." There has never been an explanation for that error either, adding to the many conspiracy theories. It was corrected days later to read "Marlowe". (There are, however, other instances when the name "Marlowe" was written as "Morley." Some sources question if Marlowe himself may have occasionally used that spelling of his name at times. Spelling was "fluid" at that time.)

*FACT*: The coroner and church reports *do* give an *inordinately detailed* description of the murder. It includes pages and pages about who was sitting where, and how they all moved about the room during the quarrel, and that Frizer's wounds were only a quarter inch deep, and Marlow's stab was about two inches deep but it killed him instantly. *Historians have long wondered* why these minutiae were so detailed and yet the names of the victim and the murderer (as well as the date) were incorrect. It is very unusual for church or coroner records to contain this type of detail, a factor which has also fueled the conspiracy theories about Marlowe's death.

*FACT*: According to the church records Marlowe *was* buried unceremoniously in an unmarked grave in the yard of St. Nicolas Church in Deptford. This fact is amazing in light of Marlowe's stature in England at that time as the country's number one playwright. It was also unusual in light of usual procedures in the sixteenth century. Though historians may not agree on the reason for this instant burial, all of them seem to agree that it *was* very suspicious, unusual, and filled with hidden meanings. *To this day no such grave has ever been found.*

*FACT*: The Constable's office *did* receive a *Writ of Certiorari* pardoning Ingram Frizer, witnessed by the Queen, within two weeks. This process ordinarily took months. It is another fact that seems to defy explanation.

*FACT*: Sir Francis Walsingham *did* state that Marlowe's death would be a case of "A wrathful God taking his rightful revenge on a vile blasphemer."

*Fiction*: There is *no* record that Sir Francis Walsingham ever instructed the Constable to question Sir Thomas Walsingham regarding the murder. If this occurred, it would more likely have been a decision by the Constable, not Sir Francis Walsingham.

*FACT*: Shakespearean quote: "An equal pound of your fair flesh, to be cut off and taken in what part of your body pleaseth me." *The Merchant of Venice*, Act I, Scene 3. Also: "A pound of flesh." *The Merchant of Venice*, Act IV, Scene 1. (In this novel the more commonly *misquoted* line is used: *The pound of flesh nearest the heart.*)

## CHAPTER THIRTEEN

*Fiction*: There is *no* record of throwing the body used in a murder plot into the Thames River.

*FACT*: *All's Well That Ends Well* is a play attributed to Shakespeare.

*FACT*: The report by Coroner Danby *did* list the wrong person as the "murderer" of Marlowe. The incorrect name (Francis Archer instead of Ingram Frizer) was later corrected by the coroner.

*FACT*: The theatre where the play *All's Well That Ends Well* would probably be presented *was* the Rose Theatre. The Globe Theatre, usually associated with the plays of Shakespeare, had not yet been built at that time.

*FACT*: Thomas Kyd *did* die in August, 1593, as a result of the torture, after being released from Bridewell Prison. His fingers *had* been broken in prison. He actually *was* thirty-six years old when he died.

*FACT*: Marlowe *was* twenty-nine years old at the time of Kyd's death.

## CHAPTER FOURTEEN

*FACT*: Coroner Danby's report and the burial records *were* word-for-word and filled with many errors. (See *Historical Facts*, Chapter 12.)

*FACT*: Ingrim Frizer's name *was* wrong, listed as Francis Archer in both the burial records and the coroner's report. No one knows why. It was later corrected.

*FACT*: The Queen *did* issue a *Writ of Certiorary* pardoning Frizer within two weeks. It usually took months for such a writ to be executed. It can be assumed that Sir Francis Walsingham must have requested this. This is another example of the type of activity that has fostered conspiracy theories.

*FACT*: As stated earlier, Poley had returned that morning from a courier assignment in the Netherlands. It *was* unusual that he would have immediately been sent to Deptford.

*FACT*: Marlowe was immediately buried in an unmarked grave in a small country churchyard. That fact *defies logic* by historians to this day. No such grave has ever been found.

## CHAPTER FIFTEEN

*FACT*: The plays written under the name of Shakespeare are – on the whole – more sensitive and lighter than those written under the name of Marlowe.

*FACT*: Marlowe's *Edward II was* based on historical facts of England's King Edward. The details about the play are accurate, including those about a monarch who casts aside his wife (Queen Isabel) for his lover (a man named Gaveston); also true are the facts that Edward's love later ebbs to the younger man named Spencer; as are the fact that his death on his own bed resulting from a red-hot spit forced up into his bowels.

**FACT**: Marlowe's *Edward II was* successful, in spite of its homosexual theme and graphic violence.

**Fiction**: There is *no* evidence that Sir Thomas Walsingham was responsible for the more sensitive style of plays attributed to Shakespeare in comparison to those written by Marlowe.

**FACT**: The actor William Shakespeare actually *did* "hold horses for the gentry while they were in watching the plays."

**Fiction**: Though he was known for holding horses for the gentry while they watched the plays there is *no* record that Shakespeare was known as "Horsy Will, the pony boy."

**FACT**: Shakespeare did have walk-ons and small roles at the Rose Theatre. At that time the Globe Theatre (which is better known now as the venue for Shakespeare's plays) had not yet been built.

**FACT**: Ben Jonson, Thomas Nashe, and Robert Greene were all respected playwrights in Marlowe's time. However, each of them had a style so different from Marlowe that it would have been virtually impossible to pass their works off as those of Christopher Marlowe.

**FACT**: It *was* true that playwrights and actors needed patrons for financial reasons and because of the law. The various troops of actors wandering all over England were considered to be vagrants and thought to be the cause of many problems in the country. *The Second Act of Congress of 1592* – the Vagrancy Act – *did* lay down the laws which read: "Unlicensed vagabonds, common players, and minstrels, not belonging to any baron or other personage of greater degree can, by law, be whipped, have their noses cut off or burned through the ear". As a result, most actors, playwrights and theatre companies searched out a patron, who afforded them a measure of protection. As a by-product of this arrangement, the lords who sponsored such companies got acknowledgements and what might be called "good public relations."

**FACT**: Thomas Kyd was one of the writers who sometimes did not have a patron.

*FACT*: It was a common belief at the time that actors frequently had an "ambiguous sexuality," as it was worded in that period. This is another example of the delicate euphoniums the English were able to concoct.

*FACT*: Theatre *was* considered a *very* rough world at that time.

*Fiction*: Sir Wriothesley, though he had a reputation as a flamboyant homosexual, was *not* known for sleeping with young boys or for having cats.

## CHAPTER SIXTEEN

*FACT*: The facts about Shakespeare's life are accurate. He had little schooling, leaving when he was fifteen. He had a wife, Anne Hathaway, and three children whom he had left in Stratford. Some biographers believe that at the time he married he was also seeing another woman, Ann Whately. However, Ann *Hathaway* was three months pregnant when they married. He was only eighteen and she was twenty-six.

*FACT*: There actually are no records of what Shakespeare did during his "lost years," 1585 to 1594.

*FACT*: In spite of the fact that some biographers ignore the fact, Shakespeare *did* have the reputation for a multitude of sexual liaisons -- all with women. There are no records of affairs with men.

*FACT*: Shakespeare and Marlowe *were* both born in the same year, 1564. In 1593 Marlowe would have been twenty-nine, as stated.

*FACT*: Shakespearean quote "The lady doth protest too much, methinks." *Hamlet*, Act III, Scene 2. (In this novel: "*Me thinkest the lady protests too much, milord.*")

*Fiction*: There is *no* record that Shakespeare insisted that he be called "William," though Shakespeare himself hardly ever used a shortened version of his name (such as "Will," "Willy," or "Bill.")

*FACT*: Shakespeare *was* accused of poaching deer from the Thomas Lucy estate in Stratford. Some historians assume that was his reason for his leaving Stratford.

*Fiction*: There is *no* record of any agreement by Shakespeare to take credit for the plays of Christopher Marlowe though such an arrangement has been the subject of theories for years.

*FACT*: Shakespearean quote: "When shall we three meet again? In thunder, lightning or in rain. When the hurly-burly's done. When the battle's lost or won." *Macbeth*, Act I, Scene 1. (In this novel, the quote is changed to *And, when shall we four meet again? In thunder, lightning or in rain. When the hurley-burley's done. When this deception's lost or won.*)

*FACT:* The plays *King Lear* and *All's Well That Ends Well* are two plays attributed to Shakespeare.

## CHAPTER SEVENTEEN

*Fiction:* There is *no* record of Sir <u>*Francis*</u> Walsingham questioning Skeres about the murder of Marlowe at Deptford.

*Fiction:* Likewise, there is *no* record of Sir <u>*Thomas*</u> Walsingham rewarding Skeres for not revealing to Sir Francis Walsingham what happened at Deptford.

## CHAPTER EIGHTEEN

*FACT*: In *Macbeth*, Duncan does look at the bleeding sergeant and did say '*Go*, get him surgeons." (*Not*: "Go *get* him, surgeons.")

*Fiction*: There is no record of anyone renaming the play *As You Like It* with the new title *Like You Like It*.

*FACT*: The comma *had* been "invented" thirty years earlier.

*Fiction*: The line: "They stole our dogs and raped our women" *does not* appear in any Shakespearean play.

*FACT*: Shakespeare *did* appear on stage as the ghost in *Hamlet*, and as Adam in *As You Like It*. The character Adam *does* have only three scenes and a total of eight lines. He *does* have the opening line of the play, "Yonder comes my master, your brother."

*FACT*: Actual Shakespearean quote: "A Plague on both your houses." *Romeo and Juliet*, Act III, Scene 1.

*FACT:* The play about Elizabeth's father *was* originally entitled *Henry VIII – All Is True*. The latter part of the title was lost somewhere along the way and is now known only as *Henry VIII*.

**FACT:** The play *Henry VIII* does not mention the King's divorce or the breakup with the Church of Rome.

**FACT:** As stated in a later chapter, Sir Thomas Walsingham *did* hire a scrivener to do some copying and rewarded him with a ring mentioned in Sir Thomas's will. It has never been determined what copying the scrivener did or why Sir Thomas waited until he died to reward the copier.

**FACT:** Queen Elizabeth *did* request that Shakespeare write a play just about Falstaff after she saw *Henry IV, Part Two*. She *did* request that it be a play in which Falstaff falls in love.

**FACT:** Shakespeare *did* have a sexual liaison with the Widow Vautrollier, and did occasionally pay Vautrollier's new husband to take money to his family in Stratford. Though not mentioned in this novel, the new husband was, coincidentally, also from Stratford, thus making it logical for Shakespeare to use him as a messenger.

**FACT:** According to historians, Shakespeare *would* stop overnight in Oxford at Mistress Davenant's Tavern whenever he did travel the two-day trip to Stratford. Historians agree that he *did* sire a son with her, whom the mistress named William. Throughout the boy's life, he claimed to be the son of William Shakespeare. Shakespeare called the boy this "godson" and left this boy money in his will, referring to him in that document as his "godson."

**FACT:** Marlowe *did* have the reputation for frequently saying "*All they, who love not boys and tobacco, are fools*."

**FACT:** Shakespearean quote: "Cowards die many times before their deaths. The valiant never taste of death but once." *Julius Caesar*, Act II, Scene 2. (In this novel the quote is changed to read: *A coward dies a thousand deaths, the valiant die but once*).

**FACT:** Shakespeare's Sonnets were dedicated to W.H. Some historians think that could have been a code for "<u>W</u>alsing-<u>H</u>am."

## CHAPTER NINETEEN

**FACT:** Sir John Falstaff *is* the fanciful knight – loveable but a buffoon – in *The Merry Wives of Windsor*.

*FACT*: The plot of the play is correct. Falstaff, a loveable buffoon of a knight, does scheme to get money from two local men by seducing their wives. The plan does go awry and Falstaff does suffer the revenge of the two women (when he is hidden in a basket of dirty laundry, cast into the Thames River, dressed as a woman and then beaten, etc.)

*FACT*: Those *are* the lines from *The Merry Wives of Windsor*:

> *To Shallow rivers, to whose falls*
>
> *Melodious birds sing madrigals.*
>
> *There will we make our bed of roses*
>
> *And a thousand fragrant posies.*

*FACT*: Marlowe's poem "The Passionate Shepherd to His Love" *was* written before he was "killed" but was *not published* until 1599, six years after his supposed "death." In the companion poem written by Sir Walter Ralegh the following year, entitled "The Nymph's Reply to the Shepherd," Ralegh seems to correct Marlowe's very romantic ideals with a realistic rewriting.

*FACT*: The lines of "The Passionate Shepherd to His Love" are different by *only three words* from those written into *The Merry Wives of Windsor*:

> *By shallow rivers, to whose falls*
>
> *Melodious birds sing madrigals,*
>
> *And I will make thee beds of roses*
>
> *And a thousand fragrant posies.*

*FACT:* The difference between the two works is centered on *only three words*. In *The Merry Wives of Windsor* the last line begins with "There will we...." In the poem "The Passionate Shepherd to His Love" those words are changed to "And I will...."

## CHAPTER TWENTY

*Fiction:* There is *no* record of any "File 13" at the Privy Council dealing with either Shakespeare or Marlowe.

*FACT*: There *actually are* more than a hundred identical or similar lines in the works of Marlowe and Shakespeare. Such a coincidence does not exist between any other two authors of that time. This is one of the most glaring arguments that Christopher Marlowe actually wrote the works attributed to William Shakespeare. It is difficult to believe that this was a coincidence of some kind.

*FACT*: Shakespearean quote: "Something is rotten in the state of Denmark." *Hamlet*, Act I, Scene 4. (Changed in the novel to read: *Something is rotten in Scadbury.*)

## CHAPTER TWENTY-ONE

*FACT:* As stated previously, there *are* more than one hundred very similar or identical lines in the works of Shakespeare and Marlowe. No other two writers of that time have such similarities. This is considered by many as a major factor in the many Shakespeare-Marlowe conspiracy theories.

*FACT*: These lines appear in Shakespeare's *Merry Wives of Windsor*.

> *To shallow rivers, to whose falls*
>
> > *Melodious birds sing madrigals:*
> >
> > *There will we make our beds of roses*
> >
> > *And a thousand fragrant posies.*

And these lines appear in Marlowe's poem "The Passionate Shepherd to His Love:"

> > *By shallow rivers, to whose falls*
> >
> > *Melodious birds sing madrigals,*
> >
> > *And I will make thee beds of roses*
> >
> > *And a Thousand fragrant posies.*

*FACT*: *The only substantial difference between the two above works is the phrase "And I will" instead of "There will we."* This coincidence is too great to be accidental

*FACT*: Marlowe *had* used parts of the poem "The Passionate Shepherd to His Love" in various works (under his own name) before his "murder" in 1593.

*FACT*: In *Dr. Faustus,* Marlowe wrote about Helen of Troy: *Was this the face that launched a thousand ships?* In Shakespeare's *Troilus and Cressida*

there is the line about Helen of Troy: *She is a pearl whose face hath launched above a thousand ships.*

*FACT*: In *Tamburlaine* Marlowe wrote *Ye pampered Jades of Asia. What can ye draw but twenty miles a day?* In *Henry IV* Shakespeare wrote *Pampered Jades of Asia, which cannot go but thirty miles a day.* The number of miles is the *only* difference.

*FACT*: Shakespeare's sonnets and Marlowe's *Edward II* both contain the line *Lilies that fester smell far worse than weeds.*

*FACT*: Marlowe's line *Yet Caesar shall go forth; thus Caesar did go forth,* is identical to Shakespeare's *Caesar shall go forth; yet Caesar shall go forth.* Only the *order* of the two sentences is different.

## CHAPTER TWENTY-TWO

*FACT*: As stated above, Marlowe's line *Yet Caesar shall go forth; thus Caesar did go forth,* is identical to Shakespeare's *Caesar shall go forth; yet Caesar shall go forth.*

*FACT*: Marlowe's line *The moon sleeps with Endymion* is identical to Shakespeare's *Ho, the moon sleeps with Endymion.* It is difficult to believe that this was merely a coincidence.

*FACT*: Shakespeare's writings *do* show great knowledge about foreign countries, the military and courtly manners. And yet Shakespeare had *never* left England, had *never* been in government service, and *never* had any occasion to learn about manners of court.

## CHAPTER TWENTY-THREE

*FACT*: Queen Elizabeth *did* actually die in 1603 and James I *did* become king of England at that time. His coronation gave a major boost to the theatre world.

*FACT*: Historians accept the fact that the majority of the sonnets *were* written to another man, referred to as a "fair youth" and "my beloved." Other parts were supposedly written to some "dark lady."

*Fiction*: Many authorities feel that if Marlowe wrote the sonnets, he would probably have dedicated them to Sir Thomas Walsingham. Though some historians acknowledge that fact, there is *no* proof of this.

271

**FACT**: It *is* factual that Londoners *did* refer to the sonnets as the "Sugar Sonnets."

***Fiction:*** The word "homoerotic" is an anachronism. The word *did not* exist at that time and Marlowe could not have used it.

**FACT**: In "The Rape of Lucrece," Shakespeare's dedication did read "*The love I dedicate to your Lordship is without end.*"

**FACT**: At that point Shakespeare *was* becoming very famous; he was earning enough money to buy a larger home and a part interest in the Globe Theatre; and he was getting a crest for his family.

**FACT**: King James I *was* a fan of witchcraft and there seems to be agreement among historians that this was the reason the author begins *Macbeth* with the scene containing the three witches, supposedly to gain the king's favor.

**FACT**: James I was a descendant of Duncan, the King in *Macbeth*. It's assumed that this was structured to gain favor for the author with the new king.

**FACT**: James I *did* actually sponsor a group of actors at the Globe Theatre and *did* call them "The King's Men."

**FACT**: The facts about the new king *are* accurate. James I was the former James VI of Scotland and the devotedly Protestant son of (the staunch Catholic) Mary, Queen of Scots. At the time of his coronation he was 36 years old and, though married, had the reputation of nibbling at the ears and fingers of attractive young men while holding court. Historians have accepted that he was homosexual.

**FACT**: James I *was* also known for not bathing and the constant habit of playing with his codpiece. Not mentioned in this novel is another fact. As James VI of Scotland, before he became King of England, he was often criticized by members of his court for his "physical display of affections" with the Earl of Lennox. However, *the Earl* was usually blamed for "drawing the King into carnal lust."

**FACT**: There actually *was* a common saying on the streets of London about the new king that 'Young men lie in his bedchamber and are his minions.'

*Fiction*: There is *no* record that Londoners said the new king was called James the First because "he got first crack at young men."

*Fiction*: There is *no* evidence that Constable Maunder ever encountered Marlowe in Scadbury Manor or that there was any reference to anyone named Winston Walsingham of Warwick.

*FACT*: Four years after the death of Marlowe, Ingram Frizer *was* still employed by Sir Thomas Walsingham.

*FACT*: *Cymberline is* a play attributed to Shakespeare.

*Fiction*: There is *no* evidence that the incident portrayed in this chapter ever occurred comparing the handwriting of Shakespeare with that of a professional scrivener.

## CHAPTER TWENTY-FOUR

*FACT*: Scadbury Manor *was* about two hours ride from London.

*FACT*: In Marlowe's *Tamburlaine* there is the line *The sun, unable to sustain the sight, shall hide his head*. It is similar, but not identical, to Shakespeare's *The sun for sorrow will not show his head*.

*FACT*: The line in Marlowe's poem 'Hero and Leander' is identical to the one in Shakespeare's play *As You Like It -- Who ever loved that loved not at first sight?* That same line is echoed a multitude of times in other Shakespearean works.

*FACT*: The sonnets *were* dedicated to "W.H." To this day, controversy continues to swirl about the dedication. Was it for "*W*riothesley, *H*enry" or "*W*alsing-*H*am" or some other person? There are quite a few candidates with those initials.

*Fiction*: Constable Maunder's first name was Henry, not Walter Henry. There is *no* reason to believe the sonnets may have been written to Constable Maunder.

*FACT*: There is *no* evidence whatsoever that there was any romantic relationship between Shakespeare and his patron, Sir Henry Wriothesley, a fact that makes the dedication of the sonnets to Sir Henry *very unlikely*.

*FACT*: One of the many sonnets which *does* seem to be written more by Marlowe than by Shakespeare, reads:

*When in disgrace with fortune and men's eyes,*

*I all alone beweep my outcast state,*

*And trouble deaf heaven with my bootless cries,*

*And look upon myself, and curse my fate.*

**FACT**: Another sonnet also seems to apply less to Shakespeare and more to Marlowe and Thomas Walsingham:

*Then haply I think on thee,*

*For such sweet love remembered*

*Such wealth brings,*

*That I scorn to change my state with kings.*

**FACT**: The following line *does* appear in *As You Like It*: "When a man's verses cannot be understood (nor a man's good wit seconded with the forward child, understanding) it strikes a man more dead than a great reckoning in a little room." Historians agree that this line does seem to refer to Marlowe's death in the back room of Widow Bull's place following the "reckoning" of the bill. This "death," of course, not only struck Marlowe literally dead but also dead as a writer. (The part in parentheses of the above line appears in the play *As You Like It* but was eliminated in this novel.)

**FACT**: As stated, historians have never been able to prove that Marlowe and Shakespeare ever met.

**Historical Fact**: Though not mentioned in this novel, Thomas Walsingham married a woman named Audrey Shelton in 1596 supposedly for her dowry. Also see the coincidental reference to the name "Shelton" in **Historical Facts**, Chapter 30.

## CHAPTER TWENTY-FIVE

**Fiction**: There is *no* record that Sir Francis Walsingham's favorite wine was Grigio (sometimes referred to as *Gris* at that time).

**Fiction**: There is *no* record of a conversation between Sir Francis Walsingham and Sir Henry Wriothesley in which Wriothesley calls him a whore.

*FACT:* Shakespearean quote: "By the pricking of my thumbs, something wicked this way comes." *Macbeth*, Act IV, Scene 1.

*Fiction:* There is *no* record of Sir Francis Walsingham sending guards to search the Scadbury Estate years after the "murder" of Marlowe.

## CHAPTER TWENTY-SIX

*Fiction*: There is *no* record that Sir Thomas Walsingham had a horse named Joshua.

## CHAPTER TWENTY-SEVEN

*FACT*: Sir Thomas Walsingham *did* use Robert Poley as his courier.

*Fiction:* There is no record of Christopher Marlowe's use of a white quill pen with a red tip.

*FACT*: Venice *is* a series of about 100 small islands three miles off the coast of Italy in the Adriatic Sea. There were, of course, no horses or carriages -- only boats. The *Campanile* tower *is* in St. Mark's Square.

*FACT*: Forks *were* invented in Venice in this period.

*FACT*: *It is factual* that women were not permitted to appear in Elizabethan theatre. By tradition the female roles were taken by young boys. It *is* true that the author of these plays did utilize this device that helped both actor and audience. After a scene or two, the women in the play would find some reason (or excuse) to disguise themselves as men. That made it easier to accept that it was a man playing a woman playing a man. This façade went on until the last scene or two when the "young man" would remove the disguise and would, according to the plot, become a "female" again.

*FACT*: In the late sixteenth and early seventeenth centuries women *did* appear on stage in Italy, Spain, and Greece. This actually was in great contrast to the procedure in England.

*FACT*: The line "For what's a play without a woman in it?" is in Thomas Kyd's play *The Spanish Tragedy*.

*FACT: The Merchant of Venice* and *Othello* are both plays attributed to Shakespeare. Both *do* take place in Venice.

## CHAPTER TWENTY-EIGHT

*FACT*: Marlowe's poem "The Passionate Shepherd to His Love" *does* begin with the line "Come live with me and be my love and we will all life's pleasures prove…."

*FACT*: Marlowe and Thomas Walsingham *did* meet when both were assigned to spy on instigators connected with a plot to overthrow the Queen. This plot was known as the Babington Conspiracy.

*Fiction*: There is *no* record of any such meeting between Walsingham and Marlowe at a caretaker cottage.

## CHAPTER TWENTY-NINE

*FACT*: Sir Walter Ralegh *did* write a companion poem to Marlowe's "The Passionate Shepherd to His Love," which was published in 1599 (six years after the "murder" of Marlowe.) Ralegh's work was entitled "The Nymph's Reply to the Shepherd," written in 1600. It did counter almost every line of Marlowe's work with similar images and parallel metrics. Marlowe's poem was naïve, innocent and youthful while Ralegh's was sober, realistic and mature.

*FACT:* The publication of the poem by Sir Walter Ralegh *did*, of course, bring attention back to Christopher Marlowe, his supposed death and his connections to Ralegh. The two works *are* considered "companion poems" to this day.

*FACT*: Sir Walter Ralegh, who was born in 1552, was twelve years older than Christopher Marlowe. The details of naming the province for Queen Elizabeth and his placing his cape over the mud *are* historically accepted.

*FACT*: The lines from Ralegh's "The Nymph's Reply to the Shepherd" *are* accurate:

> *If all the world and love were young,*
>
> *And truth in every shepherd's tongue,*
>
> *These pretty pleasures might me move*
>
> *To live with thee and be thy love.*

The last verse *does* read:

> *But could youth last and love still breed,*
>
> *Had joys no date no age no need,*
>
> *Then these delights my mind might move*
>
> *To live with thee and be thy love.*

## CHAPTER THIRTY

*FACT*: Historians agree that there is *no reason* to believe that the actor Shakespeare ever traveled to Italy.

*FACT:* As mentioned in the previous chapter, there *was* a famous plot, usually referred to as the "Babington Conspiracy," to kill the Queen.

*FACT*: Shakespearean quote: This fellow is wise enough to play the fool. *Twelfth Night*, Act III, Scene 1.

*FACT:* As stated previously, both of Shakespeare's plays *The Merchant of Venice* and *Othello* do take place in Venice, Italy.

*FACT:* At the time the two above mentioned plays were written, the source materials for each *was* written *only in Italian* – not yet translated into English. *Therefore, whoever wrote these two "Shakespearean" plays had to be able to read and understand Italian – something that Christopher Marlowe would have been able to do, but the actor Shakespeare could not do.* The above fact does not necessarily prove that Christopher Marlowe wrote these plays, but it does make a strong case that the actor Shakespeare did not write them.

*FACT*: Shakespearean quote: "Make but my name thy love, and love that still; and then thou lov'st me. Sonnet 136. (In this novel: *"But make my name thy love."*)

## CHAPTER THIRTY-ONE

*FACT*: The play The *Taming of the Shrew* does take place in Padua.

*FACT:* Padua *is* eleven miles from Venice. Scadbury *is* twelve miles from London – hence, Marlowe would have moved less distance than that from Scadbury to London.

*FACT*: Sir Thomas Walsingham's cousin, Sir Francis, would know Padua. He lived there from 1552 to 1556 doing his graduate studies at the University of Padua.

*FACT*: Sir Walter Ralegh *was* imprisoned in the Tower of London.

*FACT*: Padua *was* the home of Dante, Donatelli, and Galileo. The Cathedral of St. Anthony to this day contains the partially preserved body of St. Anthony. Today, 900 years after his death, the saint's tongue is still mostly intact.

*FACT*: Christopher Marlowe *did* use the pen name "Thomas Shelton" when he had Edward Blount publish his translation of Miguel de Cervantes' *Don Quixote*. The interesting facet here is that this "nom de plume" consists of two words, "*Thomas*," (as in *Thomas* Walsingham) and "*Shelton*" (as in Audrey *Shelton*), the woman Thomas Walsingham later married, supposedly for her dowry, when he badly needed money. The "possible future pairing one day" of these two people -- Thomas Walsingham and Audrey Shelton -- was a known fact. The question remains: Was it possible that *this is where Marlowe got his pen name*? Some historians see no other way he could have arrived at that particular name.

*FACT*: Shakespearean quote: "The fault, dear Brutus, is not in our stars, but in ourselves, that we are underlings." *Julius Caesar*, Act I, Scene 2. (In this novel "*The fault, dear Thomas, lies not our stars but in ourselves*.")

## CHAPTER THIRTY-TWO

*FACT: Padova* is the Italian word for Padua.

*FACT:* The Shakespearean play *The Taming of the Shrew* does take place in Padua.

## CHAPTER THIRTY-THREE

*FACT*: Both plays, *Two Gentlemen of Verona* and *Romeo and Juliet* do take place in Verona.

*FACT*: Montague actually *was* the family name of Henry Wriothesley's grandfather.

*FACT*: At that time, Wriothesley *had been* put into prison (but by order of the Queen, *not* by order of Sir Francis Walsingham, who was, in reality, dead by that time).

*FACT*: Shakespeare did leave London to return to live in Stratford, though the exact reason is debated. Some historians believe it was for business reasons.

## CHAPTER THIRTY-FOUR

*FACT*: It *is* true that Shakespeare never had a formal education – nothing beyond the age of 15.      It *was true* that at that time (as Sir Wriothesley explains in the novel) theatre was considered merely "bawdy fare at vulgar playhouses."

*FACT*: Shakespeare had no way of knowing precise details about Italy or court manners. It *is* true that there is no record of his having been out of the country. However, Sir Wriothesley *was* familiar with court manners, travels in Italy and military protocol. It was well-known that for years Henry Wriothesley had taught the Italian language to local aristocrats.

*FACT*: In the play *Romeo and Juliet,* the family name of Romeo *is* Montague. This was Sir Henry Wriothesley's grandfather's family name.

*FACT*: Shakespeare did spend a lot of "time" with the Widow Vautrollier and Mistress Davenant. He *was* also known for frequenting the local bordellos.

*FACT*: Henry Wriothesley *was* arrested and put into the tower of London. However, it was by order of the Queen and not at the order of Sir Francis Walsingham. At the time of Wriothesley's arrest Sir Francis was dead.

## CHAPTER THIRTY-FIVE

*FACT*: As stated in the previous chapter, Sir Henry Wriothesley *was* arrested and imprisoned in the Tower of London.

*Fiction*: There is *no* record of Wriothesley taking a cat to prison with him.

*FACT*: Christopher Marlowe actually *had* used the name William Shelton when translating the text of Miguel de Cervantes' *Don Quixote* from Spanish to English. (See *Historical Facts* – Chapter 30.)

*FACT*: Shakespeare *did* return to Stratford. The precise reason is not clear. Some believe his return pertained to business there.

*FACT*: It *is* well known that there are about 100 duplicate or near duplicate lines between the writings of Shakespeare and Marlowe.

## CHAPTER THIRTY-SIX

*FACT:* Thomas Kyd *did* write a play entitled *Hamlet* about the prince of Denmark *when he was living with Marlowe*. It was written about the year 1587 – approximately a decade before the one attributed to Shakespeare. It's another oddity that Shakespeare, actor from Stratford – whom Kyd probably never met – would pick the same historical character as a subject for a play. It would be far more credible to believe Marlowe would write it, since the two of them were living together when Kyd wrote his play. There are no copies of Kyd's *Hamlet* in existence. The play by Thomas Kyd is historically referred to as *Ur-Hamlet*.

*FACT:* Another similarity *is* the coincidence of a play by Shakespeare concerning a Jewish person living on an island off the coast of Italy (*The Merchant of Venice*) and a play by Marlowe about a Jewish person living on an island off the coast of Italy (*The Jew of Malta.)*

*FACT:* A third tie-in between Shakespeare and Marlowe concerns the fight that Marlowe's roommate (Thomas Watson) had with William Bradley. It is almost identical to the fight in *Romeo and Juliet* that Romeo's friend (Petrucio) has with Juliet's cousin Tybalt. Even more coincidental is the fact that the death of Marlowe at Deptford was similar to the other two fights/deaths. In all of these cases, the main person (Marlowe / Romeo / Frizer) is threatened and a friend takes the knife and kills the person doing the threatening.

*FACT*: Shakespearean quote: "Exceeding wise, fair-spoke and persuading." Henry VIII, Act IV, Scene 2. (In this novel: *"Exceedingly wise, fair-spoken and persuasive."*)

## CHAPTER THIRTY-SEVEN

*FACT*: Shakespeare *did* return to Stratford sometime around 1609, seven years before he died in 1616.

*FACT:* Shakespeare *had* been having sexual relations with the Widow Vautrollier. He *had* been sending the widow's new husband to Stratford with money for Shakespeare's wife and family. Though it is not mentioned in the novel, the widow's new husband was originally from Stratford and would be probably very willing to act as a messenger to his own home town. A by-product of this arrangement was that it removed the new husband from the Vautrollier home while Shakespeare was romancing his wife.

*FACT:* As mentioned previously, Shakespeare also had an affair with Mistress Davenant who lived in Oxford, a city where he would stop on his way from London to Stratford. Shakespeare would stay overnight at the Davenant Tavern each way on the two-day trip whenever he personally journeyed to Stratford. Mistress Davenant *did* have an illegitimate son whom she named William. This child always said he was the son of Shakespeare. Shakespeare referred to the boy as his "godson" and left him money in his will.

*FACT:* As mentioned previously, Anne (Hathaway) Shakespeare *was* eight years older than her husband.

*FACT:* Shakespeare *had* received a family crest and *did* buy New Place, the second-largest home in Stratford in 1596. It *is* true that it was the only brick home in Stratford.

## CHAPTER THIRTY-EIGHT

*FACT:* The Italian city of Milan *does* date back to three centuries before the birth of Christ. It is factual that the cathedral in Milan, at the time of Marlowe and Shakespeare, *was not* completed although they had been working on it for more than 250 years. It *is also true* that the church would not be finished for another two centuries *after* the lives of Shakespeare and Marlowe.

*FACT:* A messenger would have to come by horseback from the port in Genoa since Milan is not on the sea.

*FACT:* Christmas decorations would usually remain on display until January 6, the feast day of Epiphany.

## CHAPTER THIRTY-NINE

*FACT:* Shakespearean quote: "Lord, what fools these mortals be." *Midsummer Night's Dream*. Act III, Scene 2.

*FACT*: Shakespearean quote: "Shall we now contaminate our fingers with base bribes?" *Julius Caesar*. Act IV, Scene 2.

*FACT*: Shakespearean quote: "Tomorrow and tomorrow and tomorrow, creeps in this petty pace from day to day." *Macbeth*, Act V, Scene 5.

*FACT*: As stated previously Christopher Marlowe had used the pen name "Thomas Shelton," when translating the text of Miguel de Cervantes' *Don Quixote* from Spanish to English. (See *Historical Facts*, Chapter 30.)

## CHAPTER FORTY

*FACT:* Sicily, the island off the tip of Italy, *is* the southernmost part of the country. Palermo is the capital.

*FACT:* *The Tempest* does take place in Milan and Naples (both of which are areas south of Venice, Verona, and Padua), where Marlowe could possibly have been living.

*FACT: Much Ado about Nothing* is set in Messina (farther south, at the bottom of the Italian peninsula, across the straits from Sicily) – another clue to where Marlowe could have been living.

*FACT: The Winter's Tale* actually does take place in Sicily (off the southern tip of Italy, actually as far south as one can go in that country.) This is yet another possible clue to Marlowe's ventures.

*FACT*: The city of *Syracusa* (Syracuse in English) *is*, as stated, on a small island which is a few meters off another island (Sicily).

*FACT*: Henry Wriothesley *was* moved from prison to the Tower of London where he had a suite of apartments. *It is true* that this transfer was at *the request of his mother* who paid nine pounds a week for this extravagance. There is no record that his suite in the Tower of London was the area in which Mary, Queen of Scots, had been imprisoned.

*FACT*: Actual Shakespearean quote: "Ill blows the wind that profits nobody." *Henry VI*, Act II, Scene 5.

*FACT*: It is true that with the exception of historical plays, no Shakespearean works were set in London (and only one play was set in contemporary England.) Shakespeare's plays took place in other countries, many in Italy.

## CHAPTER FORTY-ONE

*FACT:* Shakespeare's plays did continue to appear after his death – eventually fourteen in all.

*FACT:* It is true that there were no Shakespearean plays set in the France, Spain or London of that day. But his plays do seem to "create a map for traveling north to south on the Italian peninsula."

*FACT:* As mentioned previously, Marlowe *had been* a spy working for Sir Francis Walsingham for eight years.

*FACT:* The word "*god*" is not capitalized since it is a generic exclamation and not referring to God.

## CHAPTER FORTY-TWO

*FACT:* A "bedsit" is the term in England for a studio apartment.

*Fiction:* There is *no* record of a spy named Burnell working for Sir Francis Walsingham, and, of course, no record of such a person meeting Christopher Marlowe.

## CHAPTER FORTY-THREE

*FACT:* Shakespearean quote: "This was the most unkindest cut of all." *Julius Caesar.* Act III, Scene 2.

*FACT:* Shakespearean quote "One that loved not wisely but too well." *Othello.* Act V, Scene 2.

## CHAPTER FORTY-FOUR

*FACT:* At that time, Sir Henry Wriothesley *was* still in prison and Shakespeare *had* left London to return to Stratford

## CHAPTER FORTY-FIVE

*FACT:* The information for the Shakespearean play *Julius Caesar* did come in part from Holingshed's *Chronicles.*

*Fiction:* As stated in a previous chapter, there is *no* record that Marlowe wrote with a white swan quill which had a red tip.

*FACT:* Shakespearean quote: "For there is nothing either good or bad but thinking makes it so." *Hamlet.* Act II, Scene 2. (In this novel, the line is changed to: *Nothing is either good or bad but only thinking makes it so.*)

## CHAPTER FORTY-SIX

*FACT:* Shakespearean Quote: "Cauldron, Cauldron, double trouble. Fire burn and cauldron bubble." *Macbeth*, Act IV, Scene 1. (In this novel: *Cauldron, Cauldron, double trouble. Cauldron boil and cauldron bubble.*")

*FACT:* King James I *did* release most of the prisoners that Queen Elizabeth had jailed -- including Henry Wriothesley.

*FACT:* Actual Shakespearean quote: "The course of true love never did run smooth." *Midsummer Night's Dream.* Act I, Scene 1. (N.B. *However, Marlowe would probably* not *have corrected the word "smooth" to the adverbial form: "smoothly."*)

*FACT:* Sir Walter Ralegh actually *did* spend much of his life in and out of prison, almost always in the Tower of London. It *is* true that he was executed (at Whitehall) on October 29, 1618.

*FACT:* As stated previously, Sir Wriothesley's mother *did* arrange for him to be moved to more acceptable and elaborate quarters in the Tower of London. She *did* pay nine pounds a week for this.

*FACT:* Shakespearean quote: "The play's the thing." *Hamlet*, Act II, Scene 2.

## CHAPTER FORTY-SEVEN

*FACT:* Sir Henry Wriothesley *was* in prison for two years. The charge *was* treason.

*FACT:* It is true that originally Sir Wriothesley was condemned to death but that Sir Cecil Burghley, president of the Privy Council, had interceded and commuted the sentence to life imprisonment. This, of course, left the door open for a release in the future.

*FACT:* Shakespeare's oldest daughter, Susanna, *had* married John Hall, a local physician, in 1607. Only Judith, the youngest daughter, remained in the Shakespeare home until Shakespeare died in 1616.

*FACT*: As mentioned previously, Shakespeare had been using the new husband of the widow Vautrollier to deliver money to his wife and family in Stratford.

*FACT:* It is surprising but true that the residents of Stratford were not aware that their neighbor, William Shakespeare, had been writing successful plays. They only seemed to know that he had been acting on the stage in London. One can't help but wonder why this is true. It seems to be one more fact flaming the conspiracy theory that Shakespeare did not actually write the plays attributed to him.

*FACT:* Shakespearean quote: "The play's the thing." *Hamlet*. Act II, Scene 2.

*FACT*: It is true that in the sixteenth and seventeenth century, a play was frequently written by a "team" of writers. Just as often a second person would rewrite work done by the original author. Since the name of the person who wrote the play was often a complicated and murky subject, the author of a work was seldom given credit at the time of the performance.

## CHAPTER FORTY-EIGHT

*FACT*: Shakespearean quote: "What wound did ever heal but by degrees?" *Othello*. Act II, Scene 3.

## CHAPTER FORTY-NINE

*Fiction*: Sir Francis Walsingham did *not* have Nicolas Skeres killed.

## CHAPTER FIFTY

*FACT*: *Midsummer's Night's Dream* is a play attributed to Shakespeare.

*FACT:* By this point in time, Shakespeare *had* returned to live in Stratford.

*FACT:* Shakespearean quote: "Life is a tale, told by an idiot, full of sound and fury, signifying nothing." *Macbeth*, Act V, Scene 5.

*FACT*: Two centuries later, the poet Thomas Gray *did* write a poem entitled "Elegy Written in a Country Churchyard." It included the verse: "*The boast of heraldry, the pomp of power, all that beauty, all that wealth e'er gave -- await alike the inevitable hour. The paths of glory lead but to the grave".*

## CHAPTER FIFTY-ONE

*FACT:* It is correct that William Shakespeare died in 1616, on his birthday, at the age of fifty-two.

*FACT*: When William Shakespeare died there *was* a very noticeable absence of *any* eulogies, tributes, memorial poems and words of praise for him. Lesser playwrights had died and garnered myriads of tributes. *But herein lies a major question*: why were there none when Shakespeare died?

*FACT*: There were a multitude of accolades penned when Marlowe "died". But there was nothing by Shakespeare, even though they could have been contemporary playwrights in London, and possibly overlapping in the years each could have been writing plays.

*FACT*: It is possible that one of the reasons considered by historians for the lack of tributes to Shakespeare was that the rest of the literary world may have separated the *writings* from the *writer*.

*FACT*: Oddly, when Shakespeare died *there was nothing from a fellow poet, or an actor, a friend, or publisher – not a single remembrance*.

*FACT*: There were no literary figures at Shakespeare's final services. By comparison, when Ben Johnson died, all the nobility and gentry were there. Most of the residents of Stratford were not even aware of the fact that Shakespeare was a playwright. They knew only that he was an actor.

*FACT*: Shakespeare *was* fifty-two when he died. The accepted cause *was* a venereal disease.

*FACT*: The first play to appear with Shakespeare's name as the author *did* appear in 1598 – five years after Marlowe's death.

*FACT*: The *first legal record* of payment to William Shakespeare as the author of a play is from the Lord Chamberlain's Men in 1594, a year after Marlowe's "murder."

*FACT*: It is true that Shakespeare left small sums of money to his children as well as to his "godson." It had always been well accepted that the son of Widow Davanant was Shakespeare's child. When Shakespeare was living in London, he made very few journeys back to Stratford. But when he did, he would always stop overnight on the way there and on the way back at a place called "The Tavern" in Oxford. Each time Widow Davanant, the owner, seemed to be able to accommodate him for the night. When she later bore a son, she proceeded to call him "William." As the boy grew up, he always claimed that Shakespeare was his father and everyone in Oxford seemed to accept it.

*FACT*: Shakespeare always referred to the Davanant boy as his "godson," and he left money in his will to that boy as well as to his own two daughters.

*FACT*: Shakespeare's will actually *was* very long and detailed, completed *only two months* before he died, indicating it was very current and should have been very accurate.

*FACT*: The myriad of details in the will did include listing *every one* of his possessions and household goods – everything – a bowl, a sword, plates, jewelry. He even willed all of his clothes – to his daughter Joan.

*FACT*: Shakespeare's will contained *no* references to books, printed copies of his plays, or partially completed works. There was *no* mention of willing his poems, plays, or other writings to *anyone*.

## CHAPTER FIFTY-TWO

*FACT:* As mentioned above Shakespeare *did* die at age 52 – on his birthday.

*FACT*: Historians agree that Shakespeare *did* die of a venereal disease.

*FACT*: As stated earlier, Shakespeare's will *was* very long and detailed, completed only two months before he died, indicating it was very current and should have been very accurate.

*FACT*: The myriad of details in the will included seemingly listing every one of his possessions and household goods – everything – a bowl, a sword, plates, jewelry. He even willed all of his clothes – to his daughter Joan.

*FACT*: It *is* true that at that time most of England considered the writings of the poet Ovid to be quite pornographic. He was another proponent of men sleeping with boys. His works were the source for

Shakespeare's poem 'Venus and Adonis,' as well as parts of the play *A Midsummer Night's Dream*.

***FACT***: Christopher Marlowe was also a fan of Ovid. It *is* true that he translated all of Ovid's "Amores" in 1599 while still a student at Cambridge. It is also true that his translation was banned and copies publicly burned as part of Archbishop Whitgifts crackdown on "offensive material."

***FACT***: It *is* a surprising fact that Shakespeare listed no books in his will. *None*. This was in spite of the great value these would have had at that time and would probably have been willed to someone.

***FACT***: The newly invented printing press would shortly make it possible for many more people to own books.

***FACT***: Among the books that one would expect to be listed in the will of Shakespeare would be the 200 or more used to derive the stories for his plays, including Holingshed's *Chonicles*, Ovid, and Plutarch. Because of all the biblical references in the writings of Shakespeare, one would also expect him to have owned a bible. *Surprisingly, he obviously did not.*

***FACT***: It *is* true that Shakespeare's will did *not* include printed copies of his plays because he obviously possessed no copies. Usually about 500 copies had been printed. In some cases they were financed by Thomas Walsingham and his friend, the printer Edward Blount.

***FACT***: The title page of the first printed quarto *does* state "Printed According to the True Original Copies".

***FACT***: As stated, Shakespeare *did not* will the rights of his plays to anyone. It is true that in some cases the plays could be the possession of the theatre where first presented, but not all of his plays would have fallen into this category.

***FACT***: In the play *Julius Caesar*, Mark Anthony *does* state in his speech over Caesar's dead body that the ruler had left all his worldly possessions to the citizens of Rome.

***FACT***: Shakespeare *is* credited with writing thirty-seven plays, two long narrative poems, 154 sonnets, and possibly much more. There is no mention in his will of bequeathing any of these works, though he does mention pots, pans, clothes, etc.

*FACT:* Shakespeare *was* born a Catholic and apparently *did* die a Catholic.

*FACT*: Sir Walter Ralegh *did* die while in prison, beheaded at Whitehall on October 29, 1618. He spent a good part of his life in and out of the Tower of London.

*FACT*: It *is* true that Sir Walter Ralegh's last words were "This is a sharp medicine but is a physician for all diseases and miseries."

## CHAPTER FIFTY-THREE

*Fiction*: The following quote is *not* from the writings of either Shakespeare or Marlowe: "Once an idea has been caged – once a voice has been silenced – the world is never the same again."

## CHAPTER FIFTY-FOUR

There are no entries for Chapter Fifty-Four.

## CHAPTER FIFTY-FIVE

*FACT*: As mentioned previously, Shakespeare *did* die in 1616.

*FACT*: Spain *was* still seething from the execution of Mary Queen of Scots, the defeat of their Amada, and the ascension of Mary's own son, James I (by then a devout Protestant) to be the head of the Church of England.

*FACT*: The plague *was* virtually always present and would mysteriously flare up every few years. Whenever the death toll in the city reached forty, all public gatherings except for church services *were* banned within seven miles of London.

*FACT*: It *is* true that the new King, James I, decided to produce his own translation of the bible that had been, until then, the sole canon of the Catholic Church. The new version was designed to become the official version of the gospels for Protestant England. This version *was* called the *King James Version*.

*Fiction*: Sir Francis Walsingham was *not* put in charge of producing the new version of the bible. He was dead by the time of the introduction of the King James Bible.

*FACT*: The king *did* show good judgment in insisting on strict oversight of the production of the new bible. Why? Because the second edition of the new Bible (produced in 1631) actually *did* have this startling typographical error. It read "*Thou Shalt Commit Adultery.*" There are still eleven copies of that edition in existence today, each supposedly worth about $100,000 each.

*FACT*: The plays of William Shakespeare *did* continue to appear for years after his death. There actually were a total of fourteen that were "found" after he died. (This chapter of the novel, however, takes place at the period after only the first *twelve* plays had been "found.")

*FACT:* *Loves Labors Lost* and *Coriolanus* are both plays attributed to William Shakespeare.

*FACT*: The Globe *did* actually burn down in 1613 when an errant cannon ball started a fire during a production of Shakespeare's *Henry VIII*. It was rebuilt the next year.

## CHAPTER FIFTY-SIX

*FACT:* Grigio wine was formerly called Gris wine.

*Fiction*: There is *no* record of a secret hiding place in the west tower of Scadbury Manor.

## CHAPTER FIFTY-SEVEN

*Fiction*: Sir Thomas Walsingham did *not* poison his cousin Sir Francis Walsingham and they did *not* die on the same night. Sir Francis Walsingham died in 1590. Sir Thomas Walsingham died in 1630.

## CHAPTER FIFTY-EIGHT

*FACT*: Thomas Walsingham *was* buried on August 19, 1630.

*Fiction*: King James could *not* have either attended or missed the funeral of Sir Francis Walsingham. His coronation was years *after* the death of Sir Francis.

*FACT:* As mentioned previously, atheism *was* a crime of treason, punishable by death.

*FACT:* It *is* true that Sir Francis Walsingham was the first Secretary of State for England.

***FACT***: The will of Sir Thomas Walsingham *did* include money to a scrivener "to buy a ring."

***FACT***: Fourteen plays attributed to William Shakespeare *did* appear after his death.

***FACT***: Shakespeare *is* often credited with writing scripts with no corrections. One possible reason for this would be the possibility that the manuscripts were recopied by a scrivener.

***FACT***: Shakespearean quote: "To sleep, perchance to dream – Ay, there's the rub." *Hamlet*. Act III, Scene 1. (In the novel, the line is shortened to: *So there's the rub.*)

***Fiction***: There is *no* record of a File 13 in the Privy Council pertaining to either Marlowe or Shakespeare.

***FACT***: This is part of a Shakespearean quote: "Who steals my purse steals trash; 'tis something, nothing; 'Twas mine, 'tis his, and has been slave to thousands; But he that filches from me my good name robs me of that which not enriches him, and makes me poor indeed." *Othello*, Act III, Scene 3. (The quote is shortened in the novel: *He who steals my purse steals nothing but he who steals my good name....*")

***FACT***: In the play *Hamlet*, in his farewell speech to his son, Leartes, who is leaving for France, Polonius tries to sum up a lifetime of advice in a few lines. This speech *does* include: "*This above all, to thine own self be true and it must follow, as the night the day, thou canst not then be false to any man.*" (*Hamlet*, Act I, Scene 3.)

***FACT***: Shakespearean quote: "Of one that loved not wisely but too well." *Othello*, Act V, Scene 2.

***FACT***: Historians believe *The Tempest was* one of the last plays written by William Shakespeare.

## CHAPTER FIFTY-NINE

***Fiction***: There is *no* record of any headstone with such an inscription for Christopher Marlowe.

***FACT***: Sir Henry Wriothesley *did* die from an unknown fever while visiting the Netherlands.

***Fiction***: There is *no* evidence of a note left by Christopher Marlowe when he died.

***Fiction:*** There is no evidence that Robert Poley or Constable Henry Maunder took care of Christopher Marlowe before he died.

***FACT***: Sonnet 72 actually <u>*does*</u> read "May my name be buried where my body is. And live no more to shame nor me nor you." (In the novel this quote is shortened to read: *Let my name be buried where my body is and live no more to shame me nor you.*)

TED BACINO has worked as a reporter on a daily newspaper, as a high school and college educator and as a director of stage musicals. He has a BA and an MS from Northern Illinois University and a KSG from Harvard. He has lived in Germany and London but now divides his time between Venice, Italy; Paris, France; and Palm Springs, California. Mr. Bacino has three children, eight grandchildren and three great-grandchildren. In 2005 he received a Star on the Palm Springs Walk of Fame, for directing theater. Some of those he directed early in their careers have starred on Broadway and some have been the recipients of Tony Awards.

TBacino@AOL.com